The Goddess Nekhebet

by

TC Carrier

Cover Artwork: Elihu Bey; ADOFO Illustrations

Published by: www.TCCarrier.com

ISBN: 978-0-9834462-8-6

In serving you, I found my destiny.

Contents

Prologue

There is an unseen power or entity that preys on us every day that remains undiscussed. It seeks to control and manipulate every facet of our lives. Its mission is to make us weak and dependent. It nurtures our shortcomings and insecurities as human beings. The weaker we are, the stronger it becomes. Its main goal is to capture our hearts, minds, bodies, and souls without us being aware of it. It is stealth. It is conniving. It is relentless. It is elegant. It is ruthless in its pursuit of total domination of our lives. You cannot touch, taste, see, feel, or smell it. But it is closer to you than you could ever imagine. It does not care if you are suffering from its rule over you. It only cares about obtaining more power in its ruthless pursuit to control your every action, deed, thought, and motive. It is jealous when you don't pay it any attention. It is insecure when it sees something else vying for your time and energy. It is violent and has temper tantrums when it doesn't get its way. It will never compromise. It will never give up. It is meticulous and strategic in its quest to bring you to your knees. It stalks your every waking moment, and even infiltrates your dreams. It will intoxicate you with its reason and eloquent words. It will seduce you with its charm and rhetoric. It will promise you the world but give you nothing in the end. It will build you up only to tear you down. It will convince you that you can't live without it, but nothing can be further from the truth.

Its main purpose is deception. It works night and day to come up with new techniques to persuade you to follow it. It needs you to be its slave. It yearns for you to worship it. It needs you to validate its existence. It will rule you by making you feel inferior. It has unapologetically killed and hurt millions of people with its insatiable thirst and hunger for flesh, blood, and total domination. It never asks for forgiveness. It never thinks the cause of your suffering is its fault. It blames you, the victim, for not recognizing that you are a slave to it. It has never cared about you but you have never questioned its motives and voluntarily give it your blind loyalty. You always have accepted it—and some of us have even sacrificed our own lives so it can continue its evil quest of domination and oppression.

It is only interested in its own self-preservation. It is ruthlessly self-centered. It is fearful and like any bully, is a coward when you stand up to it. It plays the victim role and points the finger at others. It is superficial. It needs people to pay attention to it and seeks praise from everybody. It is insecure and needs to be told how great it is every waking moment of the day. It doesn't take risks because it will always make excuses when things don't go its way. It doesn't dream or step outside the box because it is a coward behind all of its perceived power. It is the only real enemy we will ever encounter, yet we choose to put its best interest ahead of our own. It only survives because we nurture it. We protect it. We sustain it. We give it life.

Chapter One:
The Infinite Struggle

Right now, in a parallel universe, a fleet of one hundred militaristic spaceships ruthlessly inflict their barbaric destruction on all the peaceful beings in the universe. Led by Supreme Sovereign Sobek, ruler of the Yayvou, their sole purpose is to acquire more power. The Yayvou are advanced humanoid reptilians who conquer and destroy all species they come in contact with. Their sinister ships are hidden behind one of the twelve majestic and giant moons of the planet Ashanzu, and are lined up in a sharp "V" formation. This formation is their notorious and hostile signature battle cry. The Yayvou are preparing for a massive invasion to end their 666-year quest to conquer their most despised rivals, the peaceful Temkaay.

Their unique, lethal ships resemble the bottom-dwelling ocean creatures on Earth known as the stingray. The ships' exteriors closely resemble mirrored liquid mercury as they attempt to camouflage their lethal intentions in deep space while they ambush innocent neighboring species throughout the universe. Much like the ocean-dwelling stingray, the Yayvou ships travel through space using two giant fins that cut through space in an effortless waving motion. Pulsating, blood-red lights illuminate at the base of the giant fins along each ship's edges and are essential to their maneuverability.

Although these glowing lights illuminate the ships' renewable energy source, these structures are ultimately fueled by low-frequency emotions, such as fear, terror, hate, destruction, and chaos.

The tails of the Yayvou warships are positioned at the back, which helps to balance a ship's polarity and steadies the ship during battle maneuvers, much like the rudder on a sailboat. When engaged in battle, these "tails" loop over the top of the ship to reveal a cannon-like weapon that is armed with blasts of deadly red plasma projectiles.

The Yayvou plan is to exert their greatest effort to usurp and capture the Temkaays' knowledge of space travel, metaphysics, magic, and technology. The depth of knowledge these majestic Temkaay beings possess is far beyond any species in the known universe. The first and only objective of the massive Yayvou attack is to capture the Temkaay leader, Goddess Queen Nekhbet, and force her to divulge the sacred information of her highly advanced civilization. Once the Yayvou succeed in acquiring her knowledge, their parasitic culture consisting of death, slavery, and destruction will spread like a virus, seizing every extraterrestrial civilization in the universe like a plague of locusts. The Yayvou agenda will continue to prevail. Even when all the universe is conquered, they will be forced to destroy themselves; war is all they know. They thrive on destruction and violence, even if it means genocide against their own species. The Yayvou do not discriminate.

The Yayvou reptilians rely on their menacing appearance to intimidate their prey. Their demeanor is torpid, unwelcoming, and emotionless. Their piercing, blood-red eyes peer straight through any species within eyesight, and glow of blood from those they have slain. They have two long, sharp, curving black fangs protruding from both sides of their upper jaw and extending below their chin, similar to the prehistoric saber-toothed tiger. Their agile phalanges carry black, six-inch-long, razor-sharp claws; their metatarsus as well. Their tails are short—almost non-existent—most comparable to when a salamander sheds its tail; but Yayvou tails never grow back. Losing their tails is a of rite of passage into adulthood and a badge of honor. Only the young Yayvou offspring have their long tails intact. The savage species have thick, albino alligator skin and are bred to be over eight feet tall, muscular—and ruthless.

They pride themselves on uniformity and are always dressed for combat. Adult Yayvou wear black bullet-proof vests made of dragon skin that have several compartments containing numerous lethal weapons. Thick steel spikes line their protective headgear from the crown to the nape of their helmets, forming a deadly metallic mohawk. Their fingerless gloves allow their daunting claws to move freely, and are also made of black dragon skin and lined externally with sharp metallic spikes. Strapped around their shoulder is a massive gun that resembles a rocket launcher on steroids; it rests down the middle of their prickly, scaly back. On the left breast plate of their vest is a series of glowing sensors that control any weapon within a Yayvou's personal arsenal. With just the touch of a button, the Yayvou can summon a specific firearm to be automatically transported through electromagnetic frequency waves, locked and loaded, ready to expel Yayvou terror.

The more sensors one carries on their shield, the higher is the rank in their military and the more weapons they have access to in their personal arsenal. Some Yayvou have as little as six sensors and some have as many as twenty-four. Regardless of the arms they bear, every Yayvou is a walking weapons arsenal and is trained to utilize each part of his or her body and uniform in combat. Every article of their uniform carries a weapon of mass destruction, from the thick metallic spikes on the tops of their boot straps to their utility belt, all the way up to their head. One can only imagine the immense firepower of their governing leader, the Supreme Sovereign Sobek.

"Ssupreme Ssovereign, we believe we have found the goddesss queen! Sshe can no longer hide or run from uss!" Commander Ammut exclaimed in his distinctive reptilian hissing accent. "Our scoutss and sspy droness have confirmed her whereaboutss!"

"Where iss she?!" Supreme Sovereign Sobek deviously responded in a cold, deep, and calculating voice.

"Sshe is hiding on the twelfth moon, called Laun-Chi', belonging to the planet Asshanzu."

"Give me your full reconnaissance report. I want to know everything about the environment on thiss moon sshe dwellss on. I want to know the sstrengthss and weaknessess of her people and their culture sso I can exploit and conquer her once and for all! I want her neck in the grasp of my cold, sharp clawss as ssoon as possible."

"Yesss, Supreme Sovereign Sobek!" Commander Ammut motioned to one of his scouts to hand him a report. "I have the recon reportss right here, Supreme Sovereign."

The commander removed a tiny computer chip in the shape of a contact lens from the scout's right eye. He then inserted the chip into a console located inside an isolated room that was filled with multicolored crystals. The room is similar to multi-colored sand lying in what appears to be a giant sandbox.

Once the computer uploaded the data from the chip, the multi-colored sand crystals began to glow and become animated. They formed a three-dimensional map of what the scout had physically seen on the moon. The miniscule crystals started to float and swirl in midair. Thousands of multicolored crystals levitated over the sandbox and joined together to reveal a vivid and holographic replica of everything the scout witnessed in real time.

The high resolution of the colorful hologram brought the scout's report up close and personal. An automated robotic voice proceeded to narrate with detail what the scout had witnessed. The Yayvou could now see firsthand the topography and landscape where Nekhebet's queendom is located.

The moon where she resides, Laun-Chi', appears to be in a perpetual sunset state. The sun never rises above the horizon, yet the planet is very tropical, like an Amazon rainforest on Earth. There are three moons positioned low in the sky in an inverted triangular alignment. Each moon represents a different lunar cycle from the others. The plants and vegetation are fed and nourished by the , majestic, iridescent glow emanating from the three moons. The sky's luminous and celestial gradient begins with the horizon's golden hue, then changes to aqua and turquoise, and finally into shades of purple, lavender, and indigo. At the top of their atmosphere is a hypnotic, ultraviolet, iridescent glowing tinge.

There seems to be a perpetual glowing mist in the air. Because of the planet's low gravity, it rains in reverse. Water droplets rise as condensation from the many streams, canals, and rivers on the planet. The ground looks and feels like soft, lavender-colored grass that comes alive when walked upon, as if it is communicating with its inhabitants. The blades of grass glow with gratitude as they become sacred ground beneath the Temkaays' feet. The Temkaay seem to go into a meditative state when they make contact with this grass as they communicate with each stride they take. They call this process grounding.

Transportation on Laun-Chi' is an aquatic infrastructure. The tropical waterways and canals also have an iridescent glow, appearing as if the water carries a healing and regenerative energy. The Temkaay draw strength from their water. Although these waterways are used as primary transportation there are no boats, ships, or rafts. The natives simply walk on water or float to their destination via these liquid highways. They seem to communicate with the water telepathically, as the water seems to know where they want to travel and how fast they want to get there...

A once calm and calculating Supreme Sovereign Sobek became enraged by the Temkaays' majestic way of life. "Enough!" he yelled, and slammed his claws on his console. "What are the weaknessess of her people?! All I want to know iss how to destroy thesse forssaken creaturess as quickly as posssible! Enough with the tour! We are not on vacation! I'm here to plunder, pillage, and drink their blood!"

Commander Ammut hissed and signaled to another one of his scouts to hand him another computer chip contact lens. The crystals deciphered the data on the new chip and formed a different 3-D image of the inhabitants of the moon named Laun-Chi'. The robotic computer narrator continued.

The Temkaays' skin color can be described as a richly polished onyx of perfect, triple blackness. Their hue is rich and deep, like a bottomless abyss. These regal beings have an iridescent indigo glow that emanates from their skin as they move to and fro, especially on the waterways of their planet. They are all between eight and ten feet tall with very long, lean torsos, necks, and limbs, but they are still very shapely, like an hourglass. When they move, their arms and legs sway like the ocean current. Their limbs measure approximately 50 percent longer than our stocky Yayvou limbs. They are strong but not muscular, graceful but not timid, patient but not docile. A very peaceful race—but don't be fooled; they have a warrior spirit if called upon that will fight to the death.

They all possess a small circular mark behind their left ear. In this circle is a moniker or logo that is uniquely designed with a specific symbol that represents their unique assigned name and life's purpose. This tattoo-like symbol is also a telepathic portal that allows communication between the Temkaay. Yes, they communicate without speaking. It would seem as if these tattoos were strategically placed close to their ears so they can communicate as subtle as a silent whisper in meditation when they touch it to activate it.

The Temkaay have a single, butterfly-shaped eye socket in the middle of their forehead which houses a set of two corneas. The upper cornea is used to see their physical dimension, and the lower cornea is a portal that allow others to get a glimpse inside their soul and heart. The duality of their vision enhances their communication and perception. It's as if they communicate according to the level of consciousness of the given individual.

Everyone knows the true nature of their majestic neighbors, and they all seem to put each other's needs ahead of their own. They are the very definition of unity in a synchronistic and symbiotic relationship that serves the whole, as opposed to the individual. Each Temkaay embraces their special role in society and demonstrates the utmost respect for one another. A casual greeting involves the bowing of heads towards one another so they can feel each other's eyelashes flutter against their own. This is their second means of communication. When two Temkaay flutter and connect via their lower corneas, they access a direct and unobstructed path that leads to their heart, which is absent of ego, slander, fear, hate, jealousy, or contempt.

The border of the butterfly-shaped eye is elaborately decorated with finely ground powder of precious stones, such as lapis lazuli, jade, amethyst, hematite, turquoise, diamonds, and agate, which glimmers against their deep-ebony skin. Temkaay somehow can function, navigate, and traverse telepathically and intuitively. Their strong powers keep their predictions accurate, their memories strong, and their planetary perceptions keen. Although they don't see images, they detect energy through auras that contain all the characteristics and personalities of the objects being observed. They respond to light that emits from other beings. This species has mastered the State of Knowing. Above all, a most interesting aspect of the Temkaay is that this race of beings is all female!

Supreme Sovereign Sobek seemed to be perplexed about what he was hearing from his scouts. Still, he is growing even more angry and frustrated by the minute. His bloodshot eyes are now boiling. "Enough with the weak characteristicsss of thesse fragile little females! All I want to know is where I can find this so-called goddesss queen, capture her, and cut off her head once she reveals all her secrets to me! Have you ssimpletons forgotten the mission!?"

Commander Ammut trembled, but tried to hide his fear. He knew the Supreme Sovereign Sobek hated fear and could smell it. Commander Ammut hastily snatched the last chip from the final reconnaissance scout's eye, knocking him to the floor with his swinging claw and taking out his eye with it. The automated translator gave the next report.

The goddess queen resides in an enormous subterranean temple in the shape of an upside down pyramid. Ordinary Temkaay citizens inhabit the surface level of the structure. The further you travel within her temple, the higher the rank of the Temkaay that reside there. As one travels further down, the population becomes smaller, and only the most important leaders of her community live there. The queen's chamber is located at the bottom tip, and is the structure's final room. Just above her sacred royal chamber, twelve of her personal female bodyguards, the most elite soldiers in her army, are housed.

These elite female soldiers are named the Mino [Meen-No]. They are the most brave, agile, swift, courageous, and highly skilled soldiers in the entire universe. The Mino are immensely loyal to their leader. They were personally engineered and selected by Nekhebet to be her bodyguards. Upon inception, they vowed to protect their goddess queen, even at the expense of sacrificing their own lives. They are skilled in advanced weaponry and are masters of many styles in the art of hand-to-hand combat, and they are geniuses in strategic and tactical warfare. They instinctively unify to work together during battle.

One of the Mino stands above the rest. Her name is Sutol [Sut-Tul], the very best and brightest of the elite fighting regiment. Sutol was assigned by Nekhebet to never leave her side and to travel the universe with her. She is the goddess queen's ultimate line of defense. Sutol has never let anyone inflict harm upon her queen, nor has she ever failed her. She is the most loyal, courageous, and disciplined of all the soldiers in Nekhebet's army. She will fight to the death, and will gracefully annihilate any species that brings harm to Nekhebet. Sutol has held her rank for 33 years and has never thought twice about giving her life in the queen's honor; in fact, she lives for that moment.

Supreme Sovereign Sobek scoffed, "Haaaa! You mean to tell me these puny little harem prostitutes are her last defense? I am not impresssed! There is no way I'll let my massive, lethal army get beaten by a few weak female wannabe warriorss and their peace-loving goddesss. Thiss will be a lot eassier than I ever thought it would be. They have never felt the wrath and ruthlesss sstrength of the mighty Yayvou!" The reptilian soldiers all snarled and hissed and yelled out a bloodcurdling war cry in unison.

"Give my foot soldierss the desscription of thiss weak-minded, sso-called queen and her tiny little girl mascotss. Her capture and ensslavement sshall be eassy. Remember! I want her alive sso I can extract her ssecrets of sspace travel and other metaphyssical sciencess that sshe hass masstered! I can already tasste her ssweet blood dripping from my lipss!" Supreme Sovereign Sobek snarled in the face of a Yayvou scout. Commander Ammut put the last reconnaissance chip in the computer before the supreme sovereign could command him to do so. The supreme sovereign had been worked into a frenzy. He could barely contain his temper as his deep breathing showed signs of hyperventilation. The multicolored crystals activated as the computer downloaded the last chip's data.

This chip displayed the final holographic blueprint to the goddess queen Nekhebet's underground temple. Nekhebet appeared from the 3-D colored crystals. She is thirteen feet tall and more majestic than described. Her presence commands respect and attentiveness when she glides into a room. She is reportedly thousands of years old, but none of the Temkaay can verify her age. Even without hair, her beauty and regality are timeless. Her neck, arms, and legs are very long, slim, and muscular. She is the color of deep obsidian yet has an iridescent purple hue that resonates from her skin. This is her aura.

The queen wears a translucent, metallic, white gown with gold embroidery along the sides. Her garment flows freely, like the hydro-infrastructure waterways of the Laun-Chi' canals. A thin, golden headband decorates her forehead, containing shades of purple, turquoise, and royal-blue stones around its full circumference in the shape of cowrie shells. In the middle of her forehead is a gold medallion in the shape of a miniature phoenix that is soaring straight up to the heavens.

Just when you thought her appearance couldn't get any more elaborate, her distinctive jewelry is actually hundreds of organic beads, jewels, and precious metals that link together in the shape of hoop earrings and chain necklaces. They appear to be a simple coordinating jewelry set, yet each piece, each bead, has its own individual ultraviolet glow. Every strand has a complex and unique pattern that houses glowing pastel colors that rotate around the circle-shaped jewelry like they are electrically charged.

These so-called earrings and necklaces are really made of impenetrable nucleic matter and contain the genetic DNA strands of the hundreds of different beings the Goddess Queen has birthed throughout the universe. She simply chooses a strand, puts it up to her eye, flutters in a sequence of three, and she will then decide if she wants to communicate or incarnate into that particular species, regardless of where they are in the universe. This gives the goddess queen a direct link to thousands of locations, and of course, a connection to millions of beings throughout the universe.

The Yayvou widened their blood-red eyes in shock and fury as the computer unveiled Nekhebet's glorious omnipotence. Their mouths began to salivate as they thought about their lives once they obtained the queen's arsenal of knowledge and intelligence. This was the sole purpose the Yayvou were literally at her doorstep, ready to attack with all their might. The Yayvou were hell-bent on unlocking Nekhebet's secret of time and space travel, and were steps closer in their quest for universal domination.

Nekhebet was a master teacher of astral projection—known as space travel—metaphysics, and technology. Nekhebet yearned for balance in her civilization and the universe. She achieved this by promoting and teaching core messages of righteousness, reverence, honor, humility, propriety, reciprocity, and self-sacrifice. It was these qualities that Nekhebet cared about. Her mission in life was to spread balance and harmony throughout the universe in an effort to raise the consciousness of every living being contained within it. This was what gave Nekhebet her power. This was also why it had taken the Yayvou six hundred sixty-six years to solve her majestic puzzle; because her incredibly high frequency had displaced them from her vortex. Through strategic planning, cooperation with other species, and advanced weaponry, Yayvou soldiers had finally been successful in pinpointing her current location within the universe for the first time.

While Goddess Queen Nekhebet aimed to raise and accelerate the frequency of the universe, the Yayvou wanted to keep the universe's frequency low and slow. The sadistic reptilian species had come to realize that beings in the universe are more easily manipulated, oppressed, and controlled if their vibration was plummeting at an all-time low. Fear and terror were the best way to achieve this. This power struggle is the ancient, timeless battle of the eternal tug-of-war for the universe's soul between the goddess queen Nekhebet and her arch nemesis, the Yayvou.

"Enough talk!" Supreme Sovereign Sobek yelled once again in a deep, ground-shattering voice. "It'ss time to ride or die!" The supreme sovereign forcefully shoved Commander Ammut out of the way, leaving a large wound across his face. "We have no time for hisstory lesssons, strategiess, or gamess! We've already wassted preciouss time. It iss time to sspill Temkaay blood all over the universse once and for all. Their temple will forever rain death by the power of the mighty Yayvou!" Supreme Sovereign Sobek sprinted toward his lead attack ship, slashing the Yayvou scouts and soldiers to clear his path. He was oblivious, and otherwise careless to the carnage and bloodshed belonging to his own soldiers. A sea of Yayvou soldiers followed him in a parade-like fashion, all the while gnashing their teeth, salivating, shrieking, and tussling, to get to their respective ships.

Chapter Two:
The Incarnation

The goddess queen Nekhebet was in her chambers, preparing for the most important meeting of her thousands of years of existence. Moments after she collected her thoughts, she summoned her Mino daughters, who teleported to her chamber in unison, expressing similar looks of confusion and worry. The Mino daughters could sense in their queen's aura that something was not right, and their spirits felt the weight of her heart. Sutol, the leader of the Mino and Nekhebet's personal bodyguard, was the first to speak.

"My empress queen, why are you so sad, and why have you brought us here at such short notice?"

Sutol always spoke to the majestic deity on behalf of all Mino daughters. "We are all very concerned for you. Please, tell us what's troubling you, my goddess queen."

Nekhebet slowly rose from her throne and solemnly spoke to her loyal subjects. "My beloved Mino, there comes a time when things must die so that others may have life. I am afraid that time has come." The Mino exchanged looks of confusions and whispers as Nekhebet continued. "Now is one of those times. It is one of the laws of the Sacred Scales. It is constant, inevitable; it keeps the ebb and flow of the Creator in a delicate balance of harmony and sustainability. Our people are under siege by the dreaded Yayvou. I knew this time would come, but chose to keep it a secret. When all life is faced with certain death, we have a tendency to instantly forget all the great experiences we had, which leads us to be selfish, fearful, and ungrateful."

Goddess Queen Nekhebet gazed toward the temple and took notice of her Mino daughters, of whom she was very proud. "It is natural to want to hold onto life at all costs, which can cause us to think and behave in a manner we wouldn't be proud of under any other circumstances. We can wash away a whole lifetime of love, kindness, humility, and righteousness in just one lower-level moment we choose to act upon before we die. Dying a 'good' death is just as important as living a good life. For this reason, I have made my decision for the Temkaay to not fight back."

All the Mino were astonished and shocked by the words their goddess queen had spoken. They all frantically whispered amongst themselves until Sutol interrupted the cacophony.

"But, Empress Queen!" Sutol cried out. "We have all taken an oath that we would sacrifice our very lives so that you may live! Please do not deny us this opportunity."

"My precious Sutol," Nekhebet consoled, "I would never deny you your birthright. For you I have a special mission, and the most important assignment of all the Temkaay, for I will give you my precious heart for safekeeping." The goddess queen turned to the eleven other Minos. Made in her likeness, they are feminine, compassionate, and strong soldiers willing to defend the honor of the Temkaay and preservation of the universe.

"For the rest of my beloved Mino daughters, I need you all to fight like you have never fought before. I want you to think of all the Temkaay that have touched your hearts and call on them to give you strength in battle. The spirit will be stronger, more powerful, more relentless, if it fights for a cause greater than its own survival. I need you to fight off the Yayvou so I have enough time to prepare a ritual for our people's resurrection."

The goddess queen began to unveil her sacred plan. "I am going to lock myself and Sutol in my chambers in order to perform a ritual that is needed for the survival of our people. Please buy me enough time to finish. The future of the Temkaay bloodline depends on each and every one of you succeeding. Fight with your goddess queen in your hearts. Empty your minds of fear, pain, and doubt, and hold in your extremities the strength and wrath of thirteen million Temkaay ancestors who were determined to die a good death. Through you, the future Temkaay can live in peace and harmony."

The Mino grabbed their weapons and lined up in defensive formation. Their weapons of choice were the plasma shield and the double-edged plasma spear. Each Mino embellished her personal spear with exotic feathers that belonged to the Benu bird, the creature of transformation from across the universe.

Operating the plasma spear is second nature to the Mino. Shortly after their inception, each Mino is gifted with a double-edged spear and trained in its use before she learns how to walk. While growing, they are also instructed to keep it by their side, always prepared for combat. They use it with precision, and wield it similar to the Brazilian martial arts disguised as the dance called the Capoeira.

The goddess queen anointed her beloved Mino one by one, rubbing a black, oily substance on top of their foreheads as she led them out of her chamber. Each daughter beamed with a radiant glow as she approached her queen; there was no sadness. They carried themselves with gratitude, love, and honor, because they were chosen for this special moment.

As the queen anointed the last Mino daughter, Sutol closed the massive titanium door behind them and sealed the Mino out of the chamber for one last time. The slamming of the humongous, metallic door echoed down the corridors of the queen's chambers and reverberated down the halls in a haunting tone of extreme isolation and loneliness.

* * *

The Yayvou onslaught overcame the peaceful Temkaay civilians as they ferociously marched on the queen's temple. Level by level, closer and closer, they succeeded in descending to the queen's chamber, relentlessly killing and destroying everything in their path. The civilians did not put up any type of fight. They were courageous, but nonaggressive. The Temkaay consciously submitted in unity, finding stillness in their queen's orders. They were ripped to shreds, decapitated, and slaughtered during the march of death led by the notorious Yayvou leader, Supreme Sovereign Sobek.

The Yayvou reached the final level above the queen's chamber. "Thiss iss it," Supreme Sovereign Sobek said to Commander Ammut, and signaled for Yayvou soldiers to assume the position for advancing the hostile takeover.

Just opposite the barricade, the eleven Mino took turns bowing their anointed heads to one another as an act of sacrifice and solidarity. They got in formation and eagerly awaited dying in defense of the goddess queen's honor, according to her wishes. Once they sensed their opponents' arrival they erected their shields, drew their spears, flung open the doors, and voluntarily invited the Yayvou inside their death trap. All of the Mino warriors grimaced gracefully as the Yayvou rushed in blindly. The reptilians were surrounded by the majestic light-bodies with their shields and their double-edged spears. The Mino commenced to enclose their circle and slaughtered the Yayvou with their trusted spears. The Mino were calculated in their efforts. The eleven daughters ensured the narrow doorway only allowed a certain number of Yayvou to enter at a time, to preclude them from being overwhelmed and outnumbered in a Yayvou ambush. A ratio of thirteen Yayvou for one Mino is a fair fight with excellent odds in their favor.

* * *

In the queen's chamber, Nekhebet told Sutol that the Temkaay would inevitably fall and that she must arrange another plan to one day resurrect her queendom after it has been destroyed. Sutol rejected the queen's remarks while eliciting her sharpest combat choreography. "I will never let that happen." She kicked, flipped, stabbed, and twirled her spear like a baton.

Nekhebet told her that it was hopeless to fight for a cause that has already been defeated, for the prophecy had already been written in the books of the Sacred Scales. The queen commanded Sutol to be intelligent and think several moves ahead of the enemy, and not react emotionally to the adversity at hand. Goddess Queen Nekhebet continued. "They may have won this battle, but they will never win the war. We must prepare for another place and time to rise again and build another illustrious civilization." She further commanded Sutol to trust her will, and to do as she said. A tearful Sutol reluctantly put down her weapon, knelt at Nekhebet's feet, and agreed to submit to her queen's plan for resurrection as tears rolled down her face.

Danger was fast approaching. Goddess Nekhebet and Sutol heard the brazen collision of the titanium Yayvou weapons against plasma Mino armor. The eleven daughters battled with great purpose but were mercilessly slaughtered one by one, all the while showing the courage and bravery of a thousand heroes. The hellish Yayvou were getting the best of them as the Mino force dwindled from eleven to nine, then to six and to three, with each passing moment.

The remaining three Mino warriors displayed a last surge of courage, skill, and strength the Yayvou had never witnessed in all their bloody battles. Supreme Sovereign Sobek, irritated, slowly crept up closer to the Minos' chambers to put an end to this nonsense once and for all as he lost patience with his dying soldiers. He couldn't believe the sight of his fighters being slaughtered one by one by these inferior women soldiers.

* * *

Nekhebet reached to grab the hundreds of strands of necklaces from around her limber neck. She told Sutol that each iridescent glowing necklace was really a DNA strand belonging to one of thousands of species throughout the universe she had birthed. Nekhebet knew she must swiftly, yet carefully, pick one species to contact before the Yayvou careened through her chamber. Emphatically, the goddess queen turned to Sutol. "There is no time to lose. I must astral-project myself and spiritually travel to the world of one of my species. When I am there, I will reside in a makeshift temple that will be contained and protected within the womb of my many distant daughters I have created. As she makes love in her foreign world, and her male mate releases his semen inside of her, I will capture his soul and bring it with me to Laun-Chi' for safekeeping. All creatures in the universe have a unique vibration and rhythm from which their heart resonates." Goddess Nekhebet carefully scanned the glowing strands for her temporary temple, rolling the beads between her long fingers as her eyes rolled to the back of her head. "Once that is complete, I will then guide you to incarnate into his body and your spirit will take his place while I hold his soul captive here until your mission is complete.

"But in order to do this, my beloved Sutol, you must die in battle protecting me before they capture me." Sutol's tears flowed like an endless river on Luan-Chi'. She realized the immense request from her goddess queen and tried to focus amid the shaking ground, rattling barricade, crackling walls, and Yayvou battle banter. They were closer, now launching explosives, demanding their entrance. Still and with strength, Sutol listened closer to her queen.

"When you fight and finally succumb to death, you must sing this chant on your lips in order to incarnate in the body your queen has selected. This is how I will match your spirit with the proper body I have chosen for you. Here is his vibratory key; you must repeat this chant to unlock his heart so that your spirit will inherit his body. Repeat this chant while you are dying: 'Ranam Mayoho Darenge Sakyo Sayho.'

"Once you incarnate into his body, you will lose all memory of yourself, your queen, your world, and the mission I have given you. You will have to find your way by following your heart and having no fear. Remember; everything around you is just an illusion. In doing so, you will be preparing a place for me to resurrect my queendom. Remember, all you have to do is follow your heart; you will eventually find me. Do not, I repeat, DO NOT conform to this new world! There is no time to further explain. You have never failed me, and I trust you with my life and the rebirth of the Temkaay civilization."

After the sixth explosion, the Yayvou dismantled the heavy diamond door to Nekhebet's chamber. Just moments after the door flew off its hinges, a thick, terroristic cloud of red smoke entered the chamber. A pale, grotesque Supreme Sovereign Sobek climbed over the precious stones that once made up the gigantic door to the queen's royal quarters. Supreme Sovereign Sobek scanned the periphery with his naked eye, but didn't detect any life forms. He proceeded to activate one of his highly advanced Yayvou sensory lenses to see shadows through the blood-red smoke; still nothing.

He cried out, "Well, boyss! Prepare for the easiesst, fullesst feast of your livess!"

Yet again, however, the Temkaay had outsmarted the Yayvou reptilians. Even though their weapons were highly advanced, their fleet and ammunition were created with low-level intelligence and only operated on a low frequency; thus, they were rendered ineffective in the queen's chamber. This fact was omitted from the Yayvou scout's reconnaissance.

"Unleash yourselvess!" he cried out to the bloodthirsty Yayvou soldiers as they entered the temple. As the soldiers poured in, the smoke cleared and revealed the most bewildering and unsuspecting sight. Sutol positioned herself in the Temkaay defensive stance in front of Nekhebet as her queen crossed her legs and sat Indian-style on her throne with her eye closed, hands over her heart, oblivious to the annihilation around her. Supreme Sovereign Sobek was disgusted that there was only one last Mino blocking him from his most precious prize. In his sick thirst for blood, he wished there were more Temkaay females to ravage.

With the utmost confidence in her chosen one, the goddess Nekhebet continued to scan her iridescent strands to find the closest female she could astral-project to that matched one of her hundreds of genetic DNA strands she had on her person. Not only would she need to find that proverbial DNA needle in the universal haystack, but this Nekhebet female must be currently having sex with her mate in order for Nekhebet to capture his soul and replace it with Sutol's. This was the only chance to resurrect the Temkaay.

Oblivious to the Yayvou carnage and the horrendous, beastly horde snarling around her, Nekhebet prepared for her spiritual journey throughout the universe to find a womb to call her temple.

Suddenly, Nekhebet started to chant and fell into a deep trance as her eyes rolled to the back of her head. Her spirit started to travel to a distant galaxy that its inhabitants call the Milky Way. Nekhebet pinpointed the planet she'd seeded tens of thousands of years ago. It was currently called planet Earth.

The goddess queen astral-projected her spirit inside the womb of a Black woman named Janus on this bluish-green planet. In Janus's womb, Nekhebet quickly raised the frequency and vibration with a blinding, ultraviolet light that engulfed Janus's womb to suit the needs of the goddess mother. It was now the domain of Goddess Mother Nekhebet! It was now the goddess queen Nekhebet's sacred temple, even if just for a moment.

Meanwhile, Sutol was occupied with Yayvou dismemberment for the sake of protecting her queen. Sutol defaulted to a sacred Temkaay battle sequence, finding the sweet spot in her rhythm and spear. Now fighting in a hypnotic method, with no wasted movement, she effortlessly mowed down the Yayvou. She is so skilled that not a single drop of blood fell on Nekhebet, despite the Yayvou lunging at her with all their might. Their faulty equipment, blood, and innards now decorated the walls of the queen's chamber, but Nekhebet's circle remained pure, peaceful, and immaculate. Sutol had become one with her lethal weapons, using them as extensions of herself. She proved the Temkaay reputation for tenacity and for being the most elite warriors throughout the whole universe.

Supreme Sovereign Sobek watched his best soldiers get their heads handed to them in this sacred slaughter. He lost his patience. He stepped up to Sutol to reclaim Yayvou dignity. *She'ss gonna eat that little stick of herrsss,* he thought to himself.

Void of hesitation or timidity, Sutol prepared for the fight of her life. She knew that she could not be defeated until her queen came back into her body. She summoned the spirits of her Mino sisters who had died in combat to give her strength to persevere through all the adversity, fear, and pain she was about to encounter.

Meanwhile, on Earth, Janus and her husband, Hershel, yielded to one another as their hearts pounded in unison, synchronizing and vibrating at a rate where shared energy fuses into one divine symphony.

Lying on top of his wife, Hershel pressed his heart against Janus's chest. She granted his unspoken plea for complete and utter closeness by locking her feet around his ankles to force him into her blissful bond. With minuscule air pockets resting between their flesh, Janus opened her mind, heart, soul, and chocolate thighs, to grant Hershel full access to her sacred feminine mystery.

Janus turned herself inside out to expose the depths of her soul during the ritual of divine manifestation. She took Hershel by the heart to show him the most sacred place the universe has ever known. This pure, phenomenal feat took the courage, strength, and trust that only a woman can possess.

Overwhelmed by the depths of her emotions, Hershel plunged himself further into the sacred with every iota of his being. His wife's essence was intoxicating. He vacillated from one dimension to the next, from seen to unseen. Their illuminated, invisible souls ascended, dancing, playing, swirling freely above their heads. Hershel suddenly felt an intense, cold sensation that rippled through his body. His higher source commanded him to obey the rhythm of the ripple, which started at the soles of his feet, steadily climbed up his ankles and rested between his inner thighs. Janus gently sighed in Hershel's ear. It felt like a butterfly had gently landed on his earlobe to bare its intimate secrets. This was her subtle way of giving Hershel permission to emancipate his masculine spark, whose main purpose is to give life to her at the expense of its own.

Hershel was completely engulfed in the divine union and became a slave to their ecstasy. He unwittingly converted his spiritual essence into liquid sunshine that seemed to have been sucked from his loins and into Janus's sacred feminine by a force with inexplicable strength and intensity. Hershel involuntarily abandoned the human shell that once imprisoned his soul.

His higher source projected to another dimension. Hershel swirled inside liquid dark matter, tossed wildly about. He found bliss and purpose in the chaos that presented as his new reality. Because he was too helpless and weak to fight back in his condition, he let go of his ego to the unknown power. Nekhebet has resumed her temple inside of Janus's womb, and he was now her servant. She guided Hershel like a leaf on a rushing river going helplessly downstream into her temple that used to be his wife's womb.

Hershel was drained, yet joyous in his acceptance of being conquered. His journey has a purpose that he cannot comprehend, so he continued the process without any preconceived notions of where he would finally arrive.

A light emerged from behind him, and a warm sensation blanketed his soul. He was comforted by this heated blanket of ecstasy. As he neared the light, he felt the intrigue and power of a strange presence that demanded his complete attention, allegiance, and respect. Hershel's imagination got the best of him. He was already struck by the grand entity and was overwhelmed by her aura, even though her identity remained hidden.

In the distance of the abyss, Hershel saw a figure perched on a golden throne atop a hill covered in lush lavender grass. The natural scents of jasmine and honey permeated the atmosphere. The figure was surrounded by light, so he could only decipher the silhouette. The creature appeared to be about ten feet tall, in the sitting position. He remained grounded, and squinted to see beyond the light, yet was only able to make out the length and regality of her neck. Suddenly, Hershel was teleported and delivered at her feet in the fetal position. He dared not gaze into her eyes, as he feared he would perish from the intensity of her luminous beauty. Momentarily blinded, Hershel tried to clear his vision to focus on other objects around the temple.

He saw blue-greens, purple, teal, indigo, periwinkle, and turquoise. He saw gold and lapis lazuli that sparkled like the reflection off a full moon.

Without warning, Nekhebet grabbed Hershel by the hand and threw him up in the air like a rag doll. He no longer seemed like the ex-football star that stood six feet, two inches tall and two hundred fifteen pounds. Hershel had been transformed into a minute figurine of insignificant stature while in the presence of a goddess. He thought to himself, *Did I shrink, or am I this small to her?* He reconsidered his own insignificance in the unseen realm of Nekhebet. Hershel was simultaneously petrified and honored.

Nekhebet finally put him down after playing with him for what seemed like an eternity. He fully understood how weak he really was in comparison to the goddess queen. Hershel was humbled in his humiliation, but for some reason, he felt empowered.

Goddess Nekhebet finally greeted the minute human with words and debriefed him on his assignment. "Greetings, Hershel, I am the goddess queen Nekhebet, leader of Temkaay. I have come for your soul. Although you are not worthy to sit on my throne, you have earned great favor and protection in your surrender." Hershel stood completely still and starstruck. Goddess Nekhebet insisted that he should be honored, and reassured him that his spirit and body would be preserved. As his fears were erased, he was assured that his reward would come once her mission was complete. "All will be revealed in due time."

Instantaneously, Nekhebet put her left hand on Hershel's chest and lifted him off the ground. His spirit was sucked out of his body, transferred into one of the beads on her left hoop earring, and swiftly taken away back to Laun-Chi'.

Hershel's wife, Janus, was still buried under Hershel's two-hundred-fifteen-pound body. She called out to him repeatedly, though he was unresponsive and limp.

"Hershel! Hershel! You are too heavy; I cannot breathe, baby! Hershel, get off of me, quit playing!" Janus struggled to free her petite body from beneath her husband, to see him, but Hershel was still unresponsive. "Oh my God, baby! Are you all right? You are scaring me! Baby, Imma call 911 if you don't answer me. Don't do me like this, Hershel. I'm serious! Don't play with me! Don't be embarrassed when the paramedics find you butt naked..." Janus reluctantly fumbled around with her cell phone lying on the nightstand and dialed 911.

"Hello, 911, what's your emergency?"

"Somebody help me, please! My husband is unresponsive. Send somebody, quick! I live at 274 Sirius Way."

Hershel was unresponsive when the paramedics arrived. They immediately tried to stabilize his vital signs and rushed him to the closest emergency room. Janus nervously rode in the ambulance, wringing her hands, praying to God to save her husband.

By the time they got to the hospital, Hershel's vital signs had plummeted and the medical staff immediately ushered his body to the Intensive Care Unit. Janus remained in the waiting room, kneeling in the corner, praying to God.

"Dear Heavenly Father, please save my husband. It's just not supposed to end like this. Save my baby. Please, God. Save him, God."

About twenty minutes passed before the doctors returned to the waiting room with news contrary to Janus's prayers. They related having to place Hershel on life support due to his severe comatose state. She regretfully delivered the news to immediate family and friends, also praying that they didn't ask what happened to him.

Goddess Nekhebet returned to her own body in her queen's chamber on Laun-Chi'. She was just in time to witness her daughter, Sutol, battle one on one with the most diabolical, ferocious, evil monster in the known universe, Supreme Sovereign Sobek. Sutol was giving the supreme sovereign all he could handle, knowing her queen's life was at stake. She snuck a glance out of the corner of her eye towards her queen and saw that she had returned. The goddess queen shed a tear and nodded her head, symbolizing that her mission was accomplished and it was her time to fulfill her promise. Sutol shook her head no at her queen as she erroneously thought she could still defeat the mighty Yayvou, even being outnumbered 66,666 to 1. Nekhebet telepathically reassured her that her death was the only way to resurrect the Temkaay. "The vessels are in place," Nekhebet reassured her. "All will be well."

A teary-eyed Sutol reluctantly began repeating the chant her queen told her to recite at the moment of her death, but hardly surrendered. She started out in a whisper, but gradually increased her volume to a yell as she continued to fight Supreme Sovereign Sobek. "Ranam Mayoho Darenge Sakyo Sayho. Ranam Mayoho Darenge Sakyo Sayho! RANAM MAYOHO DARENGE SAKYO SAYHO!"

For some reason, she was having a hard time putting down her weapon and willfully submitting without a fight. Sutol suddenly forced her eyes closed and dropped her shield and spear. With one swift swing of Supreme Sovereign's massive blade, Sutol was decapitated and her lifeless body fell helplessly to the polished lapis lazuli floor of the temple. Nekhebet whispered to herself, "It is done," then sadly bowed her head.

* * *

Back in the ICU on Earth, Hershel's family had gathered around his lifeless body to say their final goodbyes. The doctors said Hershel's death was inevitable, so they were all making their peace with him.

At the same time, Sutol's spirit was being sucked through a long, dark portal and was racing toward a light at the end of it. Sutol's spirit continued to repeat her chant over and over again amidst her chaos and confusion inside the illuminated tunnel walls. "Ranam Mayoho Darenge Sakyo Sayho. Ranam Mayoho Darenge Sakyo Sayho. Ranam Mayoho Darenge Sakyo Sayho..."

Sutol finally reached the end of the tunnel of her long journey. Simultaneously, Hershel's heartbeat seemed to be getting stronger. Apparently, the light at the end of Sutol's tunnel was the ICU room where Hershel's body was located!

All of a sudden, Hershel started to speak, but his family could not make out his low murmurs. In a very weak voice Hershel whispered, "Ranam Mayoho Darenge Sakyo Sayho." Sutol had made her transition and was incarnated into Hershel's body on this foreign planet.

Hershel slowly opened his eyes. He didn't recognize himself or anyone in the room. His wife, Janus, threw herself over

Hershel's bed and exclaimed, "Baby, I knew you wouldn't leave me! Thank you for coming back to me. I don't know what I would have done without you! Thank you, Jesus! Thank you, Jesus! Baby, can you hear me? Can you talk?"

Hershel cleared his throat and responded in a low, raspy voice, "Do I know you? Who am I? Where am I?" Hershel's family all looked on in disbelief as their mouths dropped to the floor.

Chapter Three:
Coming To Krist

After falling into a mysterious coma three days ago, Hershel passed all of his medical tests with flying colors and the doctors allowed him to go home. Except for his chronic amnesia, he seemed to be in perfect health. But he was completely lost, and felt hopeless and confused. He didn't recognize or remember anything belonging to his former self. The medical team was optimistic about Hershel's recovery, and provided Janus with resources to help get him back on track. Hershel sat on the edge of the bed looking out the window, fully dressed and ready to go, while Janus gathered his personal effects.

The attending physician, Dr. Etsaman, lightly knocked twice before entering the slightly open door. "Knock-knock! Ah! Seems like you're all ready to go, Hershel!" he said in a robust tone with his hands in the pockets of his lab coat.

Hershel's head turned to meet the doctor's eyes. He cracked half a smile and diverted his attention back to the window. Dr. Etsaman inserted his retractable pen into his crisp, white lab coat pocket and turned to Janus. "Now, Mrs. Rison, you are going to have to show extreme patience with your husband. Please be as encouraging and understanding as possible," he said with a heartfelt tone but stern eyes. "Hershel will need a lot of support, love, and positive reinforcement. Make sure you do the things that he loved to do to help assist him in recovering his memory. It would be great if you showed him old photos, videos, cooked his favorite foods, or visit places he may have liked before he became ill."

Janus's shoulders slowly lowered in relief while she held a plastic bag in one hand and wiped her eyes with the other. Dr. Etsaman reached for the box of tissues on the nightstand behind them and extended the box to Janus with a friendly smile. "I believe Hershel has the potential to regain all his memory and can return to his former self. But because we have never seen such a unique case, his recovery is unknown."

"I understand, thank you so much," Janus responded with a crack in her voice. "Thank you for bringing my husband back from death. I will never forget having this second chance at sharing my life with him once again. I appreciate everything you have done for my husband and me and have no doubt that he will return to his former self, so help me God!" Janus took him by the hand. "God bless you and all of your wonderful staff that helped bring the love of my life back to me."

Dr. Etsaman put his hand on Janus's shoulder as a sign of comfort. "Now you two get out of here and live your new beginning. Take care of each other." He left the room and headed toward the nurses' station.

Janus rushed to the bathroom, wiped her face clean with a paper towel moistened with hot water, and recalibrated to escort her husband back into their normal lives. "Hershel, baby, you ready to— " Janus stopped abruptly in her tracks, completely astonished. She squinted her eyes as she saw Hershel was deeply entranced with a butterfly flying outside of the window. "Oh! Well, this is new," she mumbled under her breath. She picked up her beige lambskin Michael Kors purse off the recliner and grabbed Hershel's plastic bag of clothes and an assortment of medications. Janus clung to Hershel's elbow and put all her weight on him as they walked out of the hospital arm in arm. Janus held onto Hershel's arm with all her might as a means of keeping him close to her so that he would never leave her again.

Janus and Hershel came from humble beginnings but had done very well for themselves. They went from poverty to luxury within their first two years of marriage. When they graduated from college they were earning minimum wage, living paycheck to paycheck in their separate quarters just three miles apart. Hershel rented a windowless room for $300 a month in a notoriously wild party house that had a lingering scent of vomit and bottom-shelf vodka. He could afford to live in an efficiency but chose to live closer to Janus, who was living with her sorority sisters, spending $375 for a spot on the couch in their very communal living room/multipurpose area. They were miserable living apart. Not because their busy schedules only warranted time on the weekends for cuddling and catching up over 2 for $20 meals at TGI Fridays, but they weren't satisfied with their accommodations. Hershel sacrificed sleepless nights living in his expensive closet of a room, and Janus often had to share the leather, L-shaped sectional with an untimely houseguest who didn't pay a dime. Neither one of them could afford what they were paying to live in their less than ideal arrangements, and they were scrounging to make ends meet.

Janus, though hundreds of miles away from home, did not want to go against her mother's wishes by shacking up with her soon-to-be-husband who couldn't afford to put a ring on her finger. Janus knew that Hershel was a man of his word and did exactly what he said he was going to do.

On their weekly TGI Fridays outing, the couple devised an escape plan to move in together to a studio apartment for $700 a month with utilities included. They purchased living room furniture on Craigslist and moved into their studio apartment with a futon, mini fridge, and grey Rubbermaid totes containing their worldly possessions (one of which served as the television stand). Hershel paid a greater share of the rent, and Janus covered the expenses of food and furniture. Disobeying her mother didn't seem so bad, and her dream life with the love of her life was off to a great start. That is, until Hershel was offered an (unpaid) opportunity of a lifetime to intern with a major architecture firm in Atlanta. For one year he'd work without pay, rubbing elbows and fetching coffee for some of the biggest executives in the industry. Janus wasn't happy about it, but understood his attempt and need to cut his teeth in building his resume. So she took on an extra job as a receptionist in the beauty salon below their studio apartment and got a huge discount on her hair and nails services, which she loved to get done. Even though Janus had a small budget, her high-maintenance mentality took precedence at all costs. They spent their sleepless nights dreaming of expensive clothes and properties they couldn't afford.

The couple vowed to never allow material things to interfere in their relationship. They now lived in a charming home located in a middle-upper-class neighborhood in Southern California. They owned two cars; a cherry-red 2016 BMW 3 series for her, and a black 2016 Porsche Cayenne for him. They had climbed the ranks in their respective fields and rewarded themselves by investing in a lavish lifestyle.

Janus was a highly ranked administrator at the prestigious Cedars-Sinai Medical Center in LA. She has great leadership skills and a relentless drive to be successful. She made her way through college working full-time, and still earned a 4.0 GPA. She's known to her peers to never back down from a challenge, and has always overachieved in everything she set her sights on. Janus is also a devout Christian and heavily involved in the Church.

Hershel was very strategic. He saw every opportunity as having to carefully play the cards he was dealt. He didn't come from a warm, embracing, and supportive family like Janus, although she just had her mother and aunts. His childhood years were especially rough, being in and out of foster homes and stealing food out of bodegas to eat. After getting into trouble with the rabble-rousers and being labeled a juvenile delinquent, he turned over a new leaf with sports, creating a fresh, exciting life for himself. He came alive on the field, and people fell in love with his personality. He dreamed of being a pro athlete with major endorsements and investments around the globe. But he graduated from college with a bachelor of architecture instead. He spent his first two years out of school working sixteen-hour days, seven days a week, interning with multiple companies. Hershel's charm helped him foster strong relationships and references in the industry.

A former college professor took Hershel under his wing, teaching him everything he needed to know about the business of architecture, and helped him score an entry level position at one of the top firms in the country. Hershel has been with Master Builders for the span of his ten-year career. Though the company has offices located in NYC, Atlanta, and California, Hershel works in the bustling, affluent Westwood neighborhood of Los Angeles. He has designed several business and housing developments on his impressive resume, and is well-respected among his colleagues. He is known for his attention to detail and his uncanny ability to use every inch of the property's space efficiently. His meticulous skyscraper designs stand between thirty-five and fifty stories, and tower throughout seven major metropolitan cities around the United States.

Designing buildings wasn't Hershel's first option for a career, but when he involuntarily approached a fork in the road, he relied on his instincts to propel his career forward.

"Baby, we're finally back home!" Janus flung open the iron double doors of their home. "Does anything in the house look familiar to you?"

Hershel remained quiet as he surveyed the home from the foyer. His eyes darted from the photos on the wall, to the sofa, stairs, television, umbrella holder. He seemed afraid to commit fully to entering the strange abode. Janus grabbed Hershel's right hand and gave him a tour of the house.

"This is our kitchen we just remodeled. Remember when we had a huge fight about which handles we wanted to put on the cupboards?" Hershel stared in silence with his round, brown eyes. "Yeah, baby, see, you wanted the large chrome handles and I wanted the pewter spiral knobs? And well, of course you let me get my way...as usual." Janus smiled sheepishly and gently nudged him with her shoulder. Hershel had no idea what she was talking about, and just tagged along with his wife through the house. "There's more to see." She led him down the hall as they passed the dining room, living room, and arrived at the bathroom.

"Do you remember 'my' bathroom? Just to refresh your memory, it's still off limits to you, sweetheart."

Janus flashed a quick smile and wink at her husband, but Hershel didn't seem to get her sarcasm. They proceeded down the wide hallway and into Hershel's office. "And, baby, this here is where you spend the majority of your time."

Janus directed his attention to the framed pictures of buildings and certificates hanging on the walls. Hershel approached his big, dark-mahogany desk with stacks of papers and blueprints scattered atop the surface. Hershel slowly picked up one of his skyscraper blueprints and held it upright, turned it sideways, upside down, and straight again, staring at it with perplexity. He neither recognized any of the drawings, nor understood the meanings of the measurements or symbols. Janus walked up behind him and embraced him around his waist.

"You know, if I couldn't find you, I knew you would be in here. Many times I had to come get you to come to bed with me. I think you've spent more nights sleeping on top of your desk than you have sleeping on top of me in our own bedroom," she said with a subtle sharpness in her voice, but Hershel didn't see the humor in Janus's attempt at a joke. Janus inhaled deeply while resting her head on Hershel's back, wrapping her arms around his waist, hugging him from behind "Don't worry, my king; it will all come back to you." She held him for a few minutes longer, then snapped out of her daydream.

"Okay! Come on, let me show you the rest of the house." Janus walked by their master bedroom. She was hesitant to go inside, as she hadn't been in there since Hershel lost consciousness and had to be rushed to the hospital. She stood at the doorway like there was an invisible force field keeping her from entering.

"This is our bedroom, baby. This is the last place you had your memory. You lost consciousness while we were making love. I have never been more scared in all my life. Maybe this could be the first place you regain your memory...if we made love again?"

Nervously smiling, Janus grabbed Hershel's waist and pulled herself closer to him. Hershel would normally be aroused and meeting Janus's advance with a deep, passionate kiss, but he looked down at his feet and stared for a while, completely oblivious. Janus noticed his uneasiness and grabbed his hand. She led him to the backyard to their beautiful, ten-foot Grecian swimming pool surrounded by towering palm trees. Their redwood deck is adjacent to the custom siding and holds a stainless steel barbecue grill, full bar, state-of-the-art entertainment system, and sixty-inch flat screen TV. Janus and Hershel invested a lot of money into entertaining in their backyard.

"Baby, this is your world. You created all this! Designed every rock and brick just the way you wanted it. You love to cook and entertain friends. You host the big sporting events and holiday get-togethers. Do you remember any of this? Does any of this look familiar?" Hershel shook his head no without batting an eye.

Janus tried to hide her growing hurt and frustration with Hershel. She was starting to feel shunned by him, as nothing had brought his memory back. She responded by putting her arm around Hershel's shoulders. "Don't worry, baby. I got your back. I know who you are and we will get through this together. Okay? I will never leave you. You can always count on me to be here for you. You hear me? You will never have to worry. Ok? So cheer up! We have a second chance at sharing our lives together. This is the new beginning many couples wish they had. Let's go sit on the living room couch; I'll get you something cold to drink."

The couple walked back into the house. "We can relax and I can tell you the fairy-tale story of how we first met. Would you like that?" Hershel nodded his head yes and Janus escorted him to the couch. She turned on the TV for him to occupy his time while she ran to the kitchen to retrieve his favorite beverage from the refrigerator. As she opened the fridge, she saw the familiar, dark-green bottle of Heineken beer and drew it out.

Janus sat beside Hershel on the couch, opened the bottle of beer for him, and placed the beverage on a coaster on the coffee table. She noticed that Hershel was enthralled by what was playing on the television.

"WE INTERRUPT THIS REGULARLY SCHEDULED PROGRAM TO BRING YOU THIS SPECIAL REPORT. ANOTHER YOUNG BLACK GIRL HAS TURNED UP MISSING. HER NAME IS TRINITY. SHE IS TEN YEARS OLD. THIS IS THE THIRD BLACK GIRL THAT HAS BEEN KIDNAPPED THIS MONTH. IF ANYONE HAS ANY INFORMATION AS TO HER WHEREABOUTS, PLEASE CONTACT THE LOCAL AUTHORITIES IMMEDIATELY."

Hershel picked up the beer and put the bottle up to his lips and took a big sip. He was disgusted by the taste; his face puckered up and he refused to swallow the liquid. He didn't want to spit it out, as he knew it would hurt Janus's feelings. He put the bottle back on the table as if to say, what was I ever thinking to ever like this foul mess?

Janus noticed, but avoided asking him why his taste in beer had changed. Instead, she took Hershel's left hand and placed it on her lap. She interlocked his calloused, masculine fingers in between her dainty, perfectly manicured ones.

"So this is how it all began, baby." She let out a large exhale while squeezing Hershel's hand as she spoke. "We met about twenty years ago at Horizon State University. It is a Historically Black College on the East Coast. We both wanted to attend a

Black College because of the extended family atmosphere and the pride we had in our community. You were there on an athletic scholarship as the star running back on the football team. I was a Public Administration major that had to work three jobs just to pay my way through college. I guess not all of us can bench press four hundred pounds, jump like a gazelle, and run through a brick wall to get someone to pay for our education," she laughed. Hershel's full lips formed a sly, closed smile as he struggled not to reveal his amusement in her statement.

Janus felt encouraged and relieved by Hershel's reaction and went on, as she continued to break down his wall. "Anyway, we were college sweethearts, very much in love, but we didn't exactly start out that way. I got an extra job tutoring the football players on the team and you were mandated to attend study hall by your football coaches because you were struggling in your classes. I remember when I first saw your fine, chocolate self. Ooh, chile, you were like an Afrikaner warrior holding a notebook in one hand and carrying a bookbag on your back. I wondered, where does this Mandingo keep his spear? The other tutors and I secretly called you Uumbatu the Afrikaner prince!" Janus mimicked in her best African male accent. Hershel spit out the liquid contents in his mouth he was reluctant to swallow and sprayed the entire coffee table as he found Janus's impersonation hilarious. Janus yelled, "Baby, you okay?!" She laughed along with him.

"Immediately, I knew you were a big deal, the way everyone around you catered to you. Right then and there I decided that you needed to be taught a lesson that wasn't in your books. A lesson called Humility 101.

"Even though you were the star player, I knew someone had to keep you in check and I instantly decided that that person was going to be me! That's right, I was the self-appointed Hershel bubble-buster!" Janus and Hershel shared a laugh for the second time.

"Baby, I think you viewed me as a challenge because I was the only one not guzzling the Hershel Rison Kool-Aid. And you were determined to win me over as much as I was determined to not fall in love with you.

"As the season progressed, you were performing on the field as advertised. Being this was your senior year, soooo many NFL scouts were flocking to your games and practices just to get a glimpse of the Horizon U Zulu warrior who carried a football like he was invincible. You had a promising professional football career ahead of you and everyone around you knew it. They were all waiting to cash in when you signed that big NFL contract. One thing happened on their way to riches, though; the cash cow proved he was mortal and blew out his right knee in the final game of the season." Janus lifted her arm to rub his bald head.

"My poor baby needed reconstructive knee surgery and his promising, lucrative NFL career vanished right before his eyes. You couldn't run, or jump, or obliterate defenders like you did before the surgery. Soon after the surgery, when it was clear that your football-playing days were over, all the women, the entourage, all the NFL scouts and sports agents and their empty promises, disappeared almost overnight." Hershel felt saddened by the thought of being abandoned due to unfortunate events that were out of his control.

"Baby, you were never seen with less than one woman under each of your massive arms before the injury. You could've had any woman you wanted and unfortunately for me, you tried to prove that fact every day I saw you around campus. You became very depressed. One night while walking home from one of my late-night jobs, I saw you by yourself on the dark, empty football field, lying in the middle of the 50-yard line in the fetal position, sobbing like a baby. As I approached you, I could hear you sobbing the words: 'Why me?' over and over again. Without hesitation, I sat down beside you and put your head in my lap like this."

Janus softly pulled Hershel to lower his head onto her lap. Hershel rested his head on her dark-blue denim jeans as she palmed his baldness. "I took you home with me that night and we lay with each other the whole night without saying a word. That night, I knew I would never leave your side no matter what happened to you. You were worth it to me then, and you still are. Not for what you have or can give me, but for what you allow me to see in your heart that others are not privy to. I saw the best in you then and I still see the best in you now. Nobody can take that away from me." Janus gave into the emotions she'd been battling all day and was consumed by anger. Her voice deepened and she yelled at Hershel, "Not even you!" hitting him on the shoulder. She belted out an ugly and uncontrollable cry, completely overwhelmed by her current circumstances.

There was a shift in the atmosphere, and Hershel grabbed her by the arms to stop hitting him. Hershel gently lay Janus's head in his lap and massaged her scalp with his powerful, masculine hands, just as she did to him on that lonely, cold football field some 20 years ago.

Hershel spoke for the first time. "Janus, I may have lost my memory, but I will search for and find the reasons I loved you and made you my wife. Please be patient with me and one day, the man you believed in and loved so hard and with so much passion will come walking through that door and sweep you off your feet again. He will make passionate love to you over and over again. He will kneel and kiss your feet and tell you that you were the only reason and his sole inspiration to finding his true self again. This is my promise to you, my wife."

Hershel stroked Janus's fine, silky, jet-black hair as she sniffled and cried herself to sleep. She wasn't sure whether she believed him or not, but chose not to ruin the moment by remaining silent. Hershel and Janus fell asleep on their living room couch that night, wondering what the future held for them, the same as they did in college in Janus's dorm some twenty years prior.

* * *

It'd been one month since Hershel had been discharged from the hospital. Hershel revealed to Janus that he could no longer sit by her side playing the submissive "Good Christian" role she wanted him to emulate every Sunday. He used to let Janus have her way without any complaints as a way to appease her and keep the peace. Every Sunday, Janus would faithfully resume her usual seat in the front-row pew on the right side of the aisle and never missed a service. Church was more of an opportunity to show off her latest fashion ensemble with matching designer bag, hat, and shoes. But it was Hershel that was her best accessory. She made sure they wore color-coordinated outfits by laying out his suit and tie on the bed every morning before he woke up. And for years he'd sit proudly by her side dressed to the nines, quietly keeping the peace while he died inside.

Janus's perfect church image crashed and burned miserably once Hershel jumped off of their "happy go Jesus" bandwagon. Hershel believed their church only cared about its own image and what is going on within its four walls and not what was happening on the outside of them. He also noticed that Janus didn't speak of her spiritual fulfillment or the reading of the 'living word,' even though she frequently caught the Holy Ghost by running around the church during praise and worship. Hershel clarified that "church" started once you left the building, not once you entered it.

Hershel confessed to her that when he attended church, he saw the preacher as a hypocrite and a self-serving coward. They argued about the church's "building fund" because nothing had ever been upgraded or repaired since they'd been attending. Hershel questioned Janus about where all the money was going, because she was the official treasurer and handled all their financial affairs.

Janus had an undying loyalty to her pastor, and she hated when Hershel questioned the pastor. She always replied, "Why you always coming at them like that? You know I cannot tell you the church's business, Hershel." Hershel always directed his statements to the church members struggling to make ends meet while the preacher lived a lavish lifestyle.

"His wealth is at the poor congregation's expense. And you don't even care. What is the meaning of this?" Janus never had a reply. He heard the whispers and gossip amongst the parishioners talking about one another. With the truth unveiled, Hershel despised all of the two-faced people who were critical of others in the light but just as guilty as the people they accused of terrible things in the dark. Hershel noticed the pastor's sexual innuendos and loose, flirtatious advances with the majority of the women in the church, and even a few select men. Hershel was also critical of the church that was located in the "hood" but didn't reach out to the poor and dilapidated community that surrounded it. This view on religion created a wedge in the couple's already fragile marriage.

Three months went by, and Hershel's memory had not improved. Hershel became very sensitive to the energy that surrounded him. He was very aware of human behavior that was egotistical in nature. He chose not to fraternize with those who had ulterior motives or were not pure of heart. He outwardly disregarded conversation that did not promote humility, selflessness, peace, inspiration, and harmony. Even though he knew his wife's ego was suffering for his actions, his newfound integrity, character, and conscience would not let him participate in the farce any longer.

Hershel had discovered a new perception of himself that was brutally honest and of the highest character, while always showing humility. He means what he says and says what he means.

He is not ruled or persuaded by money, titles, false pride, materialism, fads, programming, generational dysfunctional behavior, addictions, falsehood, or vanity. This caused a major strain on Janus and their marriage, as Janus viewed Hershel's standards as impossible to uphold.

Hershel was hypersensitive to the energy and attention that he and his wife received. They were both good-looking, articulate, well-educated, and had successful careers; Janus knew the attention they commanded. She used to love showing off her handsome husband at church by flaunting him in front of all the single women, and didn't like attending church without him. The Risons were labeled a power couple, and members always made "perfect union" comments at church functions. Everyone knew Brother and Sister Rison had the ultimate marriage for others to aspire to have.

Little did the people know, behind the scenes, the Rison couple struggled and fought just like any other couple. Even before Hershel's amnesia, Janus had always been living a double life. They appeared to be the perfect Romeo and Juliet power couple, except they were putting on a united front of deception. Janus always placed more value on the "perception" others had of their marriage than she did the effort it took to improve her actual marriage. This defect in their relationship had been further exemplified since Hershel lost his memory. Hershel could no longer live the lie. Janus had been lying to herself and others for so long she could no longer see the truth in the dysfunction of their seemingly perfect union.

Janus despised the "new" Hershel and his double-edged sword of truth. She asked why he had to be so forthright and self-righteous. She hadn't considered leaving him, because that was against Christian teachings. But it truly disturbed Janus that Hershel couldn't just get with the program that had been working for her for the last thirteen years. This new version of her husband was turning her world upside down. Janus didn't want to have to look in the mirror and find fault in herself for not accepting her new husband's awakening. To Janus, truth was irrelevant; to her, it was all about the conspiracy of silence and continuing the lie they had created. Janus was content with justifying or ignoring each other's dysfunctional behavior. This was no longer an acceptable reality to Hershel, and Janus was pissed!

Chapter Four:
Stranger In My House

Hershel's diet had also changed drastically, which caused him to lose thirty-one pounds. He only drank alkaline water and natural juices, no more of his favorite energy drinks, soda, or even alcohol. He juiced in the morning and only ate raw fruits and vegetables throughout the day. Hershel might occasionally splurge by eating a hearty helping of lentils or brown rice, but that was as radical as he got. Hershel had been rejecting Janus's cooking and she took it extremely personal. In one instance, after hours of cooking her Sunday's Best themed meal, Janus made a plate for Hershel and called him inside to eat. He sauntered into the kitchen, took one look at her plate, and declined her gesture.

"Thank you, but no thank you. I'll just have salad instead," he said indifferently. *I'm not interested in eating that slop,* he thought.

Janus watched her husband walk to the fridge to retrieve a bottle of water and medium bowl of kale salad, and proceeded out of the door. Janus was hysterical! She untied her pink kiss the cook apron, threw it on the floor, and stormed out of the kitchen into the backyard to confront Hershel. She emerged from the kitchen shouting in rage, stomping all the way to the swimming pool where Hershel was eating.

"Hershel, what the hell!?" Hershel blankly stared up at his wife, completely unbothered. Tears fell from Janus's eyes when she noticed his indifference. "You used to love my fried chicken, mashed potatoes, pork chops, mac and cheese, greens, pot roast, steak, ham, crab legs, shrimp, and all my delicious desserts. Now all you want to eat is these bitch-ass fruits, grains, beans, and raw vegetables." Janus cocked her hand back and knocked his bowl of fresh kale into the Grecian pool. Hershel watched his vegetables float atop the crystal-blue water.

"What, is my cooking no longer good enough for you? You are so ungrateful of the time and energy I put into preparing your meals. Have you ever thought about me and my feelings? Huh? Hershel, do you hear me?" Janus leaned forward, forcefully pointing her finger into his chest. "I have slaved in this hot-ass kitchen for your ungrateful ass, and this is how you show your appreciation? Remember, Hershel; who stood by your side all these years? You have put me through hell and I am getting tired of this shit. I thought my *husband* came home with me from the hospital, not a fucking rabbit!" Her eyes darted back and forth, searching for meaning in Hershel's eyes, waiting for a reply that she wasn't going to get.

Avoiding confrontation, Hershel got up from the pool, then picked up his bowl and headed back into the kitchen. Janus trailed behind him, continuing her loud tirade.

Hershel opened the stainless steel refrigerator and took out ingredients to make another salad. He spread out red onion, green pepper, kale, and quinoa on the marble counter with Janus looking on in disgust. The room was silent but the energy was tense. The only noise was coming from the crisp crunch of the red onion being diced on the cutting board. Hershel could have cut the tension with the ten-inch chef's knife he was using.

"What the fuck is this, Hershel? You're giving me the silent treatment now?"

"Janus, we don't have to go over this again."

"I am trying to be patient with you, Hershel, but enough is enough! You don't even want to throw down on the grill! What kind of Black man don't want no BBQ chicken, pork ribs, Tri Tip, or muthafuckin' peach cobbler? Now all you want to do is juice dry-ass kale and bland-ass spinach, you salad-eating pussy!"

Her words brought Hershel's movements to a halt. He looked up from the cutting board and shot her a remorseful yet fierce look. He was appalled by Janus's utter disrespect of his manhood, but still chose not to react.

Janus broke out crying, sobbing uncontrollably. "I have bought all this food for you, Hershel, do you hear me? Just for you! The doctors told me to make your favorite dishes because it may help to recover your memory or whatever, but I got to throw all this shit away because you wanna be a damn organic-vita-vega-damn-holistic-my-shit-don't-stink herbivore!" Hershel didn't look up at her and continued to chop his salad in silence.

"Your black ass was raised on this shit but now you too good for it? You practically ate McDonald's three times a day in college and you were an elite athletic specimen; now your punk ass is withering away right in front of my eyes and I'm supposed to accept this shit?" Janus banged her fists on the counter and lunged at Hershel from around the island.

Janus aggressively grabbed Hershel by his ears, shouting, "What are you trying to prove, Hershel?! I accepted the not 'feeling' church anymore bullshit, but now you are really pushing it." Hershel wiggled himself free from Janus with all of his might, but was careful not to hurt her or himself with the sharp blade in his hand.

Janus melted onto the floor, panting and weeping. "This is the most you've touched me since we've been home. Shit, you don't even wanna touch me, let alone make love to me! Tell me, Hershel; how am I supposed to feel? What am I supposed to do?" Janus stood up at the kitchen sink and continued to break down crying.

Hershel tried to console her but Janus shrugged him off. "Just leave me alone! You promised me you would come back to me but you lied to me! I don't even know you anymore!" Janus wiped her tears with the back of her hand. "I am living with a stranger in my house that doesn't even know I'm alive! Do something about this shit, Hershel. If you love me like you said you did, fix this shit and come back to me as the man I fell in love with. Because this guy can fuckin' kick rocks!" Janus picked up the Sunday's Best plate for Hershel and threw it in the sink, breaking the porcelain saucer. "All this shit can go straight to the trash, Hershel, just like our fucking marriage." Hershel went back to mixing his salad while Janus left the kitchen sobbing.

Janus didn't bother asking Hershel to sit with her and watch their favorite TV shows anymore. Before, they would make a big bag of microwave popcorn, pour some wine, and have a blunt on standby as they made their TV viewing ritual a staple in their relationship. From *Atlanta Housewives* to *The Haves and the Have Nots* and *Empire,* Janus must now watch alone. They used to talk about all the fools, drama queens, and deranged characters embraced on these shows. They made weekly bets as to which character would upstage the other in their never-ending race to the bottom, competing in the "who can be more 'ghetto' than the rest" contest.

Hershel didn't even watch TV, period. He used to love his favorite sports teams, the Oakland Raiders and the Los Angeles Lakers and Dodgers, and would never dare miss a game. Hershel put the "fan" in fanatic! Every game day he had to be wearing his lucky socks and underwear. He was as crazy a diehard fan as they came. Hershel would BBQ every Sunday like clockwork, honoring his long-standing football tradition. He used to have a house full of his buddies, ranging from his coworkers, his old teammates from college, and his childhood friend Red. Now the house was eerily quiet on Sundays. There were no more silver-and-black jerseys, purple-and-gold memorabilia, Dodger blue caps, buffalo chicken wings, Cuban cigar ashes, or cognac. The silence started to haunt Janus as she reminisced on the ruckus

Hershel and his friends used to make. She never would have thought that she would yearn for Hershel's rowdy company, otherwise known as his obnoxious, intoxicated buddies. Even that loud-ass Red, who got on her last nerve.

When Janus hinted that a game was on, Hershel didn't even acknowledge her. Hershel had lost all interest in his formerly beloved sports. He'd developed new interests and hobbies that expanded beyond the limits of his last life. Now, when a game was on, Hershel sat in his office reading books on philosophy, spirituality, astronomy, biology, chemistry, and metaphysics. If he wasn't reading a thought-provoking book, he was on his computer searching YouTube for the latest conspiracy videos, metaphysic lectures, and UFO documentaries. Hershel also spent hours tending to the new garden he'd planted. The garden gave him a sense of pride, and he hoped that Janus wouldn't complain about him anymore. Instead, she just complained that he paid more attention to his zucchini than he did her. The garden unfortunately drove a bigger wedge between the suffering couple. On more than one occasion, Janus relieved herself in Hershel's beloved garden in a passive-aggressive show of defiance.

Hershel seemed to have discovered his talent for nurturing and sustaining life. His garden was excelling at a shocking rate. He harvested the garden and used its crops for his food and homeopathic healing concoctions. With the herbs from the garden, Hershel made his own toothpaste, deodorant, skin moisturizer, aromatherapy, elixirs, and hair conditioner. Janus refused to use his holistic products because she didn't trust that they were safe. She didn't notice (or care) that Hershel's concoctions could help them cut back spending money on toiletries and items that were said to increase the risk of illness. Hershel had his separate hygiene products that Janus refused to allow in "her" bathroom.

Janus and Hershel were living two separate lives under one roof. Not once had Hershel entered the master bedroom since "the incident." In fact, Hershel slept on the floor in his office. He told Janus it keeps him "grounded."

Janus was very unhappy and was falling into a state of deep depression. When she cooked, she only cooked for herself. She stopped trying to figure out if her food was acceptable to her estranged husband. They didn't even eat together anymore. Janus prepared her meals and went straight to her bedroom, slamming the door behind her. Hershel prepared his meals, tended to his garden, and ate outside in the backyard. He has a newfound love for nature and the outdoors. He rarely stayed indoors anymore and could be seen up late at night gazing into the starry sky—the majority of the time, butt naked. He had completely abandoned the life he once lived. He didn't use utensils anymore, and would rather eat with his hands. Of course, Janus was disgusted with Hershel's new eating habits, and dared not ask him to escort her to one of their favorite five-star restaurants for fear of total embarrassment. Janus was at her wit's end to save her husband from himself.

Janus rolled out of bed and dreadfully checked her calendar to see what the day had in store. *Oh, dear God. Is that today?* She realized that Hershel's leave of absence from work expires today. She got out of bed and made her way down the hall to Hershel's office and knocked on the door. "Tarzan, I need you to put some clothes on and play normal today." Hershel opened the door and she continued to tell him that his boss at the firm wanted him to come by the office for an update on his progress.

Janus hoped that seeing his colleagues and a familiar work environment may jar his memory. Hershel had not worn any of his suits since the day he stopped going to church months ago.

"Please, can you put on one of your work suits? I'm tired of seeing you run around the house half-naked all the damn time, especially since I ain't gettin' none."

Hershel didn't understand why Janus was so adamant about him wearing a suit. But to keep the peace, Hershel gave in to her request. "Be ready in 45 minutes or we're going to be caught in traffic," Janus said, walking back to her room.

Hershel stepped into the shower and let the warm water beat down on his lean, muscular body. He washed his body meticulously, cleaning under his fingernails one by one, in between toes, behind his ears, all with his own natural products. Thirty minutes and ten wrinkled fingertips later, Hershel stepped out of the shower and proceeded to his office to retrieve a suit. Hershel had a hard time finding something to wear because the majority of his expensive tailored suit collection was now too big. Even though he'd lost so much weight, he was in the best shape of his life. Cutting out dairy had done his body great justice, and was the cause of leveraging his body mass index to 10.3 percent. He was very lean now, with beckoning pectoral muscles, protruding biceps, and a perfectly chiseled six pack. Hershel's face was also more slender and he kept it cleanly shaved to reveal his multi perfectly white teeth. If Janus wasn't so disgusted with him, she'd be all over him like white on rice.

He found a faithful old standby hanging towards the end of his assortment; a slim, charcoal, tapered silhouette Gucci jacket with soft, rounded shoulders, slim-fitting, crisp, black dress shirt with gold cufflinks, and a black tie. He stepped into a pair of black patent leather Salvatore Ferragamo wingtip loafers. Hershel felt uncomfortable about wearing animal skin on his feet, and became saddened by owning multiple pairs of calfskin shoes. *I cannot keep these shoes. I'll give them away when we get back.*

Once completely suited, he spent several minutes staring in the mirror, trying to figure out the man looking back at him. Hershel looked anew, improved, a hybrid of the man he used to be.

Janus draped herself in an expensive, black body-con Michael Kors knee-length dress and princess-cut diamond jewels that Hershel gifted her last year for Christmas. She wore her hair pulled back away from her face to show off her large, crystal studs, and donned dark-tinted sunglasses to hide the bags under her eyes. There wasn't enough mascara and concealer to hide her new, permanently depressed face. Dark circles underneath her tired, sunken eyes had claimed the face of this once gorgeous woman. Janus was breathtaking, and could have had a career in modeling if she wanted. But her denial of reality, eating destructive foods, rejecting and disrespecting her husband, was taking its toll on her. She stood in the hallway tapping her foot and checking her phone and watch for the time. *He's making us late; what the hell, Hershel?*

Janus barged in to see what was taking Hershel so long to get ready and there he was, staring in the mirror with the open tie around his neck. It seemed like Hershel had forgotten how to tie his tie.

"That figures," Janus noted sarcastically. She turned Hershel around like a child to fix his tie. "Is there anything else you don't know how to do that I have to do for you, Hershel?" Janus rolled her eyes upward and made her way down the stairs. Hershel seemed so helpless. How could a man of his height and stature seem so feeble and weak? *He can't do shit for himself.* Janus complained about Hershel all the way to her bright-red BMW.

Hershel was visibly uncomfortable in the suit and tie. He forced his index finger between his shirt collar and neck, tugging to create enough space so he didn't pass out from suffocation. Hershel followed behind her, wondering if Janus tied his tie too tight on purpose. Janus escorted Hershel to the front door on her way to her cherry-red BMW to drive Hershel to his job. Hershel abruptly stopped in his tracks and told Janus he had forgotten something in his office that he must retrieve.

Janus pulled up to the front door. Hershel hastily ran out the front door and jumped in the car. Janus wondered why he had to go back, but thought it better not to ask him. Hershel was in the car with his suit and shoes on, and that was good enough for her.

Hershel shielded his eyes from the sun as they made their way down the street in her sleek, smooth, hot ride. Janus cued the radio for the latest Keyshia Cole album via Bluetooth voice command. The weather was beautiful in the forever sunny California, but Janus felt uneasy about the task at hand. As she made a right onto the 405 freeway towards Brentwood, Janus prepped Hershel for what was happening.

"Ok, Hershel, look; your company benefits expire today. They are no longer gonna pay for you to be off work, planting and shit. Today is an assessment of your progress and to see if you can come back to work in the same capacity you left." Janus held the steering wheel at ten and two, without taking her eyes off the road. "I'm not looking at you, but I need you to hear me good. They are going to quiz you on the fundamentals of architecture and see if your memory is still intact. They will also have you draw a blueprint and schematics of a building you have designed. If you do not show them the things they need to see to start back working for them, they will be forced to terminate you."

Using the controls on the steering wheel, Janus turned down the music just above mute, and took advantage of the gridlocked traffic to look at Hershel above the rim of her dark sunglasses. "I don't know how you feel about the situation, but I have grown accustomed to a certain lifestyle that requires you to earn the salary you made before your tragic memory loss. My life will change drastically if you don't succeed. I deserve to live in luxury, Hershel. I have struggled my whole life to get to where I am and I for damn sure am not going back to eating ramen noodles and drinking cherry Kool-Aid every goddamn day!"

Hershel nodded, but didn't respond. Janus grew weary, but increased the volume of the music to distract her from the traffic and her husband's indifference as they made their way down the crowded freeway.

Janus and Hershel arrived at the architectural firm. They passed an elaborate fountain in the lobby, and Hershel was mesmerized by the marble stone sculptures in the middle of the lobby. He stood in front of the marble masterpiece in awe, as if it was his first time seeing the two giant lions standing on their back paws, spitting water out of their mouths on an enormous, shiny metallic golden sphere. He looked like a kid in the candy store when Janus interrupted his fascination and spoke under her breath, "Hershel, you are embarrassing me! Let's go! We don't have any time to waste. We are running late as it is!" Hershel put his left hand in the water one more time as if to greet it with a handshake and then caught up to Janus. They entered the elevator car and stood silently.

Janus and Hershel got off of the elevator on the sixth floor. The hallway was covered in dark-grey carpet, and the sound of their footsteps were absorbed by it. Ten feet down the hall, they arrived at the front door marked MASTER BUILDERS INC. The tiny, round-faced secretary stood up from behind the front desk when she recognized Hershel.

"Oh my God! Mr. Rison, it is very nice to see you! I almost didn't recognize you! You have lost so much weight," she said with a wide smile and bright eyes. "It is really good to see you!"

Hershel opened his mouth to respond but before he could, Janus intervened. "We have a nine a.m. appointment with all of the partners of the firm. We are running late; so, can you tell them we are here?" she said, adjusting her designer glasses.

"Why of course, Mrs. Rison," the secretary responded in surprise. *She must be one of them,* she thought. "Have a seat and I will see if they are ready for you." She pointed to a black leather couch in the lobby and whispered to Hershel as they walked away, "I hope you come back to work soon. I am rooting for you." Hershel winked his left eye back at her as if to tell her, "I got this!" but didn't say a word.

Janus caught wind of her husband's gesture and asked if there was something in his eye. He just smiled. "Whatever. Listen, just don't bomb this, Nature Boy! You need to focus on wha—"

"The partners will see you now," the receptionist told Hershel, standing in front of her desk with a sly smile, knowingly interrupting Janus's condescending pep talk. Janus pursed her lips with irritation, looking in the secretary's direction. "You two can follow me." The secretary led Hershel and Janus into a partner's wide corner office.

The office was spacious, with sweeping views of the city skyline. There were three white men in suits—one tall, one average, one medium height—sitting behind the thick glass-and-chrome desk. They stood as Hershel entered, surrounding him while exchanging pleasantries, making sure they walked the fine line of professionalism; not showing too much emotion. One by one, they shook his hand, holding onto it while patting him on the arm, giving their regards.

"It's been a while, Rison. How's it going?" asked the medium-height gentleman as he took his seat.

"Good to see you, Hershel. We know that you and your wife have gone through a great ordeal spanning close to three months now." He was ready to cut to the chase and not waste any more valuable time. He looked at Hershel seriously while adjusting his tie. "We have given you all the time we could to help you recover and eventually resume your old position with the company. Today we will decide if we want to keep you or if it is in the best interest for us that you vacate your position with the company permanently. Do you understand what is at stake here?"

Hershel turned the tables on his bosses and responded, "Yes, I am very aware of the circumstances and I am prepared either way to accept the results of your evaluation. But before we move forward, I would like to share a design I have been working on for about a month now. If this design is not acceptable to you, then I am afraid I will no longer be working for you whether I pass your test or not," Hershel said with confidence.

Janus's mouth dropped in sheer disbelief. She could not believe what she just heard. She stumbled backwards and fell into an awaiting chair. Her heart leapt into her throat, leaving her paralyzed and speechless. All the partners of the firm looked at each other in astonishment while the two men took their seats at the large, rectangular glass table.

"By all means," the lead partner spoke. "The floor is yours." Hershel walked up to the dry erase board with the confidence of the professional athlete he once aspired to be. He proceeded to take off his socks and shoes and placed them on the boardroom table. He then commenced to close his eyes and silently whispered his coma-awakening phrase, "Ranam Maho Darenge," as he dug his toes deeper into the carpet, repeating the phrase.

The firm's partners all turned around and looked at each other, confused.

Hershel eventually reached in his left back pocket and pulled out an old, wrinkled paper with schematics on it. He began to iron the paper out on the edge of the elongated table, rubbing it back and forth, smoothing out the wrinkles. He looked like a fourth-grader who did his homework at the last minute and was now forced to face the music in front of his teacher.

Janus sunk deeper into her chair, putting her right hand against her brow as if she was protecting her eyes from the sun.

Despite the shift in the room, Hershel remained confident in his method of preparation. He commenced, "Gentlemen, first I want to thank you for the opportunity to present to you this morning. I understand you are all very busy and I am grateful for your time. As you know, I have had amnesia for the last three months. During that time, I have been receiving visions from time to time of a structure that I have never thought about or even seen before. This structure not only blends in and uses the natural resources of its surrounding environment, but also resonates on a mental and spiritual plane. There is a flow of energy that permeates all things, and we must take it into account in our everyday lives and daily activities. This energy can either work for us or against us. Once we recognize these energies, we can utilize them at an optimal level to manifest that which we will." He paused to take in the dazed faces of the partners gazing at him.

Hershel continued, "I have designed a university or college campus that allows the students to not only study their given topics, but actually live and internalize what they are learning mentally, emotionally, physically, and spiritually." Hershel looked at his wrinkled paper. He held it up to the light and began to copy its contents on the dry erase board. Hershel began to draw what seemed like an Afrikan woman lying on her back with her arms and legs extended, similar to when one makes a snow angel. Hershel then started to compartmentalize the woman's legs, arms, torso, organs, and head. The firm's partners shook their heads in unison and seemed to blow out an excessive amount of air from their lungs, as if their time was being wasted.

Janus was across the room, flabbergasted! She could no longer watch her husband embarrass himself. She threw up her hands and abruptly rushed out of the room.

Hershel was unfazed and continued to explain his design. "So what I have envisioned is each part of the building's structure directly corresponds to the energy and essence of that specific part of the woman's body. For example, let's start at the feet, ankles, and legs. This area of the college campus will house the parking structures, as well as the engineering, kinesiology, biomechanics, and physical education department. That's because the energy centers of the legs of the human body house the transportation or movement of the entire body. The body cannot get from point A to point B without the activation and utilization of one's legs. This is the natural order of the body; thus, it will enhance the natural learning process of these departments. The students will have an innate understanding of the subject area and should learn more efficiently and have a higher rate of retention."

Hershel pointed to the crotch region of the body/building and continued, "As we know, this part of the body houses the reproductive organs as a way to manifest in the physical realm. So it makes sense that the biology department, business and real estate, and banking and finance departments are located here. Subjects that pertain to man creating and manifesting outside of himself to create abundance will be housed here. Money has always had a feminine connotation attached to it. For instance, the symbol of the dollar sign is ($) Comprised of two letter I's and two letter S's superimposed over each other. It spells ISIS, the Egyptian goddess of the sacred feminine. Her name real name is AUSET, where you get the word asset from. Finances are also attached to water, which is also feminine. As in Currency, Flow Chart, Trickle Down Effect, river Banks and Money or Moon which controls the ocean tides. Ships also have female names as they give Berth in water Canals after they have seen the Dock-tor and unload their Manifests.

"Moving up to the torso, in the stomach region will be the location of the university's cafeteria and food court, as well as the restaurant management, dietary and nutrition, and hospitality departments. The place in the building where the kidneys are located will be our waste management and custodial services department. The section where the lungs are housed will be the air-conditioning and heating departments, as well as the horticultural department whose plants provide us ozygen.

"Where the heart is located will be the boiler room and where the energy generators will be located. It will also house our philosophy, spirituality, and religion departments.

"As we move up to the throat area of the building, that would be the communications and language departments and the television and radio facilities. Are you with me, gentlemen?" Hershel paused to turn around at his frustrated and confused colleagues. Without waiting for their response, he continued with his presentation.

"Next is the right arm. In this limb will be the campus police and security, as well as the athletic facilities and sports programs. The left limb will house the child care and development programs, as well as our spiritual, healing and recreation centers. As we travel up to the location of the head of the building, it will be divided into three locations. The center of the head will be where our state-of-the-art solar-powered energy plant is located. It supplies the whole campus with renewable energy. The right side of the head will house our liberal arts department, which includes art, music, dance, philosophy, chemistry, spirituality, and creativity-based studies. The left side of the head will house our logical studies, such as economics, mathematics, law, linguistics, public administration, engineering, criminal justice, and architecture and design departments.

"The campus will be located on certain longitude and latitude markers that are conducive to higher learning. The university campus building in the shape of a woman will be facing east. As the sun comes up every day to greet us, it will illuminate the building where her reproductive region is located, to signify the birth of a new day. At the end of the day, the sun will set in the area of the mouth of the building to signify the building swallowing the sun, to announce the end of the cycle. This will remind the students of the opportunity and obligation they have to be better humans and strive to know themselves and follow their heart's desires."

Hershel put down his dry erase marker only to be greeted by deadly silence, mouths agape and empty stares avoiding eye contact in the room. Hershel smiled as wide as he could as he sensed the traumatic shock in the room. Without saying a word, Hershel neatly folded his wrinkled paper, placed it back in his back left pocket, and leaving his fifteen-hundred-dollar Ferragamo shoes and socks on the boardroom table, he walked out of the boardroom barefooted.

Janus was waiting downstairs in the lobby. She saw her husband beaming from ear to ear, with no shoes, and walking as if he was on cloud nine.

They never talked to each other the whole ride home, but Janus knew her husband would never go back to the firm again. Janus was silent, lost in her emotions. She feared deep in her heart that her husband was never coming back. She knew that her life would change drastically in the near future and she had no control over it. Janus was terrified, and realized that she had to conjure up any solution she could think of to save her husband and her current way of life. She thought of the unthinkable, and hesitated to act on her insane solution. *No. No, no, no, no, I don't feel like all that shit today. But I can't do this alone. I done tried everything...literally, EVERYTHING!* Janus never thought she would stoop this low but the situation left her no other choice. Desperate situations call for desperate measures. She would have to call Hershel's childhood best friend who lived in Atlanta, Georgia. Janus reluctantly picked up the phone with her shaking hand and dialed the notorious Red's cell phone number. The phone rings three times and Janus hears a familiar voice on the other end. "Boo G., is that you, girl?!"

Chapter Five:
The Transition Song

Back on Laun-Chi', an arid silence permeated the goddess's temple where she was being held captive within a makeshift torture chamber created by Yayvou soldiers. Glowing red, plasma shackles were tightly secured around Nekhebet's neck, wrists, and ankles. The pressure was monitored and intensified in fifteen-minute intervals by Commander Ammut. Each shackle was pulling her in the opposite direction, putting extreme tension on her neck, limbs, and torso. She could be pulled apart at any moment. But before she was destroyed, the Yayvou planned to forcefully extract every minor detail and secret about the universe that the goddess held inside of her.

Supreme Sovereign Sobek entered the chamber through the newly constructed titanium doors and looked up at Nekhebet hanging from the ceiling by her arms. Supreme Sovereign Sobek interrupted Commander Ammut and in his cold, calculating, hissing voice demanded, "Commander, what iss the statuss of your mission? Have you extracted any information from this feeble old woman that iss of any ssignificance?"

"Not yet, Supreme Sovereign," Commander Ammut reluctantly responded. "It's strange behavior. She seemss to be getting more ressilient and sstronger as I increase her pain and agony thressholdss." Supreme Sovereign Sobek arrogantly approached the goddess queen, tapping his claws on his chin as he pondered a clever weakening method. "I know a way to break thiss self-righteous female. Bring those ssix remaining Temkaay babiess which we kept to prepare a feast in honor of our victory!"

One of the Yayvou soldiers left the chamber and returned with a cart caged with red plasma bars in tow, carrying six innocent Temkaay children ranging from 1 to 2 years old. Nekhebet lifted up her weak, bloody, and bludgeoned head to let out a gasp when she saw her beloved babies weeping in terror. The six babies held hands and formed a strengthening circle, even in the confines of the cage. They were fearful for their mother's life, and hoped their unity would bring her strength. Supreme Sovereign Sobek witnessed her reaction and let out a hearty, menacing laugh through his devilish grin. Nekhebet struggled to wriggle herself free from bondage but was unsuccessful. She let out a loud, foreign wail that only a mother's love can interpret. Her babies were in harm's way, and there was nothing she could physically do to improve their situation.

Supreme Sovereign Sobek interjected, "Now that I have gotten your attention, do you have ssomething you want to tell me?" Goddess Nekhebet wept uncontrollably. The supreme sovereign continued, "There is no need for uss to wasste any more innocent Temkaay livess. Think about your babiess and their future. All I need iss for you to cooperate and give uss what we want and your babiess will not be harmed."

Looking past Supreme Sovereign Sobek, Nekhebet lifted up her head to stare in her babies' eyes and stopped wailing. Instead of addressing his comments, Nekhebet spoke directly to them telepathically. *"My beautiful and loving daughters. Your mother is so proud of how brave and courageous you are in this moment of uncertainty and fear. Your mother loves you so much and will not let anyone harm you. I ask that all of you trust me in the words I am about to say.*

"We are all really in a land of make-believe right now. This is just a game to see if we are worthy to live in the real world, which is a paradise where all the Temkaay are waiting for us when we decide to end this journey. None of this is real; it is just an illusion. Trust your mama and I will make sure you are safe.

"In order for us to escape this nightmare, we must not show any fear and must recite our Transition Song we learned at birth in order for us to wake up from this dream. Do you all remember the Transition Song I taught you?"

The baby Temkaay all nodded their heads yes in unison as smiles crept on their terrified faces. They felt reassured by their goddess mother. She began to chant and the babies followed suit on cue.

"Ahh Ma Ra Ahh Sa Da Ahh Say So Ho."

They repeated the chant over and over again and got louder with each verse. The babies were now playing a game similar to patty-cake with each other, slapping each other's hands in unison to the song flowing off their lips as they chanted louder and louder. The Temkaay babies were now in full-fledged recess mode as they slapped hands up and down, side to side, diagonally, rhythmically, in unison. Their innate luminous glow became more radiant as their tiny black bodies shimmied and wiggled with glee.

Supreme Sovereign Sobek and Commander Ammut looked on with frustration and confusion. They had seen enough of the Temkaay survival show and refused to allow Nekhebet to buy any more time. Supreme Sovereign drew his blood-red plasma sword and walked over to the barred cage housing the children. "Iss this what you wanted? To see your desspicable babiess ssuffer like their pathetic mother?" Nekhebet was fully entranced and didn't reply or divert her attention to acknowledge his words. "That's it! Open it up!"

Commander Ammut removed the top of the cage and Supreme Sovereign Sobek grabbed one baby out by her neck. He tossed the plump, ten-pound Temkaay baby into the air and sliced it in half as if he were swinging a baseball bat. The impact of the sword pierced the baby's thick skin producing a loud, gushy, crushing noise. Its lifeless body landed on the jade floor of the temple, but it didn't seem to bother the other babies.

"Ahh Ma Ra Ahh Sa Da Ahh Say So Ho."

Nekhebet and her babies continued to chant, oblivious of the unimaginable and demonic behavior of the supreme sovereign. Their utter disregard for his heinous behavior angered him more and ensued a rampage. He stared directly at the cage and yelled: "Another one!"

Commander Ammut ferociously opened the cage while Supreme Sovereign reached to grab another Temkaay baby. His claws danced around the cage, struggling to snatch a chanting, wiggling baby. Supreme Sovereign forcefully sank his claws into the ankles of another baby and yanked her out. He dangled her in the air by her ankles while she continued chanting. He lowered her into his mouth and viciously bit her small head off. Blood splattered on the walls and floor of the temple and on the uniforms of the surrounding Yayvou soldiers. The remaining four babies continued chanting with their goddess mother.

"Ahh Ma Ra Ahh Sa Da Ahh Say So Ho."

The other remaining babies and Nekhebet were now deep within their Transition Song. Even as the numbers diminished, the tiny Temkaay voices grew louder while focusing on the meaningful words of their chant. Their echoing voices and hand claps overpowered the noisy slaughter.

"Ahh Ma Ra Ahh Sa Da Ahh Say So Ho."

Supreme Sovereign Sobek threw the remaining Temkaay babies against each of the four chamber walls, smashing their heads. They died instantly, their lifeless bodies falling helplessly to the jade floor.

"Ahh Ma Ra..."

The Transition Song faded into barren silence. The only noise in the room was coming from Supreme Sovereign Sobek's panting and the buzzing plasma shackles around Nekhebet. Nekhebet seemed to slip into an altered state of consciousness and was unresponsive to the pain the Yayvou thought they had inflicted upon her witnessing her babies' murders. Her head hung forward with her chin buried in her chest, but they soon discovered she was still breathing.

The supreme sovereign was furious! He grabbed Commander Ammut by the throat with one claw and lifted him off the ground. "I am holding you personally responsible for exxxtracting the knowledge and wissdom from Nekhebet's brain! You had better do whatever you can and as fasst as you can or you too will end up like thesse bloody baby partss! I will be back in ssix hourss and you better have some good newss for me!"

Commander Ammut tried to not exhibit any fear and responded in a quivering voice, "Yess, Supreme Sovereign Sobek! I will not let my emperor down. You can count on me, Supreme Sovereign Sobek!" He melted inside as he tried to convince himself that what he'd just said was true.

Commander Ammut was shaken as he fell back into his throne and pondered about his own mortality if he didn't succeed in his mission. He realized that it would not be an easy task. Commander Ammut considered how he could extract the information without Nekhbet's consent. *I have tried everything I physically can to get her to talk; what am I missing?* He paced from wall to wall, crushing the remnants of dead Temkaay babies under his heavy combat boots. "Ahh haaa!" The commander had an epiphany. "I don't need her permission or her submission to get access to her knowledge. I will do it myself! Cut her brain open and get the information I need! I can perform sscientific experimentss to retrieve and extract the information for the supreme sovereign. This is it! I've got it!" Commander Ammut felt proud of himself and was anxious to get started. He rushed back over to the control console and removed his hefty utility belt. He withdrew a thick knife handle from one compartment of his belt, and under a leather flap retrieved a sharp, metallic blade from the assortment. After assembling the tool, he climbed the ladder to the height of Nekhebet.

The commander commenced to brutally saw away at Nekhebet's skull. Her pure, luminous skin was seven layers thick and required skilled effort to excise a significant portion. With the help of a few Yayvou soldiers to swap out knives and chisels, Commander Ammut cracked her skull.

His eyes widened at the sight. He discovered that Nekhebet had three sections to her brain! He found the two familiar right and left hemispheres of the brain, which most humanoid species commonly have, but also something extra. Nekhebet had a smaller brain in the shape and size of a black pine cone tucked away between the two left and right hemispheres; it glowed an iridescent ultra-blue hue. He speculated this to be the reason she had been able to live through their torture. *Is this why Nekhebet has not been accessible? I have never heard of this newly discovered third brain. Could this be how she's been hiding?* He stepped down from his ladder and stormed over to the console to record his findings.

In Nekhebet's middle brain, her interpretation of reality was based on past experiences that brought her exclusively love, joy, bliss, and harmony for the past hundreds of thousands of years of her reincarnated DNA. Pain, fear, hate, despair, distrust, anger, doubt, or pessimism do not exist there. She compartmentalized her thoughts, worldview, and interpretation of reality into respective parts of her brain. This section contained all her joyous and profound Temkaay memories of her past experiences that had been stored in her middle brain's memory bank.

While the commander pondered how to access her middle brain, Nekhebet's spirit was ushered into the depths of it. She revisited memories of raising her beloved Sutol. The immensity of her love for the Temkaay tribe was so strong that

Nekhebet drew strength from these memories to withstand the excruciating pressure her physical body was experiencing.

Deep within the archives of her middle brain, oblivious to all that was happening in real time, Nekhebet reminisced about one time in particular, when Sutol was only six years old and Nekhebet took her favorite Mino daughter on a special field trip. Just the two of them traveled across the universe and through multiple dimensions to visit a race of beings called the Unidentified Fathers Observing Science, or "The Observers" for short. These highly intelligent beings look a lot like the extraterrestrial aliens known as the "Greys." The Observers are approximately three feet tall with long, skinny arms, legs, fingers, and feet. Their short torsos resemble a five-year-old boy who swallowed a watermelon. Their oversized heads are disproportionate to the size of their bodies and are shaped like overinflated balloons. They have oversized, almond-shaped eyes that are pitch-black with two small holes for nostrils and a small, horizontal slit for a mouth. Their skin is bleak; a pasty, greenish-gray color.

The Observers were infamous for the 1954 alien spaceship crash in Roswell, New Mexico, around the site of the Area 51 secret air force base on planet Earth.

The Observers' planet was set up like one humongous science laboratory. Nekhebet and Sutol were completely fascinated by the elaborate science experiments being administered throughout the planet's facility. There were exotic animals and plants of all colors, shapes, and sizes from the far reaches of the universe housed in their open-air zoo enclosures. A young, inspired Sutol called the massive clear domes "animal bubble kingdoms" and she told Nekhebet she wanted to explore them all.

As Nekhebet and Sutol made their way through the museum on this foreign planet, they witnessed technical marvels in artwork, elaborate machinery and technology, musical instruments, intricately design textiles and architectural structures from different galaxies that were being displayed and studied. The Observers built a massive museum where they closely examined holographic planets from different dimensions in real time. They called these experiment planets terrariums, as they appeared similar to how humans keep fish in aquariums for in-home decor. The Observers studied the life of these particular planets but were forbidden to interfere with them no matter what they witnessed, including extermination, destruction, oppression, or total annihilation. These terrarium holographs were one thousand feet high and were housed in separate rooms throughout the halls of the massive museum. Once you entered each of the exhibits, you could see the planet spinning on its axis.

Within each of the rooms there are placards located on the walls that describe each planet. The holograms are roped off to prohibit physical contact. In front of the golden ropes are handheld controllers that enable museum patrons to zoom in on the planet to see the microscopic details and inhabitants. It is also capable of zooming so far out so as to see the planet's position in relation to its galaxy, and ultimately, the universe.

Of all the exhibits, Young Sutol was most enamored with one special terrarium. She was attracted to the bright-blue and green glowing colors that resonated throughout the planet and the wispy, white condensation that blanketed it. Nekhebet told her it was The Observers' number one experiment. Planet Earth, they called it. She told her everything about the history of this special terrarium:

"Hundreds of thousands of years ago, your goddess empress seeded the Earth's inhabitants with my DNA. Before me, the Earth had only basic plant life and just other simpler forms of life on a microscopic level. When I introduced my genetic material to life on this planet, the union evolved into a race of majestic, black giants over time. These giants ruled their world and had no equal for thousands of years. They built megalith after megalith with extreme and precise mathematical precision and artistic symmetry. This was considered the golden age of my children, who established highly advanced civilizations that have never been duplicated in the Earth's short history.

"My earthly creatures' earliest concept of God, or a Higher Power, was female. I, Goddess Mother Nekhebet, was the original God prototype for these earthly beings; they praised and worshipped me with all their hearts. After I established my lineage and legacy on Earth, I was very pleased with my results so I left them at their highest state of consciousness. I then proceeded to find other planets within the galaxy that maintained an environment that was suitable for establishing another colony of beings with my beautiful genetic material and highly advanced DNA. Hundreds of years later my sworn enemies, the Yayvou, began tracking me down through the scent of my genetic signature. They ultimately found me in the Milky Way galaxy, after stumbling upon this majestic, glowing, bluish-green terrarium now called Earth. You see, Sutol, the Yayvou immediately began kidnapping my peaceful, earthly giants and they performed unspeakable experiments on them. As a result, they discovered that my offspring, the Black giants, had a very high percentage of my DNA code.

"The Yayvou are a very crafty species. They have the ability to shape-shift. Being that their DNA is majority reptilian, they secretly populated the planet, introducing themselves to Earth as a species of giant reptiles. *Dinosaurs* is what they called themselves. The Yayvou thought they could overpower your queen's giant offspring with their massive size and powerful bodies. Much to their dismay, they would become extinct, as they were outsmarted by my more prominent giant, genius warriors!

"Thousands of years later, the Yayvou regrouped and came up with another strategy to overtake my earthly Black giants. They shape-shifted and introduced a smaller species of creatures called reptiles. Now they appear as lizards, snakes, dragons, crocodiles, and alligators. With these smaller, more elusive species, the Yayvou strategy was not to overpower with might and force like the former dinosaur, but to use more subtle devious tactics; deceit, betrayal, trickery, manipulation, fear, dissention, chaos, and guile."

The young Sutol stared blankly at the planet's hologram as her mother told her complex truths too heavy for her young spirit to bear. Her eyes began to well with tears and Nekhebet wiped them away with her bare hands. She felt her daughter was ready to hear the truth about the world.

Sutol responded, "Why, Mama, would they continue to attack you if you have done nothing to them? It doesn't make any sense to me!"

Nekhebet continued. "As they occupied the smaller reptilian state for hundreds of years, the Yayvou gathered all the intelligence and information they could in regard to my earthly children's strengths and weaknesses. They learned their habits by closely learning their mental, spiritual, and physical makeup. Once the Yayvou thought their reptiles had acquired enough information, their methods continued to change. Instead of trying to conquer the Black giants at large, the Yayvou secretly began kidnapping and experimenting on the weaker, elderly, and sickly of my offspring. They were either attacked by the ankles or from behind and forced into a comatose state and dragged off into the secret Yayvou base camp on the dark side of the Earth's only manmade moon.

"They spent hundreds of years grafting the weaker offsprings' DNA and slowly combined it with their Yayvou reptilian genetics through diabolical experiments. They tried many combinations, which often resulted in grotesque features, extra fingers, misplaced tails, and premature death. Most wouldn't live longer than a week, and their efforts were becoming futile. They played around with the dosage and changed the recipe to produce their standard of perfection. The result was a weaker, immature, less spiritual, and more animalistic subspecies. They called it the Saurian, otherwise known as the Neanderthal or caveman. Coexisting with my Black giants wasn't an option for these creatures. The Saurian species separated from my race of giants because they could not ascend to the mental, spiritual, and physical heights.

"The Saurians were forced to leave the giants' land of paradise in search of refuge in the northern caves of the Caucus Mountains, which is now a region on Earth called Europe. Living in this harsh cave environment of cold, damp darkness, the Saurians lost all their pigmentation and their innate ability to be humane. Being separated from the Black giants made simple things like compassion and empathy seem like foreign ideas. Due to the harsh, wet, and frigid climate, they shed their rough reptilian skin and started to grow straight hairs all over their pale bodies and faces to protect them from their harsh environment and the sun.

"The Saurians spiraled out of control, falling deeper into the abyss of barbarism by embracing animalistic consciousness. They embraced and celebrated their dominant reptilian DNA implanted by the Yayvou. The Black giant DNA was lost; hence, their lack of community or place in the human family went with it. From birth until death, their main objective is self-survival. They have no compassion for other creatures, as they see everything as a potential threat to their existence. They go through their entire lives in a state of fear and their only objective is to get you before you can get them.

"This new subspecies the Yayvou created did not instinctively possess the intelligence, spirituality, or knowledge of their goddess mother Nekhebet. So the Yayvou forced the Saurian back into cohabiting and intermingling with my giant race of earthlings. Their goal was to befriend them and earn their trust. And because my beautiful Black giants possess compassion for the lowly and pitiful Saurian, they welcomed them back into the human family in an effort to save them from themselves.

"The two species coexisted for thousands of years— perhaps a bit too closely. My race of Black giants started shrinking from a genetic defect caused by the infusion of the Yayvou DNA into their system. In fact, the Yayvou's Saurian subspecies began breeding with the race of my Black giants! The product, or products, were several different races of beings that populate the Earth today. Through the introduction of the Yayvou reptilian brain, all humans now have what the Saurian possess. The Yayvou can still manipulate this subspecies, which possesses the majority of their DNA, in an effort to control them through their thoughts, ego, animalistic behavior, and unwavering or compromising survival instincts. The more dominant the reptilian brain, the paler the skin of the earthly human. The darker the skin of the human species, the more of my DNA is lying dormant in that earthly human.

"Earth is now presently a prison planet. It is controlled by the Shadow Demons, who are employed by the Yayvou as the wardens to the Earth prison. Their sole responsibility is to keep the planet vibrating at a low frequency. The Yayvou have now installed their weaker subspecies, the Saurian, in power, and they rule the Earth with the help of the Shadow Demons. The Shadow Demons secretly populate the Earth in etheric form. They can only be seen at the corner of or the peripheral vision of the human eye, and for just a split second. They do not maintain any specific shape and can appear like various forms of dark shadows in human form. Although they cannot physically touch solid matter around them, they are excellent at manipulating the human species from beyond the physical dimension to do whatever they see fit. This is how they manipulate and rule the Saurian to implement their will in an effort to rule Earth from the shadows.

"The Shadow Demons have the power to predict the outcome of human behavior, because they can persuade humans in the direction they want them to take. This is precisely what the Yayvou needed to help them further enslave my divine children.

The Shadow Demons became well versed on human traits, so they created a weapon to feed human egos, fears, and insecurities, absorbing all the lower-level energy waves. It coaxes humans to embrace their lower selves. This invisible ray works to the demons' benefit by keeping a species enslaved without physical chains, for if a species cannot detect any physical restraints, it presumes that it has free will and is capable of free thought and action. The Shadow Demons are an intricate part of keeping my offspring at a low frequency in order to stop them from reaching their higher selves and activating my highly advanced genetic code lying dormant inside their DNA. The Yayvou know once my offspring raise their vibration, they will activate the DNA code I infused in them so long ago. Once it is activated, there is no turning back. It will only be a matter of time before they will resume their place on Earth as rulers, as my giant, Black geniuses!

"The Yayvou can also shape-shift and possess the Saurian for periods of time without them realizing it. When the Yayvou are satisfied with their intervention, they exit the Saurian body without the Saurian's awareness of the possession. During this time, the Saurian usually has no control over his actions or words. But one day, young Sutol, I will send you to this majestic terrarium called Earth. Your mission will be the most important undertaking you will face in your entire life! My child, you will wake up my sleeping giants and claim the world back under their control. This will set the natural order of things and we will have the paradise I have dreamed for all my children throughout the universe. But until then, my sweet, young Sutol, let's learn about all the other fascinating terrariums scattered throughout this multidimensional universe. There is so much for us to explore, so much for us to learn, and so much for us to experience!"

Nekhebet led Sutol by the hand as they skipped down the long, massive corridor of the museum filled with thousands of worlds of many shapes, vibrant colors and sizes, all being studied by The Observers. Sutol nearly yanked Nekhebet's arm out of the socket as she dragged her to the next exhibit, eager to learn all she could about new and exciting worlds waiting to be explored and liberated.

While Commander Ammut was preparing to make an incision into Nekhebet's middle brain, a Yayvou scientist scanned her body from head to toe with his sensor, looking for anything that might lead to the breaking of Nekhebet's mind. The Yayvou scientist was mesmerized by the pulsating, iridescent purples, turquoise, and ultraviolet jewelry around Nekhebet's neck, ears, and wrists. The pieces of jewelry looked alive as streaks of light and electromagnetic energy danced in unison, with each bead pulsating at a different rate and frequency than the others. Upon closer inspection, the Yayvou scientist discovered that one of the bead-like structures on Nekhebet's left earring had a brighter glow and its vibration was stronger than the rest of the jewelry-like orbs. He tried to extract the bead from the goddess queen's earring but received a fatal electrical shock and was instantly turned into a pile of ash. The electromagnetic force field surrounding the beads protects them from being removed from Nekhebet's body.

This grabbed Commander Ammut's immediate attention as he stepped off the ladder to closely look at the ashes on the ground. He stood up to focus on this unique bead. He stood silent for a few minutes, completely mesmerized by the rate of its pulsating speed. The commander spoke. "I want that bead! I will give any Yayvou ssoldier a month'ss ssupply of Temkaay blood to feasst upon for the one who can capture this orb for their commander!"

Nekhebet had her own gravitational pull, which forced the beaded jewelry around her neck, ears, and wrists to revolve around her like a planet revolves around its sun. It seemed impossible for the Yayvou to snatch this bead away from Nekhebet's strong gravitational pull. Hundreds of Yayvou soldiers used their weapons, claws, and brute force to pry this bead away but all received the same end result—death by disintegration. Ashes to ashes, dust to dust.

One of the soldiers was able to penetrate this unique bead with one of his sharp weapons before he combusted and was vaporized into thin air. Commander Ammut carefully retrieved the dead soldier's weapon and saw a tiny speck of fluorescent fluid on the tip of the blade. It seemed that the weapon had scraped or penetrated the glowing bead, which had left its residue on it!

Commander Ammut immediately took a sample of the substance and went to the laboratory to analyze it, while steadily stepping over a foot-deep pile of burnt Yayvou soldier ash coming up to his ankles. Commander Ammut discovered that the material within the bead contained the DNA, or genetic information, of a race of beings coming from the Milky Way galaxy. The material specifically belonged to a race of beings labeled as human, and more specifically, Afrikaner, from a planet called Earth that is located in the third position closest to its sun.

Upon further review, the commander realized that this race of beings held the most genetic information handed down from their Queen Mother, the goddess Nekhebet, than any other beings in the universe besides the Temkaay.

Supreme Sovereign Sobek was notified by Commander Ammut of his latest findings. "Supreme Sovereign, I told you I would not fail you! I have found a clue that may unlock the mysteriess of Goddess Nekhebet! We have located a tiny capssule around her ear that was disguised as her jewelry. In the capssule is the genetic information of a race of beingss she had her last contact with before we captured her. Thiss being may hold the key to Nekhebet's mysteriouss planss. Thiss creature is located on one of our prison planetss in the Milky Way galaxy. He is an inmate at our planet known as Earth, one of the first speciess of humanoidss they call Afrikaner today. They have a high level of Nekhebet's DNA but it layss dormant and has not been activated becausse of our basse we set up on their moon, which sendss out low-frequency vibrationss that keep them in a ssstupor, having no knowledge of their power or illusstrious passt. Our alliess and caretakerss of Earth, the Shadow Demonss, have an instrument that can pinpoint thiss human on Earth through a sample of hiss DNA. I ssuggest we ssend our finesst and bravesst sscouts to hunt down thiss vermin and desstroy him after we find out hiss planss."

The Yayvou and the Shadow Demons were close allies. The Shadow Demons had set up a massive base on the dark side of Earth's moon following the orders of the Yayvou. The story Nekhebet shared with young Sutol was coming to pass. From this base, the Shadow Demons projected a low-frequency energy wave on Earth that keeps the consciousness of the planet resonating at a low vibration. The Shadow Demons managed this lower-level energy as a coveted resource for the Yayvou. The Shadow Demons maintained and harvested Earth's lower-level frequency energy and offered it up to the Yayvou, who use it as a power source for their home planet and the fleet of warships in an unseen dimension.

The Shadow Demons were slowly changing the Earth's atmosphere to toxicity to keep its inhabitants sick, weak, confused, and feeble. By doing this, they could keep the humans on the prison planet Earth preoccupied with their own self-survival and feeble bickering with one another, oblivious to their real enemy. These earthly inmates bickered and fought amongst themselves and never united.

The Supreme Sovereign responded, "Excellent work, Commander; you have done a great sservice for the Yayvou. Unfortunately, you sstill owe me more. I want you to perssonally tend to thiss matter and go hunt down thiss so-called Afrikaner yoursself! You will have unlimited resourcess from the Shadow Demonss sso there will be no excusse for failure. I still hold you perssonally responssible for thiss mission!"

"Yess, Supreme Sovereign; I sshall prepare to leave right away," Commander Ammut reluctantly agreed. "I will not fail the Yayvou or you, Supreme Sovereign Sobek!"

Shortly thereafter, Commander Ammut loaded up his ship and headed out into the universe at light speed. He arrived at the Shadow Demon base on the dark side of the Earth's moon where he was greeted by Warden Eyetes, the leader of the Shadow Demons on the Earth's secret moon base.

"Gree-tings, Comman-der Am-mut. We have pre-pared for your arri-val and your mis-sion on Earth. I have re-acti-vated our star-gate lo-ca-ted in the Great Py-ra-mid in Eg-ypt un-der-ground in a se-cret cha-mber. It is pre-pared for your use. We un-der-stand that the fu-gi-tive you are look-ing for is of Af-r-ikan des-cent. I have ca-lib-ra-ted our DNA lo-ca-tor and it should work for you within the next sev-en-ty-two hou-rs af-ter you ar-rive on Earth. Then you will be able to find his ex-act lo-ca-tion any-where on Earth. If there is an-y-thing you need, please do not hes-ti-tate to ask. We are hon-ored by your pre-sence and are at your dis-pos-al."

"I will prepare to leave immediately; there iss no time to wasste! Have the sstargate ready for my departure. I will leave at once!" Commander Ammut responded hastily.

Warden Eyetes hurriedly escorted Commander Ammut to the stargate on the moon base. He gave the commander his DNA locator ring and instructed him on how to use it. There were knobs and buttons that required it to be handled with care. Following the commander's exact orders, he gave him nothing else.

Commander Ammut stepped into the stargate naked and was immediately vaporized into trillions of subatomic particles. In a secret chamber within the Great Pyramid's stargate, Commander Ammut's atoms reconfigured themselves; this time in a shape of a small albino lizard! Commander Ammut crawled out of the Great Pyramid slithering on the hot sand toward a group of European doctors that were touring the ancient sites. One of the tourists, a Caucasian male, sat down on a bench in the shade to find relief from the desert sun. Commander Ammut crawled through the foot traffic with agility and stealth and found his way beside the man's foot, then climbed up the man's right pant leg and bit him on his inner thigh region.

Instantly, Commander Ammut inhabited the European doctor's body. Commander Ammut, now disguised as the European doctor, went back into the Great Pyramid to retrieve his DNA locator ring given to him by the Shadow Demons. Commander Ammut found the tourist group and politely excused himself from the tour.

"Comrades, I believe I have had too much sun. Please continue the remainder of the tour without me. I shall return to the hotel and get some rest." He reassured his colleagues not to worry themselves and they all wished him well.

Commander Ammut flagged down a local taxi and got a ride to the hotel. For the next several days, he isolated himself from the group by saying he had not recovered from heat exhaustion. He spent all day and night plotting his mission in order to find all the resources he would need to locate the mysterious Afrikaner who was the last known contact with Nekhebet before she was captured. Commander Ammut's mission was to ultimately kill Nekhebet's Afrikaner inmate; but only after he found out why Nekhebet sent her to a prison planet in the first place.

Chapter Six:
Red

Janus had always despised Hershel's best friend, Red Thomas. She never understood the dynamic of their relationship, and hated the way Hershel defended him. He'd always say, Red's just been through a lot, take some time to get to know him, he's misunderstood. Or the infamous, you gotta let him grow on you. Janus endured Red's smuttiness for the duration of her relationship with Hershel, and within that time, Red was only successful in making Janus hate him even more. To her, Red continued to reveal himself as a two-bit, slick, womanizing, conniving, get-rich-quick, pyramid-scheming, no-good lying bastard.

Every time Hershel and Red took their annual "brocation," Janus would go days without hearing from Hershel. She suspected Red put him up to clubbing, gambling, womanizing, drinking, and smoking; behaviors she didn't think appropriate. But Hershel gave Red his undivided attention and unwavering loyalty for the extent of their brotherhood while remaining faithful to his wife. Even though Janus thought Red was a bad influence on her husband, she was desperate for Hershel's recovery. Red was the absolute last resort.

"How's my man doin'? I haven't talked to Hersh in months!"

"Hey, Red, please forgive me, but I have some serious news about Hershel."

"Aww, shit. What done happened, Boo G.? Did he choke on a piece of your dry-ass fried chicken?" Red never let up on the wisecracks about Janus's cooking and she hated that about him too. She sat on the phone in silence before Red asked her to continue.

"Three months ago, he passed out at the house and had to be rushed to the Intensive Care Unit. He was in critical condition, fell into a coma, and was on life support."

"Oh shit!" Red interjected, infuriated and shocked. "You mean to tell me my main man was dying in the hospital three months ago and your ratchet ass is just getting around to tell me?!" Janus held the phone away from her ear while Red's voice pierced through the speaker. Hershel stared at the phone with furrowed eyebrows, surprised at the reaction.

"You got me fucked up, Boo G.!"

"Will you calm down, Red!" she said. "He pulled out of it three days later and is doing fine now. He's at the house with me right now."

Red exclaimed, "Well then, why we still talkin'? Quit bullshittin' and let me talk to dat boy!"

"Hold on, Red, there is more," Janus continued, lowering her voice. "Hershel has lost all memory of his former self. He has amnesia, and doesn't recognize me or any other person that was in his life prior to his coma. He's doing ok but just know, he is not the same Hershel we all remember. I am forewarning you, just so you're not surprised. Okay, Red?"

"Whatever, Boo G. Let me talk to him; my boy will remember me, aight?!"

"All right. I'm gonna give him the phone, and maybe you can talk some sense into him. Or hopefully he'll rub off on you.

Here he is." Janus handed the phone over to Hershel. He looked at it for a moment before putting it up to his ear. Hershel cleared his throat to prepare for the impromptu conversation with the angry man on the phone.

"Ahem... Greetings?"

"Big Hersh, you ok over there? I heard you did a Rip Van Winkle and fell asleep on us. Just like black folks to try to get out of work, you going to sleep for three days, you lazy ass! Hersh, you know who this is?" Red inquired enthusiastically.

Heat raced to Hershel's palms and waves of wrinkles formed amid his forehead. This person's language sparked an unfamiliar and unsettling emotion within him. He responded, "No, should I?"

Red hollered back, "What!? Boy, you should! We been thick as thieves since we was six years old! Quit bullshittin', Hersh. I know your ass is probably playing stupid so you can finally leave that stuck-up wife of yours."

Hershel's eyes darted up to meet Janus's, only to find the back of her jet-black hair as she stared out of the window. Hershel sank into the back seat of her BMW.

"Your secret's safe with me, big homie! This is a great excuse for us to kick it like we used to; you know, since B.B. came along," Red joked.

"Who?!"

"You know, me and you 'Before Boo G.'! Lucky for your black ass I'm in town! So Imma come up and see you tomorrow and we can take one of those infamous Rio trips. I know all that fine ass and juicy Brazilian pussy should jar your memory if nothing else will. Put Boo G. back on the phone—uh, I mean your wife. I'm going to tell her to help you get ready for our two-week 'rehab and recovery' trip."

"Red, I'm fine. I don't need to—"

"Don't worry about a thing, big dog. I will smooth it out with her and let her know it's all good. See your black ass tomorrow—and don't flake on your boy! Imma take care of you, fam. Peace."

Hershel, confused, gave the phone back to Janus.

"You still there Red?" Janus asked.

"Yeah, I'm here, Boo G. Tell you what I'm gonna do. Imma take my boy off your hands for two weeks and I promise you, he will be back to his old, normal self by the time we get back. Make sure you help him pack for two weeks. Have his passport, wallet, and at least five G's in cash."

"Ok. Now, Red, understand something. I am trusting you. I have tried everything I could and nothing has worked. I hate to say it, but you are my last hope. Please bring my baby back, Red."

Lowering her voice to a whisper she added, "I don't know how long I can take this."

"Okay, thank you. See you tomorrow. Bye."

Janus and Hershel both stood on the common ground of uncertainty as they entered the house and walked to their separate quarters. Hershel made a beeline to the kitchen for his salad, and Janus went straight to the bedroom. She didn't stop by the kitchen for a snack, by the vanity to remove her jewelry, or the mirror to wrap her hair. At this point, she felt overwhelmed, underserved, and sexually frustrated.

She unzipped her dress, letting it fall to the floor and climbed underneath the plush comforter, stuffing a pillow in between her legs. A slight smirk crept onto her face as she flirted with the idea of attracting her husband once he'd improved after his "brocation" with Red. But after realizing how foreign the idea was, she faced the grim reality; there was a great risk of losing Hershel for good. Who was to say he'd even come back? *Did I just give him a get out of jail free card? Lord help me, this is too much.* Janus cried herself to sleep thinking about the endless possibilities.

Janus tossed and turned throughout the night. She had a series of dreams about the numerous occasions Red disrespected her relationship with Hershel. She never forgave him for his hand in the malfunctions of their wedding day. The night before their wedding, Red and the groomsmen insisted that Hershel join them for a nice, calm evening in the city. Even though Hershel wasn't fond of creating suspense in Janus's mind, he wanted to take advantage of his last chance at an uncensored and unprecedented brocation, especially the night before his wedding. Red led the pack of groomsmen to Las Vegas, where they racked up a hefty limo bill, bouncing from strip club to black tie galas, making out with escorts, and of course, the food and liquor. Hershel was hungover and two hours late to his own wedding. But he stood at the altar—with bloodshot eyes and a pounding headache—willingly and happily marrying the love of his life.

Janus woke up in a cold sweat, hanging off the edge of her bed. The sound of her car alarm stirred her out of her sleep and disrupted the peace in her neighborhood. She crawled across the scratchy carpet to the window and peeked between the curtains to discover a squirrel. Nothing to worry about. *Shit, glad to know somebody around here is getting their nut.* Janus crawled back to her bed a few minutes after silencing her car alarm. She picked up her phone on the nightstand to see several missed messages and four missed calls from Red, who was calling her for the fifth time.

"Hello," Janus answered groggily.

"Hey, Boo G., it's Red. I am here at the airport. Bring Big Hersh up here; we going on a trip! Make sure you bring everything I asked you for. Our flight leaves in two hours so the quicker you have him up here, the better."

Janus answered half-asleep, "Ok, Red, we should be there in an hour. What terminal are we going to?"

"Uh...Brazilian Airlines. Terminal B. See you. Bye." Red rushed Janus off the phone before she could even respond. She shook her head while putting the phone back on her nightstand and pulled the covers back over her head. She figured Red was using Hershel's illness just so he could go to Brazil and chase women, like they used to do back in the day.

Later, while looking through the house, Janus discovered Hershel in the backyard doing some type of Tai Chi exercise in the nude. *God, puh-leezz help this man.* Janus rolled her eyes heavenward and began looking for Hershel's suitcase to pack his belongings for the trip. To her surprise, his bag was already packed and waiting at the front door. *Oh?! I guess somebody's excited. I see one thing ain't changed. Still excited about that shit-ass friend of his.*

Janus about-faced toward the bathroom to jump in the shower for a quick fifteen minutes; long enough to wash away her lingering guilt, jealousy, and concern. She threw on her old, baggy, gray Horizon State University sweats, vintage Superman dad hat, and went into the backyard to find Hershel.

"Hey, Grasshopper, it's time to go meet Red; put some clothes on." Janus noticed that Hershel was not in the backyard so she searched in the house and saw him waiting by the front door.

"Do you have everything you need?" Hershel earnestly nodded yes without batting an eye. They loaded his medium-sized suitcases into the trunk of her cherry-red ride and headed south toward the airport. They sat in silence, preoccupied with their own thoughts.

Janus nervously clutched the wheel with both hands, at ten and two. Her sweaty palms and racy thoughts made her lean on the accelerator faster. *I wonder what he's thinking. Will he return the same? Ohmygod, I'll have the house to myself. What will I do?* Janus took her eyes off the road to shoot Hershel a quick glance while he stared out into the morning abyss.

I wonder if there will be fresh-squeezed juice available on this flight. Why is Janus shipping me off to a stranger, and what exactly does she hope to achieve?

The car slowed down, yielding to the congested airport traffic.

Janus pulled into Terminal B and double-parked at the designated curb for Brazilian Air. She flagged Red down as soon as she recognized him. Of course, he was wearing one of his loud orange and green signature linen short sets, a white Kangol brim hat, topped off with an unlit cigar hanging from his lips and a pair of those famous "you know your uncle can barbeque if he wears these" leather sandals. Red approached the car as Hershel exited the vehicle.

"Is that my main man?!" Red rushed him with a big smile. "Boy, you skinny as shit! I know Boo G. can't cook, but this is ridiculous! Luckily, ya boy came just in time to save your ass from starvation." Red flung his arms around Hershel and squeezed him tightly. Hershel stood still, limp in Red's arms.

"Uh, hey, Red...I, uh...I THINK it's nice to see you."

Both of the men let out a hearty laugh and they embraced each other even tighter. Janus became resentful of their closeness, even though Hershel claimed he didn't remember much about him, either. She rolled her eyes as she got into the car and drove off without saying a word to either Red or Hershel. She thought to herself, *I ain't even get that much action since he been home. Gay-ass bromance.* Hershel and Red looked up to see Janus speeding off and shook their heads in unison.

"Big Hersh, some things you are lucky that you can't remember. Don't even trip." Hershel reached down to grab his suitcase from the curb. Red continued, "So I guess it's me and you, big dawg! Rio and bad bitches, here we come! Just like old times! Hershel and Red back on scene! Or should I say, the return of the Mack!" Red put his arm around Hershel's neck and they both walked inside the terminal with their luggage. Hershel was a little confused about who this guy was, claiming to be his best friend, but somehow he found comfort and trust in him. An easy smile crept on Hershel's face as Red led him up to the ticket counter.

"Aight, Big Dawg, we have to purchase our tickets here. How much cash you got on you?" Hershel reached into his pocket for his wallet, but before having the chance to respond, he was distracted by an alluring scent. As he looked up from the ground his eyes meet a beautiful, dark-skinned woman crossing his path while she made her way to the Air Afrika ticket counter. Hershel's eyes slowly scanned the woman's entire exterior. He first noticed her scent, then her posture, then her striking features. She stood straight up, with purpose, and she had the glide of a true royal. Her short haircut was trimmed to a perfect fade, and complimented her high cheekbones. Her eyes were round, vibrant, and illuminated her dark skin like stars in the open night sky. Without a wrinkle in her fitted navy-blue flight attendant ensemble, her long, ebony arms and shapely legs moved in synchronicity with a dancer's grace. The brass and gold bangles on her wrists and neck clinked and clanked as she made her movements. Hershel was struck!

"Aye...Big Dawg?" Red continued trying to get Hershel's attention, but Hershel was hypnotized by this mysterious woman.

"Hershel! Pay attention! There will be plenty of that where we are headed! How much cash you got on you, man?"

Hershel didn't respond.

"Big Dawg, you hear me!? We need to buy our tickets now or we are going to miss our flight! Do you hear me!?"

Hershel slowly turned around and looked at Red, still in a daze.

"I am standing in the wrong line; I have to be in that one. I don't know where it's going but I gotta go there." Hershel gave Red a concerning look.

"Boy, I already made hotel plans and reservations for Rio. We will go there next time, I promise you; but we have to catch this flight right now," Red replied.

Without saying a word, Hershel picked up his luggage and proceeded to walk to the Air Afrika ticket line.

"Aye, Hersh! Hersh!" Red called out for him to come back, but to no avail.

"Hershel, what you doin', man?!! You got me fucked up! Come back over here; I'm in charge of your crazy ass! Janus would never forgive me if I lost your black ass in the hot-ass African jungle!" Hershel kept walking. Red continued yelling in the airport terminal, causing the attendants and concierge to stare at him, but Hershel didn't turn to acknowledge him. Red reluctantly submitted to Hershel and did a quick shuffle to catch up on the way to Air Afrika's ticket counter.

"So this is it, huh? You wanna go to hot-ass Africa? Janus was right, Big Dawg, you a wild boy; but you still my fam fa life. And judging by that fine piece you were staring at, maybe Africa won't be so bad. You still got good taste, my G.; I peep she had her head on straight." Red gave Hershel a nod and a quick pat on the chest with the back of his hand. "I don't think I have ever had any of that motherland pussy. Shieeet, just like the colonel of KFC said, the African woman is God's original recipe. And you know how finger-lickin' good that chicken is! My man, I know you know what I'm talmbout!" Red cracked up laughing. "Down for whateva, right, homie? Through thick and thin I am your boy!" Red stuck out his clenched fist for Hershel to give him a pound, but Hershel didn't understand Red's gesture. He grabbed it with an open palm, like it was a doorknob. Red shook his head as he and Hershel moved up next in line at the ticket counter.

"Good morning." The woman had a dark, tightly coiled Afro with rich, cocoa-brown skin, a gap in between her pristine white teeth and a set of full, rouge-painted lips. "And where are you two handsome gentlemen traveling to?"

Obnoxiously taking the lead, Red answered, "Hey. What's up, baby girl? Whateva the next flight out is, that's where we going. Right, Big Homie?" He looked up at Hershel. Hershel smiled and nodded his head in agreement.

"You're lucky. Looks like you are just in time to catch the next flight to Accra.

"Where the fuck is Acura?!" Red rudely exclaimed with scrunched eyebrows and a twisted mouth.

"It is the capital city of the West African country Ghana," Hershel interjected. "Yes, sista, we will take two round-trip tickets to Acura, thank you." Red shook his head as he pulled out his credit card and handed it to the attendant.

"No worries, Hersh, this one is on me; but just know, you owe me big-time! When you get your memory back Imma come looking for your black ass, you best believe that!" Red purchased business class seats for additional leg room for the two of them. Out the corner of his eye, Hershel saw the same stunning Black woman exit through a restricted door marked EMPLOYEES ONLY.

Hershel whispered to the ticket agent, "Excuse me, miss, can you tell me who that lady is that just went through your employee only security door?"

"Yes, I saw her go through but to tell you the truth, I have never seen her before." Hershel looked puzzled and dejected. He had a burning desire to know more about this woman, and the meaning of her name, whatever it happened to be. He hadn't felt this passionately about getting to know someone in this new life of his.

"Okay, Big Dawg, don't trip. I'm pretty sure you will see her again. But right now, we have a Timbuktu plane to catch or some shit like that."

Hershel and Red made their way to Gate 9 to board flight number 767 to Ghana, but first had to get through security checkpoints. Red, disappointed with his destination, was dragging his feet, clumsily plopping his body and belongings around and mumbling things under his breath. He didn't even care to hide his lack of enthusiasm. Hershel, on the other hand, was as excited as a kid on Christmas morning, and happily complied with the security guards. Hershel's compliance and joy made Red even more pissed. After getting through security checkpoints, they finally proceeded to the gate for departure.

The gentlemen sat in an unoccupied row by the window.

"Hershel, I can't believe you really got me going to Africa over Brazil. What is with you, Big Dawg?"

"Red, I felt it in my stomach, this is where I need to be. I am sure Rio is nice, but I am sorry to disappoint you." Red silently stared into the orange horizon while Hershel's words fell upon deaf ears.

"I'm not trying to hear none of that shit. You lucky I done seen and liked a little bit of what Acura got to offer. Bad bitches a-plenty in the motherland." Before Hershel could respond to Red's comment, they were both distracted by the gorgeous group of brown and black women draped in Air Afrika uniforms towing their minimalist luggage to the gate. The group of women formed a melanin rainbow. The pilot was a chocolate-colored woman who followed behind two bronze women. The three coffee-colored women leading the pack assumed their position behind the counter while the other three women proceeded to board the plane. The gate attendant announced that boarding would begin in twenty minutes.

Red and Hershel were both captivated by the women, and awkwardly gained consciousness with idle small talk about the weather.

"Aye, Hersh, you think it rains over there in Acura?"

"I'm not sure, but I do know it's hot, though." Hershel didn't know what else to talk about, and Red didn't know how much of the world Hershel was familiar with.

"Looks like we're in Zone 1. Guess that means we board first?" Red said, looking down at his phone checking the time: 7:15 AM.

The coffee-bean-colored gate attendant picked up the intercom and announced: "Good morning! Passengers boarding Flight 767, nonstop service to Accra, Ghana, we will now be seating passengers in Zone 1. Please approach the counter with your boarding pass out and ready."

"This is us, Red, let's go!" Hershel and Red gathered their carry-on luggage and headed toward the Jetway. They got their tickets scanned and boarded the plane to find their seats. Red was cracking jokes and flirting with the flight attendants from the desk to his seat. He figured he might as well make the most out of this trip with all of the effort he had. The guys sat down and got settled for their long voyage to the motherland.

Hershel picked up a series of pamphlets located in the mesh holder behind the seat in front of him and started browsing the snack menu. *I wonder if their salads come without chicken.* Red had already begun picking out the things he wanted to order. As they browsed the menu, Red started to reminisce with Hershel about their friendship to see if he could recall any of their past.

"So, Big Dawg, let's be serious for a minute. You don't remember me or anything we done in our past together?"

"No, Red," Hershel answered, without taking his eyes off the food menu. "You have a familiarity to me. I am comfortable and trust you for some reason, but no, my mind draws a blank when it comes to you or anybody else I have known before my drastic memory loss." Red shook his head in disbelief.

A beautiful Afrikan flight attendant interrupted their conversation while handing them sparkling water and bags of honey roasted peanuts.

"Excuse me, gentlemen, will there be anything else I can get you two while I am here?"

Red stared at the woman googly-eyed and salacious. "Is all African women as fine as you?! Shit, all I need is your phone number and the hotel you staying at when we land, li'l mama."

The flight attendant dismissed Red's rude comment, smiling and shaking her head as she turned to head back down the narrow aisle. Red sharply turned his head to check her out from behind and elbowed Hershel. "Maaaaaan! She definitely got her head on straight! Got damn! Boy, you see dat!? Hershel ignored Red's lusty comments. "Anyway, Big Homie, let me tell you about how we became such tight friends. You know, we considered ourselves brothas, so this is hard for me to believe you don't know who I am."

"I apologize, Red; I want to know. Will you please tell me? I felt a connection with you but I have no answers."

"Don't sweat it, homie. I tell you what; we gonna get you through this. We been in many tight situations before so this should be a piece of cake." Red snuggled up with his blanket, preparing for story time.

"We met when we was both six years old. Both our parents abandoned us; ain't seen them motherfuckers since. So we ended up living in foster homes for half our lives. All we knew, big homie, was that nobody gave a fuck about us and we was the only people we could truly count on. All we had was each other. When we turned eight years old, I made you hit your first joint and awwwww, man! That shit was hilarious! Baby-lung Hersh was coughing and cryin', talmbout, 'oohh, I can't sleep!' Little man claimed you was seeing a shadow figure tryna open the bedroom window to get in and fuck with you. Boy, you was paranoid as fuck!

"You claimed you wanted to quit smoking, but I eventually convinced you that you were not a quitter! We was blood brothers, inseparable at that. The motto was, we ride together, we die together!

"When we turned ten, I introduced you to our first hustle. We used to boost candy and snacks down at the Smart & Final store and sell that shit to all the little homies at school. We got so good wit it that we started taking orders a day in advance, and was delivering that shit the next day! Partner, we was Amazon before there was an Amazon! We had the whole schoolyard on lock selling that shit! The candy shit was just a prerequisite for years later, when we parlayed our skills into selling weed in high school and slanging crack on the corner."

Red looked up to Hershel's distraught face. Hershel could not believe the things he was hearing about himself. Even though those days were long behind him, he felt an unsettling grief in his heart. Hearing the story Janus told him about his football incident and his parents leaving him to the world made him realize that abandonment was a recurring issue that his spirit had finally overcome. He did not appreciate being told such heinous things about himself, and felt a sense of relief that he was so far from that old lifestyle.

"I can tell by your face; you really don't remember shit."

Hershel picked his jaw up off the floor without saying a word.

"You good, big dog? Should I continue?"

"Yes, Red. That will be fine. I want to hear the rest."

"Aight, well, by the age of twelve we were into bitches, and I taught you the pimp game. I taught you how to lie and manipulate the li'l hoes into doing your homework, giving you money, buying you fresh kicks, and of course, how to get your felt on."

Red continued, "Basically, I taught you everything you needed to know to make it out here in these streets. So, Hersh, as long as you remember these rules, you will be fine. Fuck a memory bank; you can made history with new ones. White people do it all the time. I'm telling you, Hersh, you gone be aight. Just remember Big Red's Six Rules and that's all you will ever need to make it in life. Trust me.

"Number One: Always look out for your motherfucking self! Always and in all ways! You married now, but that don't mean shit. You come before anybody.

"Number Two: Appearance over substance. Find your way to have the finest things in life—from food to cribs, cars to bitches— and do anything you gotta do just to get it. Look the part and play the part; that's when people will believe you *are* the part. Feel me?!

"Number Three: Ain't no loyalty in this game. Don't ever catch feelings. You kinda fucked that up with Boo G., but, whatever, you starting a new life, so fuck it. Ain't no telling what's waiting for you in Acura. But back to rule number three: Fuck loyalty. Hurt people before anyone has the chance to hurt you. Everything, everybody, and every relationship is temporary; nothing is permanent.

"Number Four: Take kindness for weakness. If you see a flaw in someone's character, like they being extra nice for no fucking reason whatsoever and they just giving you a bunch of shit, exploit the fuck out of it! Everything around here is business; ain't shit personal. Bury your feelings deep down inside you and don't let them ever get in the way! Shit, if you need to convince yourself that you ain't got them motherfuckers, that's cool too. Your secret safe with me. Always have been. But whatever, moving right along.

"Number Five: He who dies with the most toys wins! Get money. Ain't no other reason why we here in this life. It ain't that hard to figure out.

"Number Six: If they can't take a joke, fuck 'em! Fuck what they stood for, and you don't gotta explain yourself to no-motherfucking-body."

Red took a break to sip his brown drink. "Mmm, this shit right here is fire! Sheesh." Hershel sipped his sparkling water and wrung his face with disgust. The Alka-Seltzer taste and carbonation was too much for him to bear.

"Remember, Hersh, we didn't sign up for this shit! Our parents abandoned us first—we did not ask for this. We are victims of this society and nobody gave a fuck about us! Why should we give a fuck about others when it was so easy for our parents to throw us away like pieces of shit they flushed down the toilet?! Ain't nobody gonna get love from us until we get the love we deserve. How we supposed to sacrifice for others when ain't nobody sacrificed for us? If I'm hungry, I'm finna eat. Period. And everybody else is just in the way of me fulfilling a basic necessity in life. Feel me, bruh? It's me and you against the world, Big Homie! We took an oath. Don't let nobody tell you no different. All we got is each other, brotha. Don't get it twisted; we in this for life. Do you feel me, homie?"

Hershel was stunned! He felt an overwhelming sadness in his heart for Red. How can pain, disappointment, and abandonment lead a man to give up on the best in himself?

"Red, I don't know about our past. It really doesn't matter. All I care about is today and what we can build on in the future. I am grateful you stood by me all those years but sooner or later, we are going to have to move on from our past. Yes, I still love you like a brother and all I want for you is the best that I want in myself. I love you, Red, and no illness, crazy circumstance, or person will ever keep me from wanting the best for you. I will always keep your best interests close to my heart. Thank you for being my only family when I didn't have anybody to love me. My love for you is eternal, and I will never give up on you or ever forget what you have done for me."

Silence fell between the two men.

"Damn, boy, you ain't gotta get all soft on me. I'm just saying we gotta stick close together no matter what. I need you to man up with your gay-sounding ass! Imma get some sleep, Sweet Cheeks; I suggest you do the same cuz when we arrive in Acura or some shit like that, it's finna be on and poppin'! Aight, goodnight, princess."

Red fell asleep peacefully and effortlessly, as if he didn't have a care in the world. Hershel said to himself, how can a man so bitter and lost sleep so soundly and with a clear conscience? Hershel stared out the airplane window as the plane rose above the storm clouds. He was so enthralled with Red's conversation he didn't realize they were flying through a storm. It seemed like there was a whole new world out there as the plane ascended above the storm and was greeted by a crystal-clear, blue sky and the warmth of the shining sun.

That's it. There are times in life when everyone is going to have to go through a storm. The trick is not to stay there and accept it as your reality, but to recognize the power one has to change reality. All we have to do is change how and what we choose to invest our time and energy in. Losing my memory didn't have to be a bad thing. Why does Janus make me feel bad about it? If we just keep being optimistic, if we refuse to submit to our lower-level environment, we can rise above the storm and be greeted by the sun shining on our faces, which grants us peace, harmony, and an optimistic perspective in our lives.

My dear friend Red embraced the storm, and it has plagued his perception of self. Red internalizes the destructive nature of his environment. He is a powerless victim to the storm and is so far in the thick of it, he isn't aware that there is a sun just above his head waiting to shine on him and take away all his ailments. I don't understand why Red thinks he's okay. Well, he doesn't know any better. I wish my friend wellness, and hopefully this trip back to the motherland brings him as much healing as it brings me. Here's to rehab and recovery.

Hershel fell into a deep sleep and dreamt about the mysterious, radiant Black woman from the airport. He saw her in an open field with grass four feet tall. The sun created a golden halo above her head, and she was surrounded by colorful butterflies as Hershel followed her through open pastures. The two didn't exchange words, just eye contact. She didn't say where to, and he didn't ask. He followed her for miles and miles.

Twelve hours later, their plane landed in Accra, Ghana. The Afrikaner women on the plane let out a high-pitched yipping sound as the plane's wheels touched ground. The loud screams startled Red out of his deep sleep and he hit his head on the overhead compartment above him. Hershel, who was already up, laughed at Red's expense.

"What da fuck was that?!" Red exclaimed as he rubbed the top of his head. Red and Hershel disembarked from the plane and went through customs. Red was pissed off at the hoops they had to jump through just to get out of the airport, whereas Hershel was like a big kid and enjoying all the sights and sounds of the airport commotion. He was excited to be in another country, especially the place where history said his roots originated from.

Red had to continuously corral Hershel as he wandered off after every turn. "Hersh, you gotta stay with me, Homie. I have never been here and I don't trust none of these brothas! Stay close to me; I ain't about to let you wander off in this foreign country. I promised Boo G. that I'd have you back safe and sound. Please, brotha, stay by my side, aight?"

"No problem, Red," Hershel responded with a big, Kool-Aid grin. "But understand, I am a grown man and can take care of myself. I may have forgotten who you are, but this country seems very familiar to me and I actually feel more at home here than I do back in the States."

"Well that's all good and everything, but I don't trust none of these muthafuckas! A man that lets flies crawl all over they face and don't try to get them off, I gotta problem with!" Hershel shook his head as they continued to walk out of the airport and searched for a taxicab. "What? That's real shit." Red walked to catch up with Hershel and said under his breath, "They some nasty muhfuckas."

"My neegahs! My neegahs!" A faint, deep, masculine voice coming from a beat-up 1976 brown, Pinto station wagon, with fake wood paneling on the side pulled up beside Hershel and Red just as they reached the curb. "Are you in need of a tahxee?"

"Who the hell is you?!" Red responded. The driver stepped out of the car and opened the passenger-side door. He was wearing a throwback Walter Peyton football jersey, a New York Yankees cap, a fake gold chain with a Jesus piece and some scuffed-up Tims.

"My neegahs! My name is Enoch, but you can call me 'Eeee.' You are my Imedeekaan brudas! Get een! I can take you wherevah you want to goeh for chep! No problem."

Red and Hershel looked at each other in amazement. Red answered, "Anyone that called me my neegah is cool with me! Y'all prolly do drive-bys on elephants and shit, huh?"

Enoch hastily responded, "We must goeh ahht once. Please geet in!" Enoch opened his trunk and grabbed Hershel's bag and threw it in the trunk as Hershel entered the back seat. He went to grab Red's bag but Red abruptly stiff-armed him. "Uh-uh, back up, bruh! I don't know you like that, playa! Don't you be runnin' up on me! You don't know me! You betta back up if you know what's good for you!"

"No problem, no problem; I don't want any trabull," Enoch responded.

Just then, an airport police officer was seen running toward Enoch's beat-up car. "Stoop! Stoop, I said! You know you are not allowed heeyah. How many times do I half to tell you!"

Enoch jumped in his car and sped away, leaving a cloud of black smoke and dust that engulfed the officer, who was no longer visible out the car's back window. Red yelled, "Haaaa! This my guy, right here! You ain't supposed to pick us up, huh? You not even a cab! I didn't know they got Uber up in this muthafucka!"

"What the fook is Oohhbah?" Enoch inquired.

Red, Hershel, and Enoch all let out a hearty laugh that brought them to tears as they continued to plummet down the road. "You aight with me, E. My name is Red. This is my partner in crime, Hershel. We are going to be in town for the next two weeks so we need you to take us to a coo hotel. Think you can handle that?"

"No problem, mahn! Eee runs Accra like Jay-Z runs New Yok! Whateva you need, just ahhsk me. I am the mahn!" Just then, Enoch rummaged through his glove compartment and pulled out a beat-up CD he put in his outdated boombox strapped to the center console with bungee cords and duct tape. Out the blown out speakers they heard the lyrics from a Jay-Z and Kanye West song.

"Neegahs in Accra!" Enoch wailed as loud as he could out the car window.

"So I bawl so 'ard mudafuckas wanna fine me. But first neegas gotta find me. What's fifty grand to a mudafucka like me? Can you please remind me? Bawl so 'ard this sheet craazee. Y'all don't know that sheet don't phase meh!"

Red was in tears and had rolled onto the car's floorboard in the back seat. Hershel was content looking out his window, taking in all the sights of the mysterious but familiar country. The arid wind slapped him across the face and he became enchanted with the scenery and the smells of this foreign land. The people were different shades of brown and ebony. They were draped in colorful attire with intricate patterns. The merchants on the street were selling fruits, wood hand carvings, paintings, and other handmade jewelry and goods.

"My man E!" Red yelled above the music, gaining control over himself. "So you the man, huh? I want you to find us the finest Afrikan pussy yo city got to offer! You feel me? Every day I need a fresh pair of bad bitches runnin' through my hotel room. Can you handle that?"

Enoch started to sing, "Ooh, we doin': Big peemping we spending chess. Big peemping on B.L.A.D.E.s We doing big peemping up in N.Y.Cee. It's just that Jiggah Mahn, Peemp C and B-U-NB!"

Enoch then turned to Hershel, who was unfazed by all the commotion that was coming from Enoch's car. "So, my neegah, what can I get foe you? Ahhss, weed; just let E know and it's yours."

"First off...Enoch," Hershel reprimanded, "please do not use that word to describe me or any of our people. That word, *nigger*, symbolizes the fall and demise of the Afrikaner king and queen, which put the continent of Africa on her knees. It describes a beaten people who have been relegated to the white man's property and defined as something less than human. I know for you, Enoch, you are infatuated with hip-hop music and Black American subculture, but understand that word was created to destroy us and our civilization. It tears through the very fabric of our families, communities, and ultimately, our nation." Enoch was eyeing Hershel in the rearview mirror as he heard an uncommon truth spilling from the mouth of an American tourist.

Hershel continued, "Without embracing, maintaining, and protecting Afrocentric culture and ideology, Black people from throughout the diaspora will be lost forever without a chance of uniting or resurrecting our people back to the time when we once ruled the world with the foundation of our consciousness based on integrity, character, morals, righteousness, and spirituality. The vibration of that despicable word is rooted in destruction and defeat. Nothing righteous or uplifting comes out of the use of that word." Red rolled his eyes in disbelief, amazed at what Hershel was saying.

"Gentlemen, do you realize what the use of that word says about you? What if Martin Luther King used it in his 'I Have a Dream' speech? It would not have had the impact that it did. What if Malcolm X said in his speech, 'Niggas, by any means necessary'?" It loses its focus and direction. It loses its connection to the human soul. It disconnects you from your heart. It neutralizes everything good that comes out of your mouth before and after it is spoken. Are we supposed to celebrate the day when our babies first learn to speak that word? It saddens me, the manner in which we allow this...this lower-level vibration to just infiltrate our community and seep into our bloodstreams and become second nature to blinking, breathing, and sleeping. Remember; all words have a vibratory frequency that can either destroy or give life. It is a cancer that needs to be isolated, contained, and destroyed. It should be offensive to all humanity, not just Black people, as it is a reminder of how one word can bring a mighty, powerful, and intelligent people to their knees! That word that you so loosely use is the absolute number one problem within our community." Hershel was off on a tangent, and Red and Enoch couldn't get a word in edgewise.

"If you research all the travesties in our community, you will find this word is prevalent. It is at the base of every iota of destructive behavior that devastates our people. Police use this word to describe us as they brutalize, maim, and shoot us! Drug dealers that sell poison to our children define themselves and their customers using this word. Black-on-Black murderers describe themselves and the people they kill by using this word. The media, radio, and movies use this word profusely and justify it as art, and our babies are just soaking it all in. If you kill that word, our people will have a chance to redefine themselves. Of course, only by tapping into their best selves. One simple decision can change the direction of your fate instead of racing straight to the bottom and becoming the epitome, the very definition of the word. Young, old, East, West, light or dark, we all need to eliminate this cancer from our community and have zero tolerance for anyone who perpetuates its lower-level frequency."

Hershel stepped off his soapbox and reverted his gaze back to the scenery on the road. Enoch and Red were awkwardly silent and said nothing else for the entire ride back to the hotel. Hershel interrupted the silence with one request.

"Enoch, one thing you can do for me is take me to the slave castles where they held the Afrikaners captive before they shipped them off to the New World to be slaves."

"Yes, sir. I will take you to the most popular one. It is called Almina. We must go early in the morning because it is a tree-hour drive."

Red interjected, "Looka here, Hershel X! That was a great speech and all, but we gone have to made a compromise. Let's do this. We can go wherever you want to go during the day. We can do alladat historical, cultural, and spiritual shit you tryna do; but when the night falls, it's Red's time to play and you must—I repeat, you MUST—go with me. We got a deal, Big Homie?"

"Yes, Red. It's a deal," Hershel reluctantly agreed.

"Yesss it is a dee-Al!" Enoch cosigned.

"Shut your monkey-ass up, E, and just drive, nigga! Ohh, uh, I mean, my brotha!" Red sarcastically told Enoch as he caught himself while glancing at Hershel, mesmerized by looking out the car window.

Chapter Seven:
Twin Flames

There was a loud series of bangs on the hotel door. Hershel was up using the bathroom and Red was knocked out, sprawled out on his bed. The knock continued to get louder. Red came to and hollered, "Who the fuck is knocking at the door in the middle of the night like the goddamn police?!"

From behind the hotel door a voice called out: "What's up, my neegahs? This is your boy Enoch here to take you to the slave castles!"

Red replied, "I told you, come by tomorrow morning, nigga! What's wrong with you?!"

Enoch replied, "It tiz the moaning; it's five o'clock. I am right ohn time!"

Hershel, hearing all the commotion, exited the bathroom and opened the front door to let Enoch in. "What's up? E, come on in; you are right on time. Excuse my friend, he's still not used to the time change. But we will be ready in thirty minutes. Come on in and have a seat."

Red finally got up and staggered to the shower to get ready to head out. An hour later, Red, Hershel, and Enoch headed out the door and got into the car, headed for the Almina slave castles.

Three hours later, the trio arrived at the slave castle off the rugged but beautiful Ghanaian coast. Enoch said that he would be back in two hours when the tour ended, as he had seen it many times before, mostly by escorting Black American tourists looking to connect with their roots.

Hershel and Red continued on and joined a large group that was waiting for the next tour. It was a crowd of European families, other Afrikaners, and a mixed bag of foreigners, all mostly Caucasian. As Hershel looked through the crowd, he noticed that everyone seemed disinterested in the tour and were preoccupied with their cell phones—even Red.

As the local tour guide continued his lecture, it seemed that he was talking to Hershel directly, as if they were the only ones on the tour. "Now we will goeh down insite the dungeon where dey kept the Ahfrican slayves befoe dey wer lowded ahn da bowt to goeh to da New World," the Afrikaner tour guide explained as the group traveled down this spiral staircase that disappeared into the darkness below. "Everybaadee, please stay cloose."

As Hershel made his descent down the staircase, the air got very thick and hot as it filled his lungs. When he reached the bottom, he had to hold himself up against one of the sweaty dungeon walls that had visible human scratch marks, as if someone was clawing for their lives trying to escape. The lone, dim light down in the dungeon started to flicker on and off as if it was losing power. It created a strobe light effect, and Hershel's breathing seemed to increase with each moment.

As the whole group made its way down the narrow staircase, Hershel moved up against a wall so the whole group could fit down there. While Hershel kept getting pushed against the clammy dungeon wall by the group, he started to lose consciousness. To avoid embarrassment, Hershel positioned himself behind a makeshift partition used to hide the tools maintenance used to fix the deteriorating slave castle. Because of the crowd, Hershel was separated from Red and passed out without anyone in the group knowing his fate.

Hershel started to hallucinate. He envisioned himself washing up on the beach shore after almost drowning. It was if he was trying to escape someone hunting or chasing him. It was pitch-black as he crawled out of the water only to fall into a deep, dark ditch. Inside the bottom of the ditch he could hear the wailing and crying of what sounded like deranged little girls, or some type of ungodly creatures with high-pitched screams. Hershel was paralyzed with fear, as he could not move from the injuries he had sustained in the freezing water and the fall into the dark pit.

As Hershel tried to suppress his moans of pain so as to not let the creatures know he was there, suddenly, they pounced on him! All at once Hershel could felt slimy, sharp nails and teeth clawing and gnawing all over his battered body as he tried to fend them off. Hershel tried to let out a scream but nothing seemed to come out. He could not move as he felt himself being consumed by these shrieking and desperate creatures.

Suddenly, there was a loud bang! It was the slave dungeon door that had been closed by the tour guide as the last tourist made it up the staircase. Hershel regained consciousness and found himself in the pitch-black, stuffy, humid slave dungeon by himself. He scrambled to get on his feet and faintly heard a voice in the dark whisper, "Don't forget about me."

Hershel was startled and scared as he tried to find the staircase, feeling around with his outstretched arms frantically in the darkness. He felt the rails and stumbled up the staircase, hitting his shins against the hard metal risers, but seemed unfazed by the pain. He could not breathe as he ascended the staircase, hell-bent on reaching the top to his escape.

As Hershel's feet clanged up the stairs, the echo resonated throughout the darkness of the dungeon. Ultimately at the top, Hershel struggled to open the metal-clad door as he fumbled and fiddled with the latch. Finally, after what appeared to be an eternity in the dungeon, Hershel managed to get the door unlatched and flung it open as he crashed on the ground in the slave castle courtyard. The rest of the group was startled, as they had their backs to the slave dungeon and were rudely awakened by Hershel's antics. They let out a bunch of shrill cries from all the commotion Hershel was causing.

Hershel finally got up and dusted himself off as he looked around the crowd with his eyes squinted, trying to protect his gaze from the bright sun's rays. Half-blinded, he made out an image of what appeared to be Red as he steadied Hershel and helped him get his bearings.

Red exclaimed, "Nigga, is you crazy?! We thought Kunta Kinte came back to life and was looking for revenge!" The whole crowd burst into laughter like the roaring ocean sea and eventually dissipated as they continued with the tour. Hershel was still half-distraught but happy that he escaped being buried alive.

The tour guide wrapped up the tour by reading a plaque that Europeans had left to commemorate the Middle Passage. It was obvious Caucasians had funded the reconstruction of the slave castle and sponsored its tours to change the narrative. The large metal plaque read: "Even though the Middle Passage and the slave trade was a horrific time in Afrikan history, it also brought the religion of Christianity to save the continent." Hershel could only lower and shake his head as Enoch pulled up with his radio blasting an old Mystikal classic, "Y'all muddha fookas ain't reddaay! Here I goeh! Here I goeh!"

Red fell on the ground clutching his stomach in agony as he couldn't catch his breath from laughter. Hershel just shook his head and climbed in the back seat. Moments later, Red regained himself and entered the front passenger seat with streams of tears falling from his face. "You dat nigga, E! This dude right here?! Right here, nigga?!" Red looked in the back seat and realized what he had said. "I'm sorry, Hersh, but this dude is lit! You gotta admit,

E's the man! Oh, I mean, my brotha!" Enoch took off for the three-hour drive back to their hotel room in Accra.

Enoch dropped Red and Hershel at their hotel and told them he would be back later that night to go out on the town. Red walked Enoch to his car while Hershel lay down to take a nap after a tiring day. "Aight, E," Red whispered to Enoch. "Remember, I want you to bring two bad bitches for me and my boy Hersh. Here's a hundred dollars; you do what you gotta do to make that happen, playboy."

"No problem, Red," Enoch responded in amazement. "I know two twins that will blooh your mind. Trust your boy, I got you! They are having a party at Labadie Beach tonight. We shall goeh dere. See you laytah toonite!"

Red talked to himself as he walked back to the hotel room. "Did that nigga say twins?! I gotta find a way to take Enoch back with me to the States!" In the background, Red could still hear Enoch's music blasting in the background from his car, "I won't deenigh it I am a straight ryeduh you don't want to fook with me. Got the poulease boostin at me, but they kaant do nothing to a Gee!"

About four hours later, Enoch arrived back at the hotel door in his finest church clothes. Hershel was dressed in leather sandals, a plain, black T-shirt, an Afrikaner necklace and matching bracelet he bought at the slave castle, and Levi's jeans. Red came out in an immaculate, white linen short set and a pair of white Jordans. His shirt was unbuttoned all the way down to his belly button and he had three gold chains around his neck with his Gazelle frames.

The trio arrived at Labadie Beach, a tourist spot and a favorite for expatriate Black people that have relocated to Ghana. There is a community there that owns Black businesses and they come to the beach from time to time to reminisce about the struggle they had in their native United States.

As they moved through the crowd, it seemed everyone knew Enoch. Every ten feet or so someone on the crowded beach was calling out to Enoch to greet him. Enoch lifted his head up and inflated his chest as he received his ego boost from the crowd. "I told you muddah fookers I run Accra!" Enoch addressed Red and Hershel as they shook their heads and laughed in unison.

Finally, they reached a red velvet rope by the bar that said VIP. Enoch called a waiter over and he instantly let them in and sat them in a back booth. Right across the booth were two beautiful, chocolate, twin Ghanaian women. They both looked like a darker version of Serena Williams but with immaculate braids in their hair. They were both wearing beautiful, form-fitting Afrikaner prints with bold colors of red, orange, yellow, and gold. They both had golden Fulani earrings dangling from their ears as if they were dancing to the sway of their hips as they glided across the room to approach Enoch's table. Enoch had a big grin on his face as both Red and Hershel's jaws dropped to the ground. "Bruddahs, let me introduce you to Setau and Synepth. They come from my village in the Kumasi region in North Ghana. They are here to be your escorts for the evening." Both the twins spoke in unison, "It is nice to meet you; welcome to Ghana."

Red immediately rose up and grabbed Synepth's hand and spun her around slowly to check her out. "OOUUUWEEEEE! You a bad bitch if you was in the States Beyoncé got nuttin on you. You fine as fuck!" Red exclaimed. "She got her head on real straight, don't she, Hersh?!"

Meanwhile, Hershel got up and greeted Setau with a soft kiss on the left cheek and asked her if there was anything he could do for her. She politely said no, and the four of them scooted back inside the booth as Enoch excused himself from the table. "I see you all are in gooud company. I have to conduct bizness; time is mooney. I will be baack to check on you later." Enoch gave a stern look at the two sisters and winked at Red and Hershel as he left the table.

Hershel asked Setau if she would like to take a walk on the beach with him and she replied yes. Hershel escorted her by the hand out of the booth and they headed towards the dark ocean beach.

"Y'all behave yourselves! Don't make Uncle Red have to come after you because y'all being ornery. Enjoy yourself, Big Homie! If she can't jolt your memory loss, ain't nobody can!" Red turned back to Synepth. "Ok, so, where were we? I remember; I feel like the Nesquik chocolate bunny cuz you rich and thick and Choc-O-Lit!"

Hershel and Setau reached the ocean shore. Hershel kicked off his sandals and proceeded to take off Setau's shoes as well. Hershel spoke. "You know, Setau, I have something to tell you."

"What is it, Hershel?" Setau inquired.

"A few months ago, I was hospitalized in the States and lost all memory. I didn't recognize my friends, family; and even my wife! I just don't feel like the person I was before the accident was actually me. I don't feel bad that I don't love my wife anymore but I feel sorry that she has lost the man of her dreams because that just ain't me anymore."

"Do not worry, my friend," Setau consoled Hershel. "Love has a funny way of showing up when you least expect it. Love is understanding and forgiving; it keeps no records of wrongs. It loves unconditionally. Hershel, love has no memory. So if your memory loss is affecting your marriage, maybe you and your wife never really loved each other. And that's ok."

Hershel responded, "You may be right, Setau. I shouldn't stress over things I can't control. You know, since I have been out here I have sensed a wisdom and intellect from the Ghanaian people that seems more wise than any Americans I know. It's like you guys have the blueprint of life built into your DNA."

"Thank you, Hershel, my friend. You will goeh on to do great things on your new journey that has been ahssigned to you by your Creator."

Hershel pondered Setau's words and asked himself, "What does she mean by that? It's as if she has knowledge beyond the physical dimension."

Just then, Setau's cell phone rang. It was her twin sister, Synepth. Hershel could overhear her on Setau's cell phone yelling about how obnoxious and rude Red is. She begged Setau to come back and save her from Red's egotistical behavior and unrelenting advances.

"I am sorry, Hershel; I have to return to the pahty and save my sister from your friend. You stay here and I will be bach befoe you know eat. I love our wahk and intimeat conversation. I want to peek up where we left ahff. Please don't go anywhere. You promise me?"

Hershel assured Setau, "Trust me, Setau, I completely understand. Go back and handle your business. I will be waiting for you."

Setau took off down the beach back towards the party. Hershel was stunned by the athletic yet graceful stride of this beautiful and divine African female specimen. He could only shake his head and smile in amazement.

In the next moment, Hershel realized he was all alone. He could feel the warm and salty African sea breeze hit his face with the soft mist of every crashing wave. He suddenly realized that there was a full moon as he looked out in the ocean and the moonlight glistened on top of the ocean water as it danced on top of the waves. Hershel closed his eyes and got lost in the moment. This was exactly what he needed, and was glad that he made the trip back to the motherland.

While Hershel's eyes were still closed, he could hear what seemed to be a faint feminine voice blowing in the wind. "Help me. Help me. Don't forget about me; I need you!" Hershel instantly opened his eyes and looked around, trying to find the source of the voice he'd just heard. He started to scan the dark waters for signs of trouble or distress. Just outside his peripheral vision, Hershel thought he saw a hand reaching out of the ocean up to the sky, then suddenly sink under the water.

Hershel panicked and started to scream and yell for help but the party was too far away and the African drummers drowned out Hershel's cries for help. He had no other choice but to go in the water and try to save what he thought was a little girl he swore he heard crying out for help while his eyes were closed temporarily.

Without hesitation, Hershel jumped into the cool ocean water with all his clothes on and swam toward the spot he thought he heard the little girl's voice. He dove under the water frequently to see if he could see her but the water was pitch-black and he could barely see his hand in front of his face. Hershel went out even further in the ocean and started to dive deeper as he became frantic to save this little girl. As Hershel continued to dive headfirst into the water with reckless abandon, he hit his head on a jagged rock on the ocean floor. He was in extreme pain about ten feet down on the ocean floor and felt himself losing consciousness.

Just then, an ultraviolet light appeared at the bottom of the ocean. Hershel could hear the goddess Nekhebet's voice: "My precious Sutol, your queen is very proud of you. You are figuring out your mission that I assigned to you. Keep showing courage in following your heart and putting other people's wellbeing ahead of your own. This gives me strength and endurance to hold out until you complete your mission. I am counting on you. I dream of the day we will be reunited again; it's just not time yet. We both have work to do. Keep fighting; your queen knows you are there. Keep fighting...your queen knows you are there. Keep fighting...your queen knows...you are there..." Hershel's limp body could now be seen facedown on the ocean's surface, moving to the motion of the current of the waves.

Setau and her sister, Synepth, ran up to the spot where she'd left Hershel. Setau sensed that something was not right and immediately scanned the ocean for signs of Hershel as she cried out to him. In one swift motion, the athletic Setau barely made out an object on top of the ocean and swam a beeline straight to it. Once she realized it was Hershel, she swam even faster.

At the same time she reached Hershel's lifeless body, Red could now be seen at the ocean shore trying to figure out what was going on. Setau turned Hershel around with his back to the water and put her arm under Hershel's armpit as she side-kicked her way back to the shore with Hershel in tow.

Red finally realized that his friend was in dire straits and dove in the water to assist Setau rescue his best friend. Setau and Red managed to get Hershel out of the water and on the wet sand of the shore. Red started to perform CPR on his friend and became emotional. "Wake the fuck up, Hersh; don't do this to me, man! You gotta fight, homie. I need your help; I can't do this alone! You can't leave me after we came all this way. Fight, Hersh, fight! Don't leave me like all the rest! I need you, homie!"

Synepth showed up with the paramedics and they took over for Red's efforts of recovery. They put Hershel on a stretcher and carried him to the waiting ambulance. Moments later, the three climbed in the back of the ambulance with Hershel and the sirens blared into the night as the red ambulance light spun round and round, emitting their red hue on all objects they illuminated.

* * *

Commander Ammut was asleep in his hotel room, still in isolation from the rest of his professional colleagues. While he was in seclusion, he had been studying the medical books, documents, and papers of the doctor whose identity he had stolen.

Suddenly, there was what appeared to be a strobe light coming from the top of his nightstand. There was also a humming or vibration that was coming from the same direction. The commotion woke up Commander Ammut, who tried to block out the strobe light with his hand from his sensitive eyes as he reached towards the object. Commander Ammut instantly sat up when he finally realized it was coming from his DNA locator ring! His target was in close proximity to him.

When Commander Ammut looked at the coordinates of his target, he realized it was at the same hospital where the group of doctors were practicing. Commander Ammut jumped out of bed, put on his scrubs and white lab coat, and headed to the hospital.

Hershel was now in the Intensive Care Unit with Red by his side. Setau and Synepth were not allowed in the ICU because they were not family. They were waiting huddled up and consoling each other in the ICU waiting room across the hallway. Hershel was barely holding on for his life, a position he knew far too well.

Red was awakened by a hand that was feverishly shaking his shoulder. Red was startled for a moment, then regained his composure as he realized where he was and the circumstances that led him there. Hershel was still unconscious, lying beside him with several tubes going in and out of his mouth, nose, and arms.

"Good morning, sir," the Caucasian doctor with a European accent greeted Red. "Why don't you go downstairs with your friends from across the hall and freshen up? They are serving fresh coffee and have warm, wet towels for you. It will allow me to run further tests on Hershel and then I will be out of your way. Please do not worry; we are doing everything in our power to make sure he gets the best care possible. He should be up in no time." The doctor placed his hand on the back shoulder of Red as if to guide him out the door in a hurry.

Red went into the waiting room and saw Synepth and Setau fast asleep, leaning on each other from their chairs. Red awakened them and they all headed downstairs to freshen up and get coffee. On their way down in the stairwell, Setau suddenly remembered she had forgotten her purse and went back to the waiting room to retrieve it. As she headed back, out of the corner of her eye she saw what appeared to be a large, albino reptilian hovering over Hershel! Setau rushed toward the ICU room and flung the door open, only to find a Caucasian doctor taking Hershel's vitals.

"Oh, excuse me, Doctor. I didn't mean to startle you. I am sorry; please, forgive me." The embarrassed Setau rushed downstairs to join Red and Synepth. "I have a strange feeling about that doctor," Setau told Red and Synepth. "I do not feel he has Hershel's best intentions in mind. I have never seen him before; have any of you?" Red and Synepth both shook their heads no.

Synepth spoke up, "I have a strange feeling about him as well. Setau, remember that boy from our village that almost drowned? The one that fell in our village well?"

"Yes, I remember him," Setau answered. "Thirty minutes later, when we finally got him out, our villagers left him for dead. It was only that elderly woman that lives on the outskirts of our village in the bush that took him and three days later, he was back laughing and playing as if nothing had ever happened."

"I have a plan. Red, let's take Hershel to the medicine woman in my village. If she can't bring him back, no one can! I do not feel right leaving Hershel here with that white doctor. I saw a spirit in him that was very evil."

Synepth interjected, "Please, Red, listen to my sista. If she feels someting is not right, it is not right. Our village is three hours away. I can call Enoch and have him meet us here in thirty minutes and we can go!"

Red took a moment, then responded, "Ladies, I'm not into all that black magic African voodoo shit. I was born in Kaiser Hospital and I'm prolly going to die in Kaiser Hospital! I want to give the white man a chance. To tell you the truth, I was kinda relieved to see him amongst all the nigga doctors in here." Synepth and Setau looked at each other, perplexed at Red's statement. Red hesitated. "But I will go along with it. I mean, Hershel wouldn't be alive if it wasn't for you going in and saving him, Setau. Let's do it!

Call E and I will work out the rest. Escaping facilities undetected is my specialty. Y'all don't know who you fuckin' with!"

The trio ran back up to the ICU to keep an eye on Hershel and prepare him to leave undetected, as Synepth called Enoch to meet them out back in thirty minutes.

Thirty minutes later, Synepth got a text from Enoch stating that he was parked at the loading dock in the back of the hospital. Synepth told Setau and Red that it was time to move.

There was a nurse tending to Hershel, so the trio had to figure out how to get him out before the alarm went off when they unhooked all those tubes that were monitoring Hershel's vitals. "Ok, ladies," Red whispered, "I am going to the top floor to pull the fire alarm. When everyone is distracted I want you, Synepth, to get that trash bin at the end of the hall and bring it in front of Hershel's room. Setau, while your sister is doing that, you have the most important job. You must carefully take out all the tubes in Hershel and put some gauze and tape over his arms where you take out his IVs. I will be back to help load him in the trash bin and we will escape through the service elevator. Any questions?" Both the sisters shook their heads no. "Coo, so once you hear the fire alarm, let's make this happen. Remember, Hershel is counting on us. I'm going to make my way up to the next floor. Setau, you let me know when the last nurse leaves the ICU and then we will spring our plan into action!"

A few minutes later, the last nurse left to make her rounds and left the ICU. Synepth positioned herself down the hall by the portable trash bin. Setau proceeded to text Red to let him know that the coast was clear.

Suddenly, the fire alarm rang throughout the hospital as lights started to flash. It was a lot louder than expected as it screeched down the hospital corridors. Everyone seemed to go into an instant panic!

Setau started to remove all the tubes and wires from Hershel's person. Once she took out his IV, Hershel's alarm went off as well. Nobody seemed to pay any mind, as the fire alarm dominated people's attention.

Red arrived at Hershel's bedside out of breath as Synepth pulled up with the trash bin. Red carefully lowered his friend into the bin and covered him with blankets and pillows. "Let's go!"

The three headed to the service elevator with Hershel in tow. Just as the service elevator doors opened, they saw the Caucasian doctor that was mysteriously at Hershel's bedside coming down the hallway. He looked peculiarly at the three, then looked down at the trash bin. The three smiled at him as they entered the elevator and the doors closed.

Commander Ammut disguised as the European doctor hastily ran to the ICU to check on Hershel.

Once the trio plus Hershel reached the loading dock, they saw Enoch at a distance, blasting his rap music and singing, "I let my tape rock 'til my tape haat. Smoking weed and bumboo seeping on pryvaut stock. Way bak when I haad the red ahn green lumba jacque with the haat to maach!"

Red yelled out to Enoch, "Is you crazy, nigga!? Get yo shit started; we gotta kick rocks! They coming for us!" Enoch started his car and screeched toward the dock. The girls steadied the trash bin as Red picked up Hershel and took him down to the car. Enoch ran over to the back seat and opened the door for Hershel to be laid down.

Just then, the service elevator opened. It was Commander Ammut! He was irate and seething. He was having a hard time holding his shape-shift as he flickered back and forth from a hideous reptilian creature and the Caucasian doctor whose body he had commandeered.

All of a sudden, Commander Ammut let out a bloodcurdling scream that sent shivers down everyone's spine. Enoch jumped into the driver's seat and hit the gas as the trio hurriedly jumped in through the open car windows, as they had no time to open the doors. Commander Ammut made a death-defying leap from the loading dock to the trunk of Enoch's car in an effort to capture Hershel. Before he could get his bearings, Enoch drove under the hospital overpass and almost decapitated Commander Ammut as the force knocked him off the car and left him in a heap in the middle of the road.

Out of danger, Enoch turned up his radio and continued listening to his rap song. "Ahn if you don't knoe now you knoe. You knoe!" The trio never again spoke as to what they saw in the Caucasian ever again.

After a long, arduous, and treacherous drive through the bush, Team Hershel arrived at Enoch's and the twins' village just as night fell. They had to first go to the chief's hut to get permission from him to allow Hershel to stay. The chief granted them permission, and the crew headed to the edge of the village in search of the secluded medicine woman's hut.

Before they could find her, the elderly woman seemed to pop up out of nowhere and appeared in front of Enoch's car headlights. In her native tongue, she spoke. "I have been waiting for the chosen one. Take her inside at once. My goddess queen has given me the task to look out for her. She has almost drowned, and I need to attend to her immediately. She is very weak, I know. Leave us alone and come back in three days. Now, go!"

The trio looked at each other, confused, as she referred to Hershel as a woman. They took Hershel inside and left him with the medicine woman. It had been a long day and they hadn't seen their family in a long time. Visiting would have to be short, as they were exhausted and their number one goal was to make sure Hershel recovered completely. The moon lit up the village at night, as there were no streetlights—nor running water, for that matter. But there seemed to be a peace in the village under all the stars. This was the prime place for healing, not some cold hospital that has no compassion, love, or empathy. Red finally realized that Hershel was exactly where he needed to be.

Three days went by and Red had not been able to see Hershel since the time they first dropped him off. Red had been extremely quiet and reserved since their arrival. The twin sisters had been taking care of him, and the whole village had adopted him as one of their own. Since Red didn't have any change of clothes, he had to borrow traditional Afrikaner wear and walked around the village in his wrapped kente cloth and leather sandals. The girls teased Red and said they noticed a difference in him since he had arrived. They even noticed that he hadn't used the N-word since he had come to the village! Red seemed to show more humility and was not as abrasive and obnoxious as he had been since he'd arrived in Ghana. Red even spent most of his days teaching English to the kindergartners of the village. Red had never wanted children, but since he had been in the village, he couldn't seem to get enough of them.

Today was the day Red would finally see Hershel. He didn't know if he was dead or alive, as he hadn't had any contact with him or the mysterious medicine woman. The trio got word that the medicine woman wanted them to come by her remote hut at one in the morning. They all agreed to meet up a half-hour prior and drive to her hut on the outskirts of the village.

Meanwhile, the medicine woman was working feverishly in her hut. Hershel was sprawled out butt naked in her hut, lying atop a red-and-white colored kente cloth with unique designs, patterns, and images on it. There were candles all around Hershel as his sweaty, black skin glistened in the candlelight. There was a smell of incense that permeated the hut, and Hershel was covered with thousands of cowrie shells all over his body. The woman was singing a familiar chant as she shook a brush made of feathers over the top of Hershel's body. The medicine woman drank a flammable liquid and spit it over the top of Hershel's body. The liquid caught fire in midair as it came in contact with the flame of the candles and the whole hut lit up in the middle of the night. "Ra Ma Sa Sa Say So Hummmmm...Ra Ma Sa Sa Say So

Hummmmm...Ra Ma Sa Sa Say So Hummmmmmmm..." The medicine woman continued her chant and rituals over Hershel for hours at a time.

Suddenly, Hershel started to cough violently, as if he was choking. When this happened, the medicine woman chanted louder and faster, and blew more of the flammable liquid over Hershel's body. "RA MA SA SA SAY SO HUMMMMMMM!" Without warning, Hershel started to dry heave and eventually a giant, white snake slithered out of Hershel's mouth. The medicine woman cut off his head as soon as he exited Hershel's mouth. Hershel started coughing uncontrollably as the medicine woman sat him up and rubbed his back. Hershel had tears streaming from his eyes and was overwhelmed with gratitude and appreciation. He thanked the medicine lady for bringing him back, but realized she didn't speak English.

As she spoke to him in her native tongue, Hershel seemed to have a translator in his head that deciphered her foreign language. The voice told Hershel, "I have done my duty for the Great Mother. I always knew you would come. I am entrusting you with this mystical red-and-white kente cloth. It will always cure you of whatever ailments you have no matter how severe your illness seems to be. It will only have the power to cure you three times, and then it will no longer protect or heal you. Do not let anyone else use it. It is only for you, and may lose its powers if it comes in contact with others.

"You have a very important mission ahead of you and our ancestors have all prophesied the day you would return. My job is done; the rest is up to you. Beware of the white reptilian, for he will be your downfall if you ever let your guard down. Stay fearless. Stay diligent. And most importantly, practice humility." Without warning the old, decrepit Afrikaner medicine woman exited her hut and entered the bush under the moonlight, never to return again.

Hershel also steadily gathered himself and carefully put his clothes on and gingerly exited the hut. Just as he raised his head out the doorway of the hut, Enoch, Red, Setau, and Synepth arrived to greet him. No words were said, just tears of joy and group hugs. After about thirteen minutes, Hershel addresses the group. "It's time for me to go back to the States; I have work to do."

The next morning, bright and early, Enoch took Red, the twins, and Hershel straight to the airport in Accra to catch the first flight out. Enoch gave Hershel and Red a pound and wished them well. Enoch told them to stay in touch and if they ever came back to Ghana to look him up. They both agreed, and Red gave Enoch his prized Air Jordans as a token of his appreciation. Enoch was ecstatic, and immediately sat down on the curb so he could try them on right then and there.

Hershel and Setau hugged each other and closed their eyes tight so as to try to stop the tears as they got lost in each other's embrace. Synepth and Red shared an awkward hug as they patted each other on their backs and tried not to get too close to each other.

"Ok, you two," Red interjected, as it seemed Hershel and Setau would never let each other go. "We have a plane to catch, Big Homie."

Hershel spoke to Setau. "I will never forget you. You have not only literally saved my life, but you gave me a reason to live. I owe you more than you will ever know and one day, I promise I will repay you."

"No worries, my Hershel. You are here to do great things," Setau responded. "Promise me you will always follow your heart and show compassion for those less fortunate than you. I am certain that we will meet again."

Red and Hershel walked into the terminal and looked back to see Enoch and the twins waving back at them. All Hershel had was one brown bag with his red-and-white kente cloth in it and

Red was emptyhanded, as he had left all his possessions he'd brought with Enoch. "Well, Big Homie, it seems like you don't need to get your old memory back as fast, as you are creating new ones! Looks like you got a do-over in life. I kinda envy you for that. Let's get on this plane and get back to our miserable lives."

Hershel turned to Red and said, "You know what, Red?"

"What's that, Hersh?"

"Setau had her head on straight, didn't she?"

Red burst out laughing, "That she did, Big Homie. That she did!" Hershel and Red boarded their flight as Enoch and the twins watched them take off standing beside the outdoor perimeter fence of the airport.

While on the plane, Hershel went to sleep almost instantly. Red stayed up for a little while longer, nursing his drink, before he got sleepy. Red asked the flight attendant for a blanket because the plane was getting cold. The flight attendant informed Red that there was a shortage of blankets and there weren't any more. Red tossed and turned, trying to find a position that was comfortable, but it never lasted too long. Half-asleep, Red knocked Hershel's bag out of his sleeping hands. His red-and-white kente cloth fell on the airplane floor. Red picked it up and covered his body from head to toe and instantly fell asleep like a newborn baby.

At that moment, Hershel had a crazy dream about Red. Hershel instantly dreamed of Red back in the days when they first met in the foster home. Hershel found out that Red's mother dropped him off there when he was six years old because Red was the spitting image of his father, who date-raped his mother in college. She could not stand to see him because when she gazed in her son's eyes, she saw the man that took advantage of her trust, drugged her, and brutally gang-raped her and left her to fend for herself.

While in foster care, Hershel discovered that Red was molested by one of the foster care chaplains that came to preach the gospel every Sunday without anyone knowing it. Hershel now understood Red's disdain for women and his macho attitude as to why Red always thought he had to prove his manhood and always felt disrespected by the slightest occurrence. Red was very disrespectful to all women and very anti-religion—or any authority figure, for that matter.

When the plane touched down, Hershel was startled out of his deep sleep by Red sobbing uncontrollably. Hershel tried to console his friend and they wound up being the last two passengers left on the plane. Finally, Red pulled himself together and they both walked off the plane with Hershel supporting his friend by holding Red up around his waist and Red's arm over Hershel's shoulder.

As they disembarked from the plane, a flight attendant rushed to the two men. She had found Hershel's magical kente cloth on the floor by Red's seat. Hershel retrieved his cloth and realized that Red had used it. Hershel now realized that his good friend was now healed of all his past traumatic incidents he had experienced as a child.

No one spoke to each other on the ride home. Once they reached Hershel's house, they both embraced without saying a word. No words needed to be said. Red turned around and walked to his car as Hershel entered his doorway and closed his door. Tears welled up in Hershel's eyes and they involuntarily ran down his cheeks. Hershel instinctively knew that this was the last time he would ever see his childhood friend again. "Goodbye, my friend," Hershel spoke to himself. "You are now free to live your life for the first time in a long time. Rise above the storm and don't ever look down."

Chapter Eight:
Me & Pu

Hershel continued to stare at the ceiling of his bedroom in a restless and anxious state. He turned and looked at the clock on the wall to his right, only to notice it was glaring right back at him with its glowing scowl. The clock continued to stare back at him, silently antagonizing his insomnia with its unapologetic and relentless display of 3:33 AM. Hershel quietly excused himself from the bed he occupied with his wife. Janus was sound asleep and dead to the world.

As Hershel reluctantly ruffled the sheets in his escape, Janus let out a sigh and rolled over to her side of the bed, threatening to wake up from her slumber. Hershel was in stealth mode as he picked up his luggage by the closet that he'd taken on his recent African trip. The suitcase was still packed, as he hadn't had time to sort out his belongings; he had been back for only a few days.

Hershel set the suitcase in the hallway outside the bedroom door as he tiptoed to the bathroom, holding his handy Swiss Army knife his friend Red gave him in one hand and his wallet Janus bought for him in the other. Hershel stood over the bathroom sink and looked at his reflection in the medicine cabinet mirror looking back at him. He got lost in the gaze of the man looking back at him, whom he didn't recognize. It had been months since he'd lost his memory and he was still no closer to knowing who he was since that tragic day.

Tears started to well up in Hershel's eyes. His vision became blurry from the accumulation of liquid obstructing his view of the mirror in front of him. Finally, the weight of the burden of Hershel's tears released themselves down both sides of his face in a race to the bottom of his chin. The image in the mirror began to come more into focus. Hershel felt he had no other choice but to kill the person he saw in front of him so he could have a clean slate with no prejudice, no preconceived notions, no expectations from others or deeply ingrained programming as to what everyone else told him he is.

Hershel commenced to take his Swiss Army knife and held it under his chin. He held it there for what seemed like an eternity and then gently put the knife down to the sink. Hershel slowly pushed the blade back in the knife and carefully pulled out the scissors. He turned his wallet upside down and emptied its contents into the sink. Out fell his driver's license, social security card, and all his credit cards—and even a fat wad of $100 bills his wife and his friend Red gave him for his trip. Hershel proceeded to cut up all the contents in the sink into tiny little pieces with his Swiss Army knife.

Minutes later, Hershel looked down at the sink only to discover a mound of confetti made out of cut-up plastic cards and $100 bills. Hershel wiped his eyes clean, walked out of the bathroom, and gently peered into his bedroom to look at Janus one more time. She looked so peaceful in her sleep as the moonlight peered through the bedroom window and caressed her face ever so gently. If only he could have given her the peace she seemed to be experiencing now.

He silently closed the bedroom door and disappeared into the dark hallway. Hershel grabbed his suitcase by their bedroom door and headed toward the front door. He stopped at the threshold of the door and abruptly grabbed a pen and paper from the mantel.

My beloved Janus,

I know I will never comprehend the pain you must be in, to look into your husband's eyes, the man you vowed to spend the rest of your life with, and not have him recognize and reciprocate the love you once shared. It must be agonizing to watch me so closely but feel so distant as this stranger walks around in your house, wearing your husband's clothes, sounding like him, looking like him, but he might as well be miles and miles away. My deepest condolences and sympathy to you, as I apologize from the bottom of my heart that I cannot be him anymore.

It breaks my heart to leave you, but my heart tells me I must go. It is now time for me to find out who I have become. I can no longer serve you in the capacity of your husband. I do not want to keep torturing you with my presence and perceived incompetence and heartlessness. I'm not leaving to run away from a difficult situation, but moving towards the solution to the painful predicament we both find ourselves in. I hope one day you will find in a man everything and more than you saw in me. I know you will be rewarded for your patience and understanding for your undying love and vulnerability but as of now, things will feel worse before they can get better.

It was never my intention to hurt or disappoint you. It was never my intention to let you down and disappoint you. Maybe one day we will meet again for the first time and you'll embrace me for the man I have become. Thank you again for putting up with me and believing that I would return to you. It hurts my heart that I couldn't return your husband back to you. I will always be grateful for what you did for me and will never forget you. Please do not blame yourself. This is not your fault. This is how it has to be and the sooner we both embrace it, the better things will be. I love you.

Hershel set the pen and paper gently back on the mantel. The front door creaked as he consciously tried to made as little noise as possible. First he squeezed his suitcase through the small opening, then he stepped through with his left foot first, closely followed by his right. Hershel gingerly closed the door behind him.

He instantly felt the cold rain attack his body from above. It was too late to go back in, as he had already locked himself out. *Maybe I should have thought this through more clearly? Maybe I shouldn't have been so spontaneous in my decision to leave so abruptly?* Hershel thought to himself. It didn't matter now. There was no turning back.

Hershel lived in a rural suburb that had no sidewalks along the highway. With the torrential downpour, the visibility from passing cars was very bad. Hershel started his journey down the road holding his suitcase over his head to protect him from the rain, but to no avail. Five miles into his trek, Hershel was soaked from head to toe.

Suddenly, a dark object came out of the woods on the other side of the road and darted directly toward him! He couldn't make out what it was; it could be a raccoon, possum, skunk, or something more dangerous. It was almost on Hershel now, as he spontaneously lowered his suitcase to his chest as a means of protection.

Just as this vicious creature was ready to pounce on Hershel, he noticed it was just a soaking-wet little puppy running up to greet and play with him. Hershel picked the little guy up as the puppy tried to lick the rain off of Hershel's face. Hershel was glad he had a little companion to keep him company on his new venture.

Without warning, the puppy squirmed out of Hershel's arms and dashed into oncoming traffic! Without thinking of his own safety, Hershel threw his suitcase and ran after his friend, putting himself in danger. Hershel scooped up the dog with one hand, narrowly escaping the puppy being killed, but as Hershel jumped out of the way of the oncoming car, the car clipped Hershel's right ankle. The car's impact flipped Hershel three or four times in the air and he landed on his face on the side of the road with all his belongings in his suitcase scattered all over the road. Hershel's face was bloodied and full of gravel as passersby stopped to give their assistance. The puppy was nowhere to be found.

The driver exclaimed, "It wasn't my fault! What is this gut doing out here anyway?! He just came out of nowhere and ran in front of me like he was trying to get hit! This was not my fault! Is he dead?! Did I kill him?! Look what he did to my car?! Who's going to pay to get this fixed?!" In the background, red and blues lights started to light up the night sky and a faint siren in the distance sounded like it was getting closer and closer.

* * *

"Greetingsss, Ssupreme Ssoveriegn Ssobek!" Commander Ammut reported to his master. "I have tracked the sspecimen acrosss the Atlantic Ocean to a place called Loss Angelesssss. I retrieved hiss contact information from the Egyptian hosspital he wass in. Thiss iss the place where he ressidesss. It iss only a matter of time before he iss in my grassp! I am on my way there now to apprehend him, Ssire!"

Supreme Sovereign Sobek replied, "Do not fail me thiss time! My patience is wearing thin, my pathetic Ammut. Whether you capture him or not isss irrelevant to me at thiss point. I jusst want to sssmell blood on my clawss. You jusst make ssure it iss not yourss!"

"Yess, Ssire! Commander Ammut exclaimed with a sense of false pride and confidence. "I will not fail you thiss time! Give me two more dayss Earth's time and I will lay hiss pathetic body at your feet ass you ssit on your throne!"

"And if you don't, it will be your body that I crush at my feet!" Supreme Sovereign Sobek interjected.

Beep-Beep. Pause. *Beep. Beep-Beep.* Pause. *Beep. Beep-Beep.* Pause. *Beep...*

Hershel's groggy eyes finally opened up to a bright light shining directly above him and the sound of an all too familiar song of a heart rate monitor connected to him at his bedside. Hershel found himself back in a hospital bed but this time with a cast on his broken right ankle, elevated above his head, and a shredded face covered in gauze, the skin of which was ripped to pieces by the gravel on the side of the road where he lost consciousness. The television blurted out a familiar sound.

WE INTERUPT THIS REGULARLY SCHEDULED PROGRAM TO BRING YOU THIS SPECIAL REPORT. ANOTHER YOUNG BLACK GIRL HAS BEEN REPORTED MISSING. HER NAME IS ASHAY. SHE IS TWELVE YEARS OLD AND HAS BEEN MISSING FOR TWO DAYS. THIS IS THE SIXTH BLACK GIRL IN THE LAST THREE MONTHS THAT HAS GONE MISSING WITHOUT A TRACE. IF ANYONE HAS SEEN HER OR KNOWS HER WHEREABOUTS, PLEASE DON'T HESITATE TO CONTACT THE LOCAL AUTHORITIES. THANK YOU.

An unfamiliar voice startled Hershel from his half-asleep state. "Well hello there, sleepyhead. Glad you decided to stay with us. You were in a car accident last night and broke your ankle and injured your face pretty good. You are very lucky that's all you broke. Everyone calls me Nurse Mary; I am your primary caretaker, so just ring your buzzer if you need anything, sweetheart.

By the way, what were you doing out there in the middle of the night in the pouring rain?"

Hershel responded, "Did the dog live? Did anyone find the little black puppy?"

Nurse Mary responded, "Chile, I think that's the morphine talking. The police thought you were trying to commit suicide because witnesses say you just darted out in front of traffic like a madman. No one mentioned anything about a black dog in the police report. Later on today you will be transferred to the Mental Health Ward for a mandatory 72-hour hold to make sure you don't want to harm yourself. Just rest, baby; you safe now. Nurse Mary is going to take care of you now."

Hershel, in a panic, blurted out, "Did anyone find my suitcase? I have something of great value to me in there! Please tell me they found it!"

Nurse Mary calmly responded, "Far as I know, the majority of your belongings were either lost or destroyed. It was a mess out there on the road. I only saw one article of clothing that they brought in. Look, it's right there on your nightstand in the white plastic bag."

Hershel's heart jumped in his throat as he tried to swallow to keep it from leaving his body. Hershel was very sore, so his movements were very deliberate and methodical. Finally, Hershel reached the bag and pulled it close to his face so he could see its contents. The tattered red-and-white kente cloth was a sight for his sore eyes! Hershel sobbed uncontrollably with joy as he buried his tattered face into the cloth. Nurse Mary silently excused herself from the room.

The next day, Nurse Mary told Hershel today was his moving day. "Young man, before we can move you, I need to ask you some questions. Do you feel up to answering them?" Hershel slowly nodded his head yes. "Great!" Nurse Mary responded. "First, I need to know what your name is." Hershel was quiet and looked around the room, unengaged. Across the room he noticed a stack of magazines that had been donated to the local hospital. The top magazine appeared to be a Christian magazine whose cover read, JESUS CHRIST; THE REAL SON OF MAN?

"Mr. Man!" Nurse Mary shouted, startling Hershel. "Are you paying attention?! I asked you what your name is, sir."

Hershel's whole reason for leaving and walking on the side of the road that led him here was to escape that name. He no longer wanted to be addressed as Hershel anymore. As far as he was concerned, Hershel died the moment he left the house. Getting instant inspiration from the Christian magazine cover, JESUS CHRIST; THE REAL SON OF MAN. HE INTERPRETS AS; KHRIS-TIAN SOL-O-MON he told Nurse Mary, "My name is Kris Solomon. I am homeless and don't have an address. All I own is this kente cloth in this plastic bag. I don't have any identification or money. The only means that I have are in my heart and mind. I do not have any family or friends. It is just me."

Nurse Mary answered, "Don't worry, young man, just fill out this questionnaire as best you can and don't worry about a thing. We are here to help you. By the way, your new crutches came in. It will be a while before you use them so I will keep them behind your door for you. It is one PM now. I will be back in an hour to transfer you to the Mental Health Ward and they will give you all the help you need. There is nothing to worry about, baby. You are safe with Nurse Mary on the job!" With that, she stepped out to attend to other patients.

The new Kris Solomon instinctively knew that if he allowed them to take him to the Mental Health Ward, it was all over for him. He felt a sixth sense of urgency that he must leave before they came back. Kris Solomon gathered enough strength to take his right ankle out of the suspended sling over his bed and swing it around to the side of the bed so he could sit up. The pain was excruciating as the blood in his right leg poured down into his tattered ankle. He bit down on his kente cloth as he managed to get up on his left leg and gingerly hop toward his room door to retrieve his crutches.

Kris Solomon realized he still had the IV in his arm and knew he couldn't take it out too soon, as an alarm would sound and Nurse Mary would come in his room to check on him.

Just then, there was a blaring alarm in the main hallway. The PA announced a Code Blue in the room opposite to Kris Solomon's. He saw this as his last chance to escape. As all the nurses were running around frantically trying to assist the patient in the room across from him, Kris Solomon carefully pulled the IV from his arm and tied a piece of gauze around it to control the bleeding. With both crutches under his arms and his red-and-white kente cloth firmly placed in his mouth, he carefully peeked out his door, looking both ways down the hallway. The medical staff was preoccupied performing CPR and other medical procedures on the neighboring patient in the room across from him. This allowed him to slowly exit his room into the hallway, get on the elevator, into the main lobby, and walk out the front door undetected. With ankle throbbing and ass hanging out of his hospital gown, Kristopher Solomon once again entered the cold rain, only to get baptized by it again and again.

Meanwhile, an albino Komodo dragon slithered onto the front step of Janus's house. It was Commander Ammut! He shape-shifted back into the European doctor whose body he'd commandeered in Egypt. The commander posed as one of Hershel's doctors and was doing a follow-up home visit to check on his progress.

Commander Ammut rang the doorbell. There was no answer so he rang it again, this time with so much force that it shattered the doorbell's glass!

Janus finally reached the door with puffy eyes from her constant crying since Hershel left. She looked through the peephole and yelled out, "Who is it?"

Commander Ammut told Janus through the door, "Hello, Januss, this iss Dr. Sscaless. I am one of the doctorss on your hussband Hersshel'ss rehabilitation team. I am making a home visit to check up on him. Is he home?"

Janus's hair stood up on the back of her neck from the creepy lisp the doctor had but she opened the door to get rid of him once and for all. Janus replied, "Hello, Doctor; I am not familiar with you, but my husband no longer lives here. He has left me, and did not say where he was going. He is not coming back, so there is no need to call or come by here anymore. Have a good day."

Just as Janus closed the door in the doctor's face, Commander Ammut managed to stick his hand in between the door and the door frame. In his hand was his business card. Janus was skeptical of the doctor's motives and was too distraught to entertain any more conversations having to do with her husband who had just abandoned her without a trace and without saying goodbye.

Commander Ammut pleaded with Janus, "I undersstand your frusstration and hurt; thesse casess can be very difficult and challenging to all involved. My ssinceresst feelingss goess out to you all. Pleasse do not hessitate to call me if you hear back from Hersshel or disscover his whereaboutss. There iss still hope for your hussband. All iss not lost, no matter how bad thingss seem."

Janus reluctantly took the card from his pale hand as the commander pulled his hand back so Janus could shut the door. Janus looked at the card and looked out her front door peephole only to discover that the doctor had disappeared from her porch! Commander Ammut had already shape-shifted back into the albino Komodo dragon and had slithered into the brush.

Janus's focus returned to remembering the doctor's hand as he slipped her his card from the crack in the door. She now recalled the scaly, pale skin the doctor's hands had and what looked like jet-black, filed, sharp fingernails when he handed her his business card! Janus's hair once again stood up on the back of her neck as she got the shivers. She placed the card facedown on her husband's Dear John letter on the table by the door and walked back to her bedroom to resume her wailing session.

Commander Ammut's DNA locator finally went off! Only six miles up the road was Hershel's last location within the last 24-hour period. The commander surveyed the area and found out that Hershel had been to Our Lady of Immaculate Conception Hospital. Commander Ammut started to salivate uncontrollably as he was so close to finding Hershel! Because of the storms and pouring rain, his DNA locator seemed to have a 24-hour delay. No worries; Commander Ammut made a beeline to the hospital in the pouring rain. He also had trouble shape-shifting in the rain, so he made the trek as the albino Komodo dragon and took the back roads to avoid detection. The commander was not happy, and relished the day he could return to his species a hero.

As it continued to storm outside, Kris Solomon was shivering, his hospital gown soaked. He desperately looked for shelter from the rain; any place would do. Finally, he found shelter under the Highway 13 overpass. Kris Solomon threw his crutches down and covered himself with his soaked magic kente cloth. Within the next 30 minutes, the magic cloth became dry and surprisingly warm. Kris Solomon slept like a baby amongst the trash, dirt floor, rodents, and rocks he called his bed. To him, it felt just like the comfortable bed he shared with his estranged wife.

Sometime in the middle of the night, Kris Solomon started to have a curious dream. He dreamt about the adorable little black puppy he'd saved that night he left his house. In his dream he envisioned the tiny black puppy inside a cage in a local pet store. The puppy was behind the glass window and crowds of people were drawn to her. It was like there were no other animals in the store.

A young couple immediately flagged down the pet store owner and told her they wanted to purchase the darling puppy.

Three other families around the cage also confirmed that they also wanted to purchase the precious pup. The store owner was bewildered as to what she could do to satisfy everyone without them tearing down her store. She told the families that she had more puppies that looked just like her for half the price if they wanted to purchase them instead, and they would be coming in next week. None of the families budged, as now their children were starting to get antsy and whiny, and some fell out on the floor to start their tantrums.

Just then, a well-to-do gentleman approached the pet store owner and whispered something in her ear. Suddenly, she led the man to the back of the store. The mysterious man spoke. "It is my daughter's fifth birthday today," the wealthy gentlemen explained. "We were in here the other day and my little girl immediately fell in love with that dog." The wealthy man pulled out a stack of $100 bills and waved them in the store owner's face. "How much will it take to take that puppy home with me right now?"

The owner told the man, "Well, about that much you waved in my face!"

The wealthy man put the $1,300 in the woman's hands. "Oh, I almost forgot; I need you to do one thing for me."

"Sure, sir, anything; how may I help you?" the pet store owner eagerly replied.

"Can you clean her up and dress her in some nice pink bows, a pink collar, and paint her toenails pink as well?"

"That should be no problem," the store owner responded.

"Excellent! I will have my assistant pick her up at one PM today, just in time for my sweet baby girl's birthday party."

"Yes, sir!" said the storeowner. "You will be extremely happy!"

"I know I will," said the confident, wealthy man as he exited the front of the store, where his chauffeur opened the shop's front door for him and he disappeared into the back of his limousine. The pet store owner came out the back of the store to give the noisy crowd of families surrounding the beautiful black puppy the news that she was not for sale anymore. Angrily and reluctantly, each family slowly exited the pet store in rage and disgust, still arguing with anyone who would listen about their unfortunate circumstance that had just taken place.

The pet store owner delivered right on time and just like she said she would. When the pet store owner arrived at the family residence with the puppy in tow, all the little girls and boys at the party dropped what they were doing to touch and pet the precious black puppy that stole the hearts of everyone who laid eyes on her. When the pet store owner took her out of her portable carrying case, the whole party crowd let out an AAAAWWWWWWWWWW!! in unison. True to the pet store owner's word, the puppy was fitted with a pink collar with matching sparkling pink rhinestones! All of the puppy's nails were painted meticulously in hot pink. The ebony puppy also had one single pink ribbon tied on the top of her head that bobbled up and down as the puppy bounced around in her arms.

The daughter was so excited to see what her big birthday present was going to be and snatched the poor puppy away from the pet store owner's hands. Unfortunately, the girl was so ecstatic she almost squeezed the life out of her new friend. She told her father that the dog was the best present she could have received in the whole, wide world. She vowed she would love her new best friend forever and ever! All of the children gathered round to pet the newfound love of her life. The puppy did not seem overwhelmed as it soaked up all the love the children could dish out. The father sat back with his arms folded, wearing a proud grin. He knew that the only thing in life that he wanted was to make his daughter happy, even if it meant spoiling her rotten.

As time passed, the little girl neglected her favorite birthday present. She forgot to feed or give her puppy dog water. Her kennel remained dirty and was not cleaned regularly. She treated her like a stuffed animal and didn't realize that her dog could feel pain when she held her too tightly or threw her around her room. The beautiful puppy was now treated like an old, used toy that had lost all of its excitement and fun. The dog was literally tossed aside for the new and bigger toy the five-year-old's short attention span was now fixed on: the child's father had bought her a toy pony and her puppy was left to be an afterthought of good days gone by. The puppy's pink bows were now dirty, tattered, and worn. Its pink rhinestone collar was broken, and missing stones were scattered throughout her kennel. The hot-pink nail polish had seen better days and was scuffed up to the point you could see more nail than polish. The puppy was now neglected and left in her pen, sometimes for days, without being given any sustenance, love, attention, or affection.

One night, the puppy's kennel door was left unlatched. The daughter neglected to lock it all the way in her haste to go play with her pony. The puppy wiggled its nose between the door and the latch and pushed the door open just enough for her petite, black body to escape.

Just then, the housemaid working in the kitchen opened the back door to take out the trash for the night. She opened the door and then proceeded to grab the large, white trash bag and bear hugged it; her vision was impaired and she couldn't see past her shoulders down to the ground. The puppy suddenly rushed between the housemaid's legs and disappeared into the brisk, cool, rainy night without anybody being the wiser.

Kris Solomon was awakened at sunrise by a stray black chihuahua/terrier mix, a toy-sized dog with tattered, pink bows, frantically licking the left side of his face in an effort to try to heal the wounds on his face from the accident he was in! Kris Solomon was startled at first but then saw that the petite dog meant him no harm but was trying to comfort him. *Wait a minute?!* Kris Solomon thought. *Could this be? No, it can't, can it?* Is this the same dog that he saved that left him with a broken right ankle? *It is! It is!* Kris Solomon started to put things together. "Ok, this is why I dreamt of you! You must've come in the middle of the night and crawled under my kente cloth with me. That's why I had the dream! It was your life story. I am so sorry, li'l lady; you never know what others go through, even animals. I guess that's why we should never judge one another. You don't have to worry about that anymore, you are with me now. I am so happy to see you alive, but what is that smell?!?! PEEE-YUUU! It's you!" Kris Solomon's nose was instantly assaulted by the stench of his friend. It was obvious to Kris Solomon that this stray dog had been on the streets for quite some time. He looked for any tags or collar on the dog but could not find any. The dog was very loving and seemed to want to stay with Kris Solomon. He asked the dog, "What should I name you? Do you have any suggestions?" The dog rolled over to show her stomach in submission and panted her approval for Kris Solomon to give her a new name.

"Ok, stinky girl. The first two letters of what I uttered when I smelled you were P and U. Let's put them both together. You are now named Pu. We family now, Pu! Kris Solomon and Pu on a great adventure to find the meaning of our lives! Look out, world; an unbeatable duo has just been unleashed!" Pu wagged her tail and jumped on her hind legs to show her approval.

Kris Solomon and Pu were now inseparable. They would share everything together, including shelter, clothing, food, water, and even their thoughts. Kris Solomon told Pu, "You are all I got in this world. You are the only one that loves me unconditionally! Even though we have just met, you have been the most loyal friend that I can ever remember. Now, let's go find you some soap and water to take a bath!"

Pu immediately coerced Kris Solomon into following her and he conceded to his new best friend. Kris Solomon's ankle was no longer throbbing and he was getting pretty comfortable being on crutches. Kris Solomon tolerated his ankle injury because he didn't want to risk his Kente cloth's magic powers running out on him. Pu went behind an alleyway into Chinatown, where a row of

Chinese restaurants dumped their food in the garbage. Pu pointed to one particular trash bin. When Kris Solomon opened it, he found a concealed plastic container full of yesterday's lunch special. A Chinese cook was in the restaurant kitchen's back door watching the whole thing without saying a word. Kris Solomon was startled by this strange man watching him dive into his restaurant's dumpster. The restaurant cook nodded his head in approval and gave Pu and Kris Solomon a friendly wink. The dynamic duo took the surprisingly warm food to a park across the street and shared their meal.

After they finished eating, Pu took off down the street in a major rush. Kris Solomon could barely keep up with Pu on his crutches. "Hold up, li'l girl!"

Kris Solomon hollered as he stumbled about. Pu was now in the backyard of a house that had been condemned and boarded up. Pu was drinking from the water spigot that was dripping fresh water. Kris Solomon turned on the faucet and out flowed fresh water to drink and more importantly, bathe his new best friend in. In the white plastic bag where Kris Solomon stored his kente cloth, hidden underneath the cloth was a small, clear bag from the hospital that had items for hygiene. Kris Solomon pulled out a bar of soap, toothbrush, toothpaste, deodorant, and even hand sanitizer!

After Kris Solomon washed himself and his newly beloved friend behind this abandoned house, Pu unexpectedly took off again down another street. Kris Solomon reluctantly limped behind her on his crutches. This time, he could feel the bruises developing under his arms from the weight of his body being supported by the crutches under his arms. However, he could not stop or slow down for fear of losing his best friend.

About a mile later, Pu stopped at a clothing donation bin in a strip mall parking lot. Kris Solomon found himself a nice backpack in the clothes pile someone dumped in front of the bin and gratefully filled it with shirts, pants, socks, and underwear that seem to be tailor-made and customized for him personally. Kris Solomon even found a doggie sweater for Pu, but Pu graciously declined as she growled at Kris Solomon when her tried to put it on her. Pu's "foo foo" toy dog days were over now. She was a roughneck from the mean streets now! Pu was a real, genuine ride or die chick!

For several weeks, this became the normal routine for Kris Solomon and Pu. Life was not hard; in fact, it seemed to flow once you learned to get out of your own way.

* * *

Commander Ammut shape-shifted from his Komodo dragon state into his European doctor form behind a bush at the Our Lady of Immaculate Conception Hospital parking lot. As he rose up, he brushed himself off and got ready to enter the hospital lobby in his doctor scrubs. For some reason, his DNA tracker could not track his prey anymore. It would be impossible for a human to not be detected by it. All humans have a reptilian part of the brain located in their brain stems. It is this unique signal that each human inevitably gives off when that part of the brain is activated. It is impossible for any human being to deactivate their reptilian brain, as it is needed for the very function of their egos and self-survival instincts. A human is bred to live with this function at this basis of its core when faced with a fight-or-flight situation. Had this man somehow found some way to bypass this portion of his human brain? Commander Ammut was puzzled. At least he knew Hershel's last whereabouts, and he was now standing in front of the building where he was last detected. Soon, all of Commander Ammut's hardships would be a thing of his past and he could return a hero to his own race and resume his rightful place on the right-hand side of the most notorious and feared creature in all the known universe. All he had to do was locate and capture this feeble and weak human specimen and take him back with him.

Commander Ammut followed his tracker to the ninth floor and proceeded to enter Room 904.

"Excuse me, Doctor. My name is Nurse Mary. Is there anything I can help you with?"

"Yess, nurssse, I am looking for a patient named Hersshel. He may go by another name. He iss a Black male in hiss thirties. He is about ssix feet two inchess tall and about two hundred ten pounds. He hass an athletic build, and may have amnessia."

"Yes, Doctor," the nurse answered. "We had a patient come in a few days ago who fit that description. Unfortunately, he disappeared a little over a day ago, before we had a chance to move him to the Mental Health Ward. He came in as a possible suicide patient who broke his ankle after he jumped out in front of a speeding car."

"So you mean to tell me you let him escape?!" Commander Ammut snarled.

"Doctor, we don't run a prison here. Let me remind you that this is still a hospital where we treat people who are ill or injured," Nurse Mary rebutted.

"Are you lecturing me, you pathetic female vermin?"

"Excuse me, Doctor? What is your name? I haven't seen you around before. Let me see your ID badge."

Commander Ammut swiftly grabbed Nurse Mary by the throat with one claw and dragged her into the empty room Kris Solomon once occupied. The commander shape-shifted into his real reptilian body to do his dirty work. He lifted the helpless nurse three feet off the ground and snapped her neck with one twist. Her limp body immediately crumbled onto the bed. The commander covered her body with the hospital bed sheets.

In one swift motion, the commander jumped out the room's ninth-floor window, spilling glass everywhere. He landed firmly on top of a parked car in the hospital parking lot. Commander Ammut shape-shifted back into the albino Komodo dragon and disappeared into the woods behind the hospital with his tail thrashing violently.

Chapter Nine:
Sacari

One night, while Pu and Kris Solomon were walking their normal route, on their way home Kris Solomon felt compelled to turn down a different street than they normally went down. Kris Solomon had made a makeshift home across a fence on the other side of the railroad tracks, and this new route seemed faster. As they began their detour along their new path, they found themselves down a street flooded with heavy prostitution activity. Kris Solomon, forever humble and non-judgmental, was not intimidated by what he saw and continued down the busy street oblivious to all the devious sexual deeds around him. Everywhere he went, the ladies of the night would stop what they were doing and pay the dynamic duo all their time and attention. The women could not resist petting, snuggling, and picking up Pu! They were enamored by this jet-black puppy that reminded them of their own innocence lost so long ago. To them, subconsciously, Pu represented the little girl in them that believed she could become anything in this world, who believed she would always be protected and provided for. The naive, sweet little girl before she was betrayed, traumatized, and abused by grown men who took her innocence as a sign of weakness and preyed on her. The beautiful little girl who used to celebrate her femininity before her mother looked at her as competition and brainwashed her into feeling she didn't deserve to be loved, and the abuse by men was somehow her fault.

From that day forward, Kris Solomon and Pu continued to use this route as their normal path. A few weeks later, the pimp of one of the younger women stopped Kris Solomon and Pu dead in their tracks. "Look, trick-ass nigga! If I ever catch you and that black rat you got walking down my street while my bitches are working, me and you are going to have a serious problem! Wherever you going, you best take the long route cuz you fuckin' wit my money and that can't happen! Let me catch you round here again and I'll bust a cap in yo square, mark ass, you feel me?!"

Kris Solomon humbly replied, "Sir, I mean you no harm. My dog and I made camp on the other side of those train tracks." He pointed to the end of the street. "You see, all around the tracks is a fence that goes about a mile in both directions, but right there is a hole that we can slip through. We will be careful from now on and keep it moving to not bother you or the women on this street. Please forgive us; we meant no harm. We don't want any trouble."

The pimp lashed back, "Foo, didn't you hear what I said, nigga?! You lookin' at trouble!" He took out his Glock tucked under his belt by his lower back and put the cold, steel barrel on Kris Solomon's temple and pressed it firmly to where Kris Solomon involuntarily moved his neck to his opposite shoulder from the force of the gun. Pu started to bark uncontrollably.

Just then, one of the prostitutes ran to Kris Solomon's rescue and begged the pimp to put down his gun. "Bitch!" The pimp took his gun away from Kris Solomon's head and out of nowhere, pistol-whipped the prostitute with one vicious strike to the side of her head. The prostitute's body instantly became limp and collapsed into a heap on the filthy ground.

At that exact moment, Kris Solomon's eyes rolled into the back of his head. He had a vision of Sutol that seemed to go in slow motion. At the same time he acted out the same moves in real time that she was executing with perfect precision! Simultaneously, Pu was going off barking uncontrollably, but Kris Solomon could not hear her. He was deaf to the world around him. He could only see the saliva foaming up in her mouth as she spit her rage at the pimp in what seemed like an eternity.

With his high sense of awareness, Kris Solomon swiftly dropped down to the ground and caught himself with his left hand at the last second to support all his body weight. He then did a pirouette and stretched out his right foot that had the cast on and swept out the right leg of the pimp from under him, instantly shattering the pimp's ankle upon impact. In one fluid motion, Kris Solomon raised his body upright, then did a backflip off his good left leg, which brought his right foot with the cast over his head and connected with the pimp's hand, instantly shattering it and launching the gun 60 feet up in the air!

The crowd that had gathered around was stunned and speechless from what they just saw. The prostitutes' Johns in their cars sped away in all directions in reckless abandon. Kris Solomon calmly gathered up the badly injured prostitute and carried her away with Pu at his side. Throughout all the commotion and adrenaline rush, Kris Solomon did not realize he broke off his cast in the fight and was walking on his right ankle with no ill side effects. Somehow, his ankle had miraculously healed.

While he held the prostitute with one arm close to his chest, he wrapped her head wound with his kente cloth in an effort to stop the bleeding. She was oblivious to all this, since she had been knocked out cold and was unconscious and unaware of what had taken place. He carried the woman for over a mile until they reached an all too familiar place, Our Lady of the Immaculate Conception Hospital. As he carried her into the ER, the hospital staff rushed over and they lay her on a hospital gurney and wheeled her into the back to perform their urgent triage.

Before they had a chance to take her away, Kris Solomon removed his blood-stained kente cloth from her head and placed it in his back pocket. He had tucked Pu into his inner side pocket of his jacket where no one could see her. She had fallen asleep from all the commotion and was quiet as a church mouse. Kris Solomon smiled at her and closed his jacket ever so gently and rested his head on the wall on the side of his ER waiting room chair. He lifted his feet up on his chair and tried to tuck them under himself to get comfortable. His eyes started to get heavy as he stopped fighting to keep his eyelids open. He dosed off once again, oblivious to his Emergency Room waiting area surroundings and the other sick people staring at him ever so curiously.

Kris Solomon saw a beautiful, innocent Black girl named Sacari. She must have been approximately six years old. She was wearing her favorite yellow dress with the white ruffles sticking out underneath her dress hem. She was wearing her beautiful natural hair that was perfectly divided down the middle of her scalp and placed into two symmetrical Afro-puffs with yellow bows tied around the base of both of them. She had on white patent leather shoes that shined in the sun with her ruffled, white lace ankle socks. Her favorite thing to do was to play in the park with her beloved daddy as he lifted her up on his strong, muscular shoulders and walked around. She felt like a princess on her throne as everyone looked up to her when they saw her. She loved her view, because in her mind she was perched on top of a castle balcony high on a hill on top of the world!

She loved the attention everyone showed her as she stood out among the crowd wherever her daddy took her. When she was not on her daddy's shoulders, her daddy would also gently push her ever so high on the park swings as she kicked up her feet so her toes could dip in the fluffy, cotton-candy clouds above her.

Her daddy would also wait patiently at the bottom of the park slide, ready to catch her as she zoomed down the metal, spiral tube, laughing and giggling uncontrollably without any fear because her daddy would never fail to catch her. He daddy was always there and never, ever, let her fall down and hurt herself. She would climb on his back as he walked on all fours in the park grass as she pretended he was her royal horse, only fit for the princess to ride. Little did young Sacari know that her daddy had bad knees and would be in excruciating pain, but he would do anything to please his precious daughter, even at the expense of his own life.

When they eventually returned home after a long, adventure-filled day, her daddy would run her bathwater to the exact temperature that she liked and filled the tub with extra bubbles, just for her. His secret for making extra bubbles was to sneak in the kitchen when Mama wasn't looking and steal the Palmolive dishwashing liquid and squeeze it in her bathwater before her mother knew the wiser. He would bathe her and wash her hair, always making sure that the shampoo never got in her eyes. After her bath, he would oil her body and her scalp and put her to bed, always with a loving bedtime story. Just as she fell asleep, he would kiss her ever so gently on the forehead and tell her, "I love you, baby, and always will. You will always be Daddy's li'l girl."

One day, Sacari woke up and Daddy wasn't there to greet her and clean the "sleepy dust" out the corner of her eyes as he had always done in the past. Young Sacari went in her mama's room searching for her daddy. Sacari inquired, "Where is my daddy? He didn't come to get me this morning." Sacari's mother was visibly upset. Sacari could tell that she had been crying because of her bloodshot and puffy eyes. Her mother told her that her daddy was never coming back and to never bring him up again or even say his name!

Six-year-old Sacari was crushed, and couldn't understand why her daddy would leave her without telling her or taking her with him. She started to question herself, thinking that maybe she was to blame for her daddy leaving so suddenly. Sacari grew up unable to forgive herself for her daddy's mysterious absence, as she thought that she was to blame for him running away. Every night before Sacari went to bed she got up on her tiptoes and peered outside her bedroom window to see if this was the night her daddy would appear and come back into her life, but Daddy never came.

Two months went by. Sacari's mother brought home a strange man and told her, "This is your new daddy!" She did not like him. He didn't do all the things her real father used to do. He smiled at her but not the way her real daddy smiled at her. His smile scared her as he looked at her the way her real father never did. He bought her gifts but she felt scared when he tried to hug her. She lived in fear with this strange man in her house but could not tell her mama because she would get mad at her for chasing away another man in her life.

One night, Sacari was staring out the bedroom window waiting for her daddy to come back as she always did. The strange man snuck up behind her and covered her mouth. He told her not to scream and that they were going to have a special, secret relationship that she could not tell a soul about or he would kill her or worse yet, tell her mama she did these evil things he was going to force her to do. With no one there to protect her and no one to turn to, Sacari agreed with the "conspiracy of silence" as he repeatedly had his way with her.

That night after the strange man violated her, Sacari had a dream. She felt herself falling into this bottomless pit. It was pitch-black, where she couldn't even see her hand in front of her face. She fell and fell and fell, almost as if she was flying, but could felt gravity sucking her deep down into this abyss.

Finally, she crashed down on some jagged rocks at the bottom of this pitch-black tomb. Her body was broken, battered, and limp. Her will was defeated. She could not move and was paralyzed by fear and her own mortality. All she could do was sleep and hope that one day she could heal enough to want to keep living.

Several months passed, and she was still frozen in fear, traumatized by the eventful fall. She still couldn't see anything in the bottomless pit and it was lonely, cold, damp, and eerie. She sobbed continuously as she cried herself to sleep every night.

One day, Sacari heard a soft voice in the darkness. It was a little girl's voice, similar to hers. She was comforted by it, as she now realized she was not alone in her pitch-black prison. The voice befriended her. It told her that it was her long-lost twin sister named Lowe! Lowe told her that she was going to take care of her now. She didn't have to worry about a thing. She was going to protect her and never let another man harm her or make her do such painful, shameful, and degrading things. Lowe told her that she was the only one that loves her and she can't trust anyone but her. Lowe told her that they need to stick together now and never go against each other. She told her that she could do this for her but only under one condition. "I am not able to get out of the bottomless pit by myself, so you are going to have to carry me with you." She told Sacari that even though she was not healed, she could do it. Together, they could scale the slimy, jagged-edged walls of the abyss and climb out together.

Sacari reluctantly agreed to carry Lowe out with her and began her arduous journey to get out of the gloomy, cold, dangerous pit of darkness. Many more months passed and somehow Sacari, with her battered and broken body, had summoned enough courage and strength to climb out of her abyss with Lowe clinging to her back. When Sacari finally climbed out of the pit, she passed out in a state of exhaustion and went into a coma-like sleep for what seemed like days.

When Sacari finally woke up, she didn't realize how much time had gone by. She seemed to be back in the bottomless pit she fell into. She could not see, as her eyes were blindfolded. She could not hear, as her ears had been plugged. She could not talk, because there was a gag in her mouth. She could not move her arms and legs because her hands and feet had been tightly bound together. It felt like she was in the pit she just climbed out of because the air was chillingly cold and damp, just as the floor was in the bottomless pit.

She struggled to get out, but to no avail. It seemed like days went by before someone took off her blindfold and ear plugs. It was Lowe! Sacari looked at Lowe in terror and her eyes spoke for themselves, asking her, "Why did you do this to me?"

Lowe told her, "Remember the promise I made to you? I will never let another man harm, hurt, or use you ever again. I have to keep you in this cave as a way to protect you. This is for your own good. This is what must be done. You will get used to it in time, but find comfort that no man will ever get the opportunity to leave you, disappoint you, abuse you, or lay a finger on you ever again; I can promise you that!" Lowe rolled a giant boulder in front of the cave entrance so that no one could enter or see that Sacari was now her captive. Sacari felt the light dissipate and then disappear as the boulder sealed in her doom, where not even light could penetrate her prison.

One day while Sacari was in her prison, she could felt the warmth of a small streak of light penetrate her dark dwelling and kiss her forehead like her father used to do before she went to bed. It felt warm, healing, and comforting to her and made her smile. She got hope from the touch of the light on her body and it seemed to energize her. There must be a crack in her cave prison that Lowe does not know about! Sacari now got hope from the light and her cell didn't seem as menacing as it did before the light.

Lowe sensed that Sacari was acting different when she encountered her. Lowe fed off of fear, hate, jealousy, greed, and the ego. This new emotion from Sacari took Lowe's power away from her and she was not having it! The binds seemed to loosen up on their own. Her gag was not as tight as before. Lowe was enraged! So this time, Lowe stayed in the cave with Sacari and rolled the giant boulder at the cave's mouth from the inside, so she could investigate what was going on with her captive and how she was loosening her restraints.

Like clockwork, at noon, the sliver of light crept through a tiny crack in the cave and ever so gently kissed Sacari on the forehead with its warmth, comfort, and healing touch. Lowe witnessed this and went off! She immediately cursed the light and chased the light out of the dreary, dark cave and covered up the hole through which it came in. Lowe slapped Sacari to the ground in defiance and asked her, "How can you betray me after all I have done for you?" Lowe immediately removed the boulder from the cave and slammed it shut behind her. She climbed on top of the cave and yelled at the sun with all her might. She belittled the sun and told the sun how horrible he is. She cursed the sun and antagonized him by attacking everything the sun loves. She said the sun burns, kills, and destroys life just by its very nature. She berated the sun and lashed out at it, disrespecting the sun for the very thing the sun loves about itself.

The sun became enraged and full of fire as it started to burn hotter and hotter. The sun looked like it was on the verge of exploding from Lowe's disrespect and castration of it. The sun became blinded by its anger and in one weak moment, lashed out all its rays at Lowe to show its discontent. At that moment, Lowe removed the boulder from Sacari's prison and hid behind it to shield her from the sun's retaliation. This left Sacari's exposed body vulnerable to the sun's angry blast of masculine energy directed at Lowe. Sacari was burned over her entire naked body by the sun's violent, masculine energy. Just before the sun realized what it had done, Lowe sealed the cave with her and Sacari in it and wore a devilish grin, pleased with her devious plan that worked to perfection.

The sun could not believe what it had done and was frustrated that he had been deceived by Lowe to hurt the one thing he wanted to heal, protect, and love. The sun was mortified because he could not tell Sacari that he was tricked and that his anger wasn't directed at her but at her twin sister, Lowe. The sun felt so bad that he stopped shining and thought that maybe Lowe was right. Maybe he is worthless. Maybe he does destroy life and is manipulative and the scum of the Earth. Maybe Sacari is better off in her cave without him shining on her.

Days went by, and eventually the sun recovered from his wounds and vowed that he would never let Lowe come between him and Sacari again. So the sun continued to shine on the cave, hoping that one day his masculine rays would find a way to penetrate Sacari's dark dungeon in an effort to save her from her evil twin sister, Lowe. Each day the sun prayed and begged for Sacari's forgiveness and to give her understanding that he loves her and would never harm her intentionally. He hoped that she would come to realize that her true enemy is not him, but her evil twin sister, Lowe. Until that day came, the sun vowed to always keep shining on Sacari's cave, looking for the smallest crack to tell her he was sorry and wanted her to know that she was worthy of being saved, even if it cost the sun's own life.

* * *

"Excuse me, sir! Sir, can you hear me? Sir, you cannot have any pets in here!" It was the next day, and the ER receptionist noticed Pu peeking out from Kris Solomon's coat pocket.

"Huh? Oh, excuse me, I am sorry. I didn't mean to break any rules," Kris Solomon responded, half-asleep.

"That's ok, sir, but you have to remove your dog immediately!" the receptionist reiterated.

"How is my friend?" Kris Solomon inquired. "The lady I brought in here last night with the head injury."

The receptionist clutched Kris Solomon's elbow and guided him toward the exit. "You mean the, uh, pros— I mean, the young lady in the red dress? She is in ICU and is still in a coma. Are you family?"

Kris Solomon replied, "I am just her friend and very concerned for her."

The nurse escorted him outside and looked around to see if anybody was listening. "It doesn't look too good, sir. She took a pretty severe blow. Even if she pulls through, she may not have all her faculties. If you are family with an ID, you can visit her in the ICU anytime you want.".

"I don't have any identification," Kris Solomon said, defeated.

"No worries, just come to me this time tomorrow and I will escort you to see her. But remember, you have to leave your dog at home."

"Thank you, miss, I appreciate you," Kris Solomon gratefully responded. "She needs all the support she can get. We will see you tomorrow." The receptionist walked away hastily, as she had spent too much time away from her desk. Kris Solomon took Pu out of his coat pocket and placed her on the ground. This time she didn't take off but stayed in stride with Kris Solomon, letting him know that it was his time to lead them.

It was day number five since Kris Solomon took the young lady into the ER. He arrived in the back of the hospital by a maintenance shed. He told Pu, "Okay, Lil' Mama, you know the drill. You have to stay behind this shed until I get back. You got your food and water so you should be fine. I will only be gone for an hour or two. Be good, and I will see you when I get back, ok?" Pu let out three loud yips and proceeded to go behind the shed and lay down. The last three days, the lady at the reception desk had been surprisingly absent. Kris Solomon wondered if she ever had the intention of keeping her word; or was she just trying to get rid of him? Kris Solomon hoped that this would be the day he'd see her and that she'd keep her word to escort him to see his friend.

As he entered the Emergency Room, he caught the eye of the receptionist. She was here! She nonchalantly gestured him with her eyes and neck to meet at one of the side doors down the hall from her desk. "Hey, you! I am sorry I haven't been here but I had a family emergency. Please forgive me. My name is Carol, by the way. What is yours?"

"I am Kris Solomon," he answered.

"Nice to meet you, Kris. I don't think I have met anybody so formal! Good news; I checked on your friend. Her name is Sacari Lowe. She is conscious now and seems to have all of her faculties. She is actually free to check out any day now. They are just waiting on somebody to pick her up, as she is not allowed to leave the hospital unattended. Can you take her to her house?"

Kris Solomon was relieved and elated at the same time that his friend had recovered. "Oh, of course, of course I can help her! That's why I am here!"

"Good," the receptionist said. "Let's get you a name tag pass and I will give you her room number and then the rest is up to you." The receptionist put the name tag over Kris Solomon's heart and couldn't help but feel how solid and muscular he was. She was involuntarily compelled to leave her hand there for two seconds longer than needed, gravitating towards his heart's warm and healing energy. Carol caught herself as she cleared her throat. "Now go down this hall, to the elevator on the left. Take it to the second floor and she should be in Room 269."

"Thank you, Carol." Kris Solomon spoke with gratefulness in his voice.

"It is my pleasure, sir. Promise me you will take care of her. She needs you now more than ever," Carol responded. Kris Solomon placed his left hand over his heart and gave her a little bow of his head as he turned away and walked down the long, cold hospital corridor.

Beep-beep. Pause. *Beep. Beep-beep.* Pause. *Beep. Beep-beep.* Pause. *Beep.* Before Kris Solomon entered the room that familiar song greeted him at the door. He walked in the room left foot first and saw his friend laying in the bed smiling at him as if she knew he was coming to get her. In a whispery, weak voice she said, "What took you so long? I've been waiting for my superhero to come get me and carry me away from here! My girlfriends told me what you did for me. I don't even know your name, my black knight in shining armor!"

Just then, Kris Solomon realized the little girl in his dream that first night he slept in the ER was her! It made sense now. He put his magic kente cloth around her head while she was unconscious. "Hey, Sacari," Kris Solomon bashfully answered. "My name is Kris Solomon. I'm the one that should be thanking you! You literally saved MY life! It was the least I could do to return the favor. I'm glad you are doing better. Your chariot awaits you outside to whisk you away. Actually, I have to call a cab; but don't worry, I got you!"

"How do you know my name?" Sacari looked puzzled. Kris Solomon hastily picked up and fumbled with her medical chart at the foot of her hospital bed. "Uh, uh, it says it right here. S-a-c-a-r-i Lowe. Yeah, that's it," Kris Solomon stuttered. "Right here!"

"Calm down, superhero. I was just messing with you!" Sacari joked while laughing. Just then, a nurse came in with Sacari's discharge papers. Kris Solomon gathered up her belongings and grabbed her wheelchair. "I told you your chariot awaits!" Kris Solomon joked around. They both had a good laugh as the nurse unhooked her IV and she carefully sat down in the wheelchair.

Kris Solomon rolled her down the hallway, into the elevator, down to the lobby, and out the front door of the all too familiar hospital. "Wait here, Sacari, and soak up this warm sun on your face. I'm going to call a cab—and I have another surprise for you when I get back. I will just be a minute," Kris Solomon explained. He went through the lobby to call a cab, then exited the hospital through a side door. He then made his way to the back of the hospital to go get his faithful companion.

When Kris Solomon whistled by the dumpster, Pu jumped out from behind the dumpster and jumped into his arms! Kris Solomon walked toward the front of the hospital with Pu hidden behind his back. Once he saw Sacari in her wheelchair with her eyes closed, soaking up the sun, he gently dropped Pu in her lap. Pu immediately reared on her hind legs, put her paws over Sacari's heart, and commenced to give her a tongue bath.

"Hey, little lady! I normally don't let dogs lick me in my face but for you I will make an exception." Sacari chuckled from the soft, moist tongue-lashing Pu was giving her. As Sacari and Pu continued their "cupcake" session, the taxi pulled up. Kris Solomon put Pu in the car first, then helped Sacari out of her wheelchair and into the taxi. He closed the door behind her, went to the other side of the car, and let himself in. Pu happily greeted him again.

The taxi driver asked, "So, where to?" Kris Solomon and Sacari met eyes in an awkward moment. Sacari broke the silence and told the taxi driver, "My place." She gave the taxi driver directions to her house as she scooted closer to Kris Solomon and lay her head on his broad, strong shoulder. Pu looked at her as if to say, "You can get close, but not too close! Know your boundaries. And stay in your lane." Sacari and Kris Solomon looked at each other and smiled at what they just witnessed. "You just gonna have to learn to share, Miss Pu!" Sacari said in a matter-of-fact tone. Sacari and Kris Solomon laughed in unison.

As the taxi pulled up to Sacari's studio apartment, Kris Solomon saw a bunch of Black men just hanging out in front of her complex. "Look who came back from the dead!" the crowd taunted as Sacari exited the taxi with Kris Solomon holding the door.

"Baby, you sure can take a punch!" another male shouted. The crowd broke out in laughter.

"I bet you could go one round with Mike Tyson. My money would be on you!" They all broke down laughing while reaching for anything they could find to stay upright, as they seemed to lose their balance. Kris Solomon was starting to seethe. His jaw became tight and a vein in his forehead became engorged with blood. Sacari could feel his anger bubbling up from a place she really didn't want to see materialize.

She shouted to the crowd of men, "Hush! If any of you were real men, you would have stepped in to help me. All you coward-ass, clown niggas move out the way before you see how a real Black man protects a Black woman!" She then whispered in Kris Solomon's ear, "Don't pay them no mind, baby, they are not worth it."

As Sacari entered the front of her apartment building, the crowd of Black males made room for them as they parted like the Red Sea clearing an unobstructed path. Pu also growled at the crowd as they passed, letting them know, "Don't start none, won't be none!" All of the men's hard stares and glares at Kris Solomon had no courage behind them. They were empty promises of a threat they could not keep. He was not impressed, and kept on moving toward the entrance door and up the stairs, as the elevator seemed to be in a permanent state of repairs.

As they entered Sacari's apartment, #369, she almost tripped over the pile of mail the apartment manager had been slipping under the door since she had been gone. "Make yourself comfortable, Kris. If you need to take a shower help yourself, it is over there. I am starving, and tired of that hospital food, so I will be in the kitchen drumming up something for us to eat." Kris Solomon contemplated for a moment. Did she say a shower? That word was so foreign to him now, as he had been washing himself with that cold water spigot in the back of the old abandoned house. Hot water was definitely a luxury to him.

Kris Solomon made a beeline to the bathroom, disrobed, and climbed into his liquid cocoon. He stayed in there for over an hour baptizing himself in the hot, steamy goodness that seemed to melt away all the old off of him.

Suddenly, there was a bang on the bathroom door that woke Kris Solomon out of his meditative state. "Hey, Negro, are you all right in there?" Sacari sarcastically shouted.

Kris Solomon opened his eyes from being lost in his own thoughts as the hot water massaged his face. "Yes, yes, I'm fine. I'm getting out now. I'm sorry about that; I didn't know I was in here that long."

Sacari responded, "Well, if you stay there any longer, we both gonna be out in dem streets when I can't pay that high-ass water bill you runnin' up! Get dressed, it's time for dinner. By the way, is Pu housetrained? You know I don't play that."

"She is fine!" Kris Solomon reassured her through the bathroom door. Sacari had laid out their meal on a little table with two chairs that didn't match. The table was set by a window with a spectacular view of a dilapidated brick wall of the warehouse next door to her apartment building. She had a 99 cent store candle lit at table side and had paper plates and plastic cups and napkins from assorted fast food restaurants.

Kris Solomon pulled out her seat and Sacari wondered when was the last time any man had done that for her, if ever? They both enjoyed the modest meal made from Sacari's old scraps that hadn't spoiled since she was in the hospital. Kris Solomon told her that was the best and most nutritious meal he had ever had because it came from a place within her that wanted to show her appreciation and admiration for the man who thought she was worthy of protecting. Kris Solomon could not stop praising her for the delicious meal he'd just had. Sacari unknowingly made small of his praises and dismissed them, as deep down in her subconscious she was not allowed to feel good about anything she accomplished.

Sacari cleaned off the table and threw the dishes in the trash. Pu had fallen asleep on the couch. Sacari took Kris Solomon's hand and led him to her bedroom area where she sat him on the bed. Sacari took off all of Kris Solomon's clothes and laid him down. She then took off all her clothes and lay on top of him with her head on his chest. Gradually, she could feel his heart beating stronger and more rapidly. She knew that he was feeling her and had given her permission to slowly lower her head, kissing his body on the way down to his waist. As she passed his belly button, Kris Solomon's body started to quiver uncontrollably. He immediately sat up and folded his legs Indian-style.

"Sacari, would you allow me to try something different with you?" Kris Solomon softly pleaded.

"Kris, I had no idea you was a freak! What you have in mind? I'm all yours, superman!"

Kris Solomon explained, "No, nothing like that. I haven't had sex in a while, but I am more sensitive to energy. I just want to explore the energy piece and not get straight to the physical. You know, there are millions of worlds out there that we have yet to tap into or explore. Will you let me show you?"

Sacari nodded her head yes in agreement. "Take me to the moon!"

Kris Solomon continued, "But first I want to apologize for all the men who have hurt you. For all the men in your life who betrayed your trust and love. For all the men who abused and traumatized you. From the deepest part of my heart, I am so, so sorry for all the pain you had to suffer in silence. For all those lonely, sleepless nights you cried yourself to sleep. All those nights that you went to bed terrorized and had to sleep with one eye open for fear of abuse. To have to live your childhood in fear and terror at the time you should take for granted your safety and security. For your father who left you and never came back. For all those times boys and men caused you pain because you weren't able to say, 'Imma tell my daddy!' so they would leave you alone. Your father loves you very much, Sacari. He did not want to leave. He betrayed your mother one time and she didn't forgive him for it. She would hold it against him for the rest of his life. She knew the best way to punish him was to take the only thing he really loved that loved him back with equal fervor. That was you, Sacari. I am so sorry. He is at fault, no doubt, because he should have walked through fire to be with you, but his ego was fragile and your mother broke him. Words cannot explain my sympathy for what you had to endure. No human being, let alone a six-year-old baby, should have experienced the horror you had to endure."

Sacari immediately started to sob uncontrollably and lashed out at Kris Solomon. "Who told you this! How do you know? Have you been stalking me? Who the fuck are you? Who sent you to fuck with my head!" Sacari raised her hand and with all her might, slapped Kris Solomon dead in his face. He did not flinch. In fact, he pulled Sacari closer to him.

He now had forced Sacari to straddle him with her legs crossed behind his lower back. He was supporting the small of her back with his powerful left hand with his fingers spread widely apart, covering her whole backside. She could not move as she tried to fight and pull away. His right hand was between Sacari's shoulder blades, supporting her as her body jerked violently from the wailing and purging of this deep-rooted energy that had been stored in her most sacred space since she was six years old. Sacari tried to fight, but Kris Solomon's grasp on her was too strong. Finally, after 13 minutes of Sacari's struggling to break his grasp, she let go and submitted because of pure exhaustion. Kris Solomon started to breathe deeply and with intention, inhaling and exhaling in an exaggerated manner. A little while later, Sacari succumbed and found herself in rhythm and synchronicity with Kris Solomon's breathing. They were one.

"Sa Ku Ma Ku Gee Cha...Sa Ku Ma Ku Gee Cha...Sa Ku Ma Ku Gee Cha..." Kris Solomon went into a trance, swaying gently from side to side and continued to repeat his chant with Sacari on his lap. "Sa Ku Ma Ku Gee Cha...Sa Ku Ma Ku Gee Cha..." Next, he removed his left hand from the small of Sacari's back. He motioned his hand over the back of his head and then brought it back over Sacari's head and down to her lower back. He then directed Sacari to take her left hand, move it over the top and back of her head, bring it back over his head, and place it at the small of his back. They did this motion two more times to each other and returned their hands back to their original positions.

Kris Solomon then placed his left hand over Sacari's heart and told her to place her left hand over his. They both stayed still as they closed their eyes, only to find out their own heartbeats had begun to beat in unison with one another. They were one. Kris Solomon then placed his right hand over Sacari's left hand, which was over his own heart. He told Sacari to place her right hand over his left hand, which was placed over her heart.

A surge of energy entered their bodies, starting at the base of their spines and shooting ultraviolet light up the spine and out the top of their heads. This ultraviolet light was so bright it lit up the pitch-black room and also woke Pu out of her slumber in the other room as she raised her head from her blanket. The internal light seemed to heal every cell in Sacari's translucent body as it took inventory of what she needed on a cellular level to heal. It was cleansing. It was nurturing, fine-tuning, cleansing, balancing, and purging every individual cell in her body, refining her mind, body, and soul!

Sacari's body went limp in Kris Solomon's arms as she swirled in and out of consciousness. He then lifted her up from on top of him and gently laid her on her back on top of her bed. He once again began his chant, "Sa Ku Ma Ku Gee Cha...Sa Ku Ma Ku Gee Cha...Sa Ku Ma Ku Gee Cha..." Kris Solomon took the back of his left hand and gently caressed the top of Sacari's head and ever so gently moved his hand down the right side of her body. He did this three times, never rushing, always using the same pressure all the way down to her feet and not letting his hand lose contact with her body. He was very precise, very deliberate in his actions. He was fully present and focused on protecting and providing for Sacari in this moment.

He did the same thing, this time with the back of his right hand, all the way down the left side of her body in the same loving and caring manner. He did the same thing to her face, then her feet, paying attention to every beautiful feature that made Sacari uniquely who she is. Kris Solomon now placed his hands over Sacari's heart, but making sure he did not touch her. His hands were about an inch from touching her. He placed his hands together as if to make a diamond shape in the middle of them with his palms down. Miniscule and warm ultraviolet sparks came between his hands and Sacari's heart, activating its vibration.

Sacari let out a gentle sigh as she arched her back in an effort to get closer to Kris Solomon's hands. He then placed his hands in the same position over Sacari's womb and even more sparks started to fly. This time, Sacari couldn't control herself. She started to wail in a song instinctive of being pleasurable or painful. The more Kris Solomon held his intent over Sacari's womb, the more she gushed her sacred liquid from between her legs. Ten minutes went by before Sacari succumbed and passed out from sheer exhaustion. Her bed was soaked from having purged a lifetime of abuse, trauma, fear, low self-esteem, and the inability to forgive herself or her perpetrators. Kris Solomon had helped her release all the energy she was carrying that did not serve her greater good. Kris Solomon had helped her connect her womb back to her heart and not her ego. She was now ready to express her feminine energy in the most sacred way without fear and no regrets, just like she used to when she was a little girl. This was where her power lay. Not in her coldness. Not in her sophistication or ability to manipulate and suppress her true feelings. Not being street smart or conniving, self-sufficient and ruthless. But in her innocence. In her ability to love with no fear. To accept and always see the good in others. To show empathy and kindness. To be vulnerable. To put others ahead of herself and be willing to sacrifice for a cause that is greater than herself. To take difficult things she encounters in life as lessons to make her better and not a victim trapped and paralyzed by fear from that experience. She had been programmed since she was six years old to believe that the very things that made a woman strong were her weakness. Like kindness, nurturing, trusting, dreaming, creating, forgiving, self-sacrifice, having faith, hope, and the greatest of these, believing in love. She now believed she was worthy of love because she had become love once again.

As Sacari slowly came out of her slumber, Kris Solomon held her hand to help her sit up. He told her to stand up and face him. Sacari, still groggy and lightheaded, steadied herself as she got on her feet to face him. In one fell swoop, Kris Solomon lifted Sacari by her buttocks up to his waist. She naturally wrapped her legs around him and buried her nails in Kris Solomon's shoulder blades so as to hold on for dear life! She felt safe, loved, and supported for the first time since her father left her.

Unwavering for the next 45 minutes, Kris Solomon supported her weight long enough for Sacari to relax and trust that he wouldn't drop her. When this took place, Kris Solomon whispered in Sacari's left ear, "My masculine energy will always support and protect you, just as I am doing now, even when I am not in your presence. Know that I am willing to die so that you may live. Know that my ultraviolet light is a veil over your entire body. No one will ever harm you again. No one that does not have your best interests can harm you, unless you give them permission. You have a gift, Sacari. That gift is infusing the best in you into the food you create. If you follow your heart, it will take ten steps toward manifesting its desires. Go to culinary school. Don't worry about money, time, pitfalls, bills, or any other things keeping you from your heart, for they are not real. They are illusions of programming that you have created in your head. In order for you to manifest your heart's desires, you must be willing to give up your former life. You must be willing to kill your ego that has tricked you into believing that it is you. Walk out on faith, my precious Sacari. The only one that can stop you now, is you.

"Remember, my sacred masculine energy surrounds you; it runs through you and it is bonded to you. Call on me in times of despair. Think of me when fear and doubt try to creep into your head and I will be there to protect and provide for you, just as I am supporting you now."

Sacari had fallen off to sleep again. Kris Solomon carried Sacari with him, as she was still straddling his body. He went to the linen closet with her in tow. He pulled a new set of sheets out and replaced the old ones on Sacari's bed, doing all this while still supporting Sacari with one arm. He placed Sacari gently on the bed and headed towards the bathroom.

He returned to the bedroom with a hot washcloth and softly wiped Sacari's inner thighs and yoni. He then placed her comforter up to her chin and gently kissed her softly on the forehead. "I give you my love and light to protect and provide. A part of me dies so that you may thrive." He went into the living room only to see Pu wide awake, wagging her tail and ready to go. Kris Solomon quietly gathered his backpack in one hand and Pu in the other. He looked at the clock on the wall and it showed the all too familiar 3:33 AM staring back at him. Kris Solomon opened the front door and walked out consciously, not wanting to alert Sacari of his exodus. He looked back one more time, bowed his head, and with his left hand, touched his heart. He tenderly shut Sacari's front door behind him and disappeared into the night with Pu leading the way down the dark, dimly lit street.

Chapter Ten:
Kora

As our dynamic duo walked the streets in the wee hours of the AM, Pu was amused by a paper that had been picked up by a strong gust of wind and was hurtled in the air in a delicate dance as it flipped, dove, and swayed to and fro in midair. The paper seemed to have a mind of its own as it somersaulted in the air, climbed up again and flipped and twisted as if it was on a string never touching the ground. Kris Solomon was amused as Pu ran and jumped in the air to snatch the paper out of the sky but always missed it just by a hair. Just when you'd think the paper would fall harmlessly back to the ground, another strong gust of wind would catch it and take it even higher in the night sky!

The dance between the mysterious paper and Pu went on for 15 minutes straight as this mysterious paper seemed to defy gravity. Next thing you know, Pu and Kris Solomon found themselves in a railroad yard chasing this elusive flying leaflet. The paper flipped again, barely missing the ground, and landed gently inside a train car that was just now slowly taking off.

Pu, oblivious to her surroundings, jumped inside the train car, pursuing the paper, and clutched it in her mouth as the train picked up speed. Kris Solomon became aware of the situation and hastily ran after the train with Pu on board as it gained momentum.

The train continued to gather speed down the dark tracks as Kris Solomon was now in a full-blown sprint to catch the train.

Pu appeared at the door of the train and started barking profusely, encouraging her friend to catch up with her. With one last-ditch effort, Kris Solomon leapt off the ground as high as he could and desperately dove for the train car's entrance. He narrowly gripped the bottom floor of the train with both hands. As the train rumbled faster down the tracks, he lost the grip from his right hand and his feet were dragging on the jagged rocks that surround the train tracks. Kris Solomon's legs were slowly being sucked under the train, where the steel wheels of the train car were increasing momentum as they angrily gained velocity going down the tracks.

Kris Solomon's eyes rolled into the back of his head as everything now seemed to be in slow motion. Pu was barking uncontrollably, but Kris Solomon could not hear her or the deafening sound of the rumbling train. With Kris Solomon's free right hand, he grabbed his left wrist that was holding onto the train car for dear life. He seemed to do a one-arm pull-up with his left hand, trusting that it wouldn't slip off the train and leave him for dead under the train on the tracks.

Once Kris Solomon's head and shoulders were above the train car floor, he swung both his legs over the back of his head with all his might and executed a perfect backflip and landed on his feet inside the train car in a warrior-like stance, ready for combat. Pu immediately jumped in his arms as if to say, "I knew you got this, Big Fella!"

As Kris Solomon started to relax, he fell into one of the dark corners of the train to get some well-deserved rest. Pu patiently waited for him to get settled in before she crept into his lap, using Kris Solomon as a makeshift bed for the night. Kris Solomon welcomed his loving companion and started to pet the back of Pu's neck when he discovered she was holding something in her mouth. It was the piece of paper that was the culprit for them being on this speeding train headed to God knew where!

Kris Solomon retrieved the paper from Pu's mouth and uncrumpled it so he could see what it said. *"Missing! Ten-year-old Black girl named Damiana. She is four feet tall and weighs 85 lbs. She has been missing since the beginning of the month. She is very shy and loves to read. If anyone has seen her, please call us or the local authorities immediately. Damiana, if you are reading this, please call us and come home, baby girl. Your family loves you and misses you so much. Please help us bring our daughter home. Reward will be given to the person who finds her or knows her whereabouts."*

Kris Solomon put the paper down and lay his head on the back of the train car's cold, steel wall and dosed off almost instantly. Pu had already beaten him to the punch and was already sound asleep in Kris Solomon's lap. The train's hypnotic rumble and synchronized movement down the tracks guaranteed that they would both get a much-needed good night's sleep.

Arf! Snarl! Arf! Snarl! Arf! Arf! Kris Solomon and Pu were suddenly awakened by a savage Rottweiler snarling, seething, and foaming at the mouth one inch away from Kris Solomon's nose. They were awakened by a 150-pound beast and a group of three pissed off, burly, large, white men who patrol the railways. Kris Solomon and Pu were beaten and thrown off the train in the middle of the night. The three men threatened Kris Solomon that if they ever saw him again trespassing on their private property they would not treat him with their nice hospitality they had shown him this time.

After Kris Solomon gathered his bearings, picked the gravel out of the side of his face, palms of his hands, and knees, he scanned the area to see where he had landed. As they climbed up a ravine that separates the train tracks from the main highway, they saw a sign in the distance. As they continued their trek up the road, the sign came into focus. It said, "Welcome to Oakland." They now realized they'd traveled over 400 miles and were in Northern California.

About an hour later, Kris Solomon and Pu found themselves in a seedy part of downtown Oakland. They asked a man on his early AM deliveries on the street if he knew where the nearest homeless shelter was and he pointed them in the direction of a nearby church about six blocks down the road.

Kris arrived at the church and saw a long line wrapped around the block of people lining up to get something to eat for breakfast. He assumed this was the place. Kris Solomon bypassed the line as they directed him inside the building at the main office where newcomers register to be placed on their list for a bed for the upcoming night. Kris Solomon glanced over the paperwork and saw one of the stipulations of securing a bed was he must attend mandatory church services before he would be allowed a bed. Kris Solomon politely set down his application and pen and turned around and walked out the front door with Pu secured and hidden in his coat pocket. He would rather sleep on the streets than be dictated to and infringed upon in regard to his beliefs.

Once again, Kris Solomon and Pu were awakened by a stranger standing over them. This time it was from a beautiful smile and caring eyes bearing gifts for them. They were awakened by a beautiful spirit. "Greetings, Beloved! My name is Kora. I am a volunteer worker that drops off socks and blankets for those in need. May I give you a care package?" To her surprise, Pu popped her head out of Kris Solomon's chest pocket and started to lick Kora's hand as she gave Kora her instant approval! "Why hey, Lil' Guy! I didn't see you coming! It looks nice and cozy in that space you crawled out of!"

Kris Solomon cracked a smile, as Kora's aura was very healing and loving. "Thank you so much, sista, we really appreciate your generosity. You never know how something so small or trivial can change a persons' life. Give thanks." Kris Solomon stood up, put his left hand over his heart, and bowed down to Kora.

"Well ain't you the charmer!" Kora replied. "If you two are looking for some extra money, I could use a strong man like yourself to help me carry my tent, chair, tables, handmade jewelry, and natural body care products to the flea market every day. I may not be able to pay you two what you're worth, but I am an excellent cook and you can shower and wash clothes at my place if you like."

"Say no more, huh, Pu? We are there! Just give us a time and place and we got you!" Pu barked three times to cosign with Kris Solomon.

"Great! It's a deal. Meet me at the Ashby Bart parking lot in Berkeley every day at six AM. And we will put you right to work! How are you two doing on a place to stay? Did you check out the homeless shelter at the church around the corner?"

Kris replied, "Yes, we checked it out yesterday and it wasn't a good fit so we decided to leave and wound up here for the night."

"I understand," Kora replied. "Everything ain't for everybody. It's just a shame that anyone would put stipulations on what hoops they want you to jump through knowing that you are desperately in need. I tell you what I am going to do, Brotha Kris Solomon and the magnificent Pu. I have a garage that needs to be cleaned out and organized. It is not much, but if you help me straighten it up you can have a little space to call your own—on a temporary basis, of course."

"I think me and Pu won't let you down. We will take you up on that offer and turn your garage space into the Taj Mahal! We are so grateful for you, Kora. We are so humbled by your beautiful heart!" Kris Solomon overwhelmingly exclaimed.

Kora answered, "Bet; that's a deal. Meet me at this address at seven tonight and I will show you the space. I have to continue handing out my care packages so I have to leave you now and complete my rounds. See y'all tonight!"

* * *

It'd been three weeks since Kora had met the dynamic duo. Since the two of them arrived, her business had been thriving. Kris Solomon created a work space for Kora in her garage. He built shelves and a work space specifically for her jewelry making. He collected all her crystals in glass jars and labeled them on a shelf he made specifically for them. He attached her spools of copper, brass, and sliver wire in specific dispensers. He made drawers and labeled them according to all her jewelry making supplies and tools. For her body care products, he created a separate storage space specifically for all her raw butters and oils. He created a label-making area and a place to store all her glass jars, bottles, and lids. All her mixers, blenders, juicers, and other appliances were in their proper place designed for optimal precision. Kris Solomon had even installed shelves and compartments in Kora's vintage van for easy access and set up of her pop-up tent and tables at the shows and festivals she did all around the Bay area. Her sales had tripled in the time since he had arrived, and it couldn't happen to a nicer person.

Kris Solomon had even changed her configuration on how she set up her tent and displays at her shows. "Kora, when we set up your booth we want it facing due east, with the rising of the sun. The sun will shine on your jewelry and will show the luster and brilliance of each precious stone and copper housing. The morning sun gives life to the new day, and so it shall rejuvenate the life frequency in all your crystals. As the sun reaches its peak at high noon, directly above us, it will activate the best in all your customers. If they feel their best, they will want to look their best and adorn themselves with your beautiful creations. As the sun sets in the west, the universe reflects in everything that has happened throughout the day. It is in a state of gratitude and appreciation. So will your customers be. They will want something phenomenal to match the consciousness of the magnificent things they accomplished that day. Their hearts will be open; thus, they will be more in tune with knowing your worth and the products you have manifested.

"Besides having your booth facing due east, you want it to be located on the corner of the aisle. To the master mason, the cornerstone is the most important piece in any building, monument, or structure. As it is laid down, it sets the precision and accuracy of the entire structure. And so it will be with your booth. When you set up your display tables, you want to make sure they are set up in a way to invite energy flow at its optimal level. People are energy, and you want them to flow and not become stagnant or inhibited. Once their Chi is open, they are more connected to their hearts and won't base their decision to make a purchase on fear or an impoverished mentality.

"Also, Kora, do not rush or pressure your customers to make a purchase. This lowers the vibration and gets them in a fight-or-flight state of mind. Money cannot be exchanged for goods and services if their hands are clenched in a defensive mode. The best way to hustle in the universe is to sit still and be in a state of humility, gratitude, and appreciation."

All her life, Kora had put others ahead of herself. It was just in her nature. She always saw the best in people, even when they didn't see the best in themselves. She left her heart open and exposed with no fear of being hurt, betrayed, or abused, and somehow, she always seemed to be protected. She was always looked after. She was never in need, and lived a life of abundance and prosperity.

Kora never worried or stressed over paying bills. Never worried about her rent being paid or how she was going to make ends meet. It was like she lived life knowing she had a winning lottery ticket in her back pocket that she could cash at any time. It seemed like she had this protective force field around her that no one that meant to do her harm could penetrate. She lived life like an innocent little girl running through the flowers, laughing and singing, without a care in the world.

She is extremely engrossed in her femininity and expressed it every chance she got. She is a nurturer. She is a healer. She is a caretaker. She is creative expression with no boxes or boundaries. She is forgiveness. She is a breath of fresh air. She always uplifts. She never doubts or judges. She does not hold grudges. She always believed in the best in humanity and because of this, she never failed.

"You know, Kris Solomon," Kora pondered, "you are an amazing man with many gifts to give to the world. How did you get to this place? You are one of the kindest, most talented men I have ever met. What is your story? If you choose to share with me. I am in awe of your sacred masculinity."

Kris Solomon responded, "I appreciate you, Kora. In the last six months, my life has been turned upside down. I have died twice and come back to life. My memory has been erased of any previous life I have had six months prior. I went from making six figures to living on the streets. I have lost it all, only to gain more of my life's purpose. I have let the universe dictate what I should keep in my life and what I should let go. I know that I came here with conviction and purpose. There is a mission that I was sent here for that is a matter of life and death, but not just mine; hundreds of thousands of lives are counting on me. There is something that is aching just outside my five senses that we call our reality. It gets stronger every day. It is relentless yet elegant in its message for me. I was chosen, and for that I must be extremely valuable and I am learning my worth every day.

"I have learned not to be distracted by the mundane programming of this world. It is designed not to have our own best interest but to serve an entity that grows stronger by our fears, our insecurities, our egos, and animalistic passions and desires. We are programmed to be motivated to acquire nothing but food, shelter, clothing, transportation, avoiding pain, and seeking pleasure. This is not why I came into this existence. These are all tools used to distract man from following his heart with no fear in order to find his life's purpose. It is a struggle every day, as the programming is relentless. It never stops. It tirelessly works night and day to control your heart and mind. I refuse to succumb to the illusion of this world that so many humans have made their complacent reality. The best way to enslave a people is to not have them know they are slaves. It is the battle of our subconscious minds that controls our behavior without us even knowing it. Our subconscious mind communicates through images and symbols. This is how the programming starts. He who controls the images and symbols from the time you get up until the time you go to bed becomes your master. One thing I do know, Kora, is I know who I am not."

"I am so happy for your enlightenment, Kris Solomon! It is time! I have a sister up north about 300 miles from here. Here name is Indigo. She owns a farm in the woods up there that is surrounded by magnificent nature all around her. She has dedicated her life to collecting, nurturing, and categorizing natural and organic seeds. Organic seeds are becoming extinct. Once they are gone, they are lost forever. Everything is genetically modified these days so she is literally preserving nature for future generations to resurrect when the time is right. I know she would love to have you and Pu, as I know she can use a helping hand. I will call her and give you directions to her farm. I think you being in nature will help you find clarity in knowing your purpose as you continue to follow your heart.

"But before you go, I want you to share a special tea with me that I made from a rare, purple lotus flower that my sister, Indigo, found high up in her pristine mountains. It called to me today and it wants me to share it with you. I have dried out the leaves and have kept it exposed to moonlight for the last three years, waiting for the right time to partake of it. It chose you. It told me it will bring clarity and focus on your life's journey. It has a special message for you. A message that will clarify who you really are and your life's purpose.

"I have prepared myself to administer this special tea ritual that I was called to give to you. I have fasted for the last seven days and have only worn white clothing throughout that time, as instructed. I am here for you, Kris Solomon. Please trust me with all your heart and you will see what others can't show you. You will hear what others simply refuse to. You will smell what others won't. You will taste what others can't. Because where you are going, the lotus flower told me, your five senses won't help you. I will be your guide in the midst of the darkness. The solitude. The chaos. The fear. I will never leave you. I will never give up on you. I will never forget you. Quiet your mind in times of confusion and you will hear my faint whisper in the eye of the storm. I will guide you when it seems like you are trapped. I will give you hope when all seems lost. I will give you strength when you think you can't go anymore. I will never fail you. I will never leave you, even when it seems that you have been forsaken. Meet me upstairs in the bathroom so we can begin."

Kris Solomon bowed his head to the same level as Kora's heart and placed his hands together in front of him as if to pray, his fingertips touching his lips. Kora extended her left arm out to Kris Solomon. He gently grabbed her hand with his left hand and allowed Kora to guide him up the stairs to the bathroom.

Kora proceeded to run his steaming bathwater. She added fresh mint, hibiscus, lavender, calendula, and damiana as well as eucalyptus, peppermint, and tea tree essential oils. She also plopped in the bathwater shungite, amethyst, lapis lazuli, rose quartz, and aquamarine crystals.

As the infused elixir filled the tub, she directed her attention to Kris Solomon. He was waiting patiently, like a baby waiting for its mother to bathe him. She pulled his shirt up over his head. She then unbuckled his sandals and gently slid them off his feet. She proceeded to take off his pants, leaving him exposed, and gently led him to his oasis to get baptized.

As she lowered him into the tub, the water rose ever so close to the tub's edge but did not spill over. Kora lit thirteen candles, all strategically placed around the tub, and turned off the bathroom lights. The bathroom had now transformed into an illuminated, sacred portal into the unseen realm.

In the darkness, Kora started to chant a familiar song that resonated with Kris Solomon. "Ahh Ma Ra Ahh Sa Da Ahh Say So Ho. Ahh Ma Ra Ahh Sa Da Ahh Say So Ho. Ahh Ma Ra Ahh Sa Da Ahh Say So Ho." Kora repeated this chant over and over until Kris Solomon got lost in her melody and went into a trance as his eyes rolled to the back of his head. Kris Solomon eased his head underwater, and now Kora's chants became heightened in the water. "Ahh Ma Ra Ahh Sa Da Ahh Say So Ho. Ahh Ma Ra Ahh Sa Da Ahh Say So Ho. Ahh Ma Ra Ahh Sa Da Ahh Say So Ho."

Kris Solomon was content staying underwater as long as he could, as it reminded him of the safety and nurturing of the womb.

Finally, Kris Solomon came up for air after what seemed like 30 minutes of holding his breath. Kora put one of her body care products on a loofa to cleanse Kris Solomon. It was a liquid black soap base infused with lavender and tea tree essential oils and shea butter extracts. She stood him up in the bath and lathered him up from head to toe, leaving no crevice on his body neglected. She took an abalone shell from on top of the bathroom sink, filled it with water, and poured it over Kris Solomon's head to rinse him off. She repeated this process until all the soapy water was completely off his body.

She then took another one of her products, a body oil, and moisturized his skin from head to toe with her hands. It was made up of argon, black seed, coconut, and sweet almond oils infused with white sage leaves, copal, palo santo, frankincense, and myrrh resins. Kora was very particular in her preparation for Kris Solomon's journey.

Finally, his skin was met by Kora and a huge, fluffy, black towel with which she dried him off. After she wiped him from head to toe, she led him to her bedroom. On the bedroom floor was a *merkabah*, a circle and other sacred geometry patterns made up of copper wire, cowrie shells, and crystals. She led Kris Solomon to the middle of the circle and they both sat down facing each other with legs folded in front of each other.

Kora poured her steaming lotus tea into one copper cup decorated with more crystals and sacred geometry symbols all over it. She raised the cup to Kris Solomon's lips with both hands and gently tilted it toward his mouth. Kris Solomon spread his lips ever so slightly and allowed the warm liquid to enter his mouth and run down his throat. Kora told him to take three big gulps, so he finished the tea with some excess dripping down the side of his mouth.

Kora then positioned herself behind Kris Solomon and spread her legs to straddle him from behind. She told Kris to relax and lay back. His head fell gently into her lap. She proceeded to trace geometric shapes and patterns on Kris's face with her left middle finger as she chanted, "Ahh Ma Ra Ahh Sa Da Ahh Say So Ho. Ahh Ma Ra Ahh Sa Da Ahh Say So Ho. Ahh Ma Ra Ahh Sa Da Ahh Say So Ho." Gradually, Kris's eyelids got heavier and heavier as he gently dozed off in her arms.

BAM! BAM! BAM! BAM! BAM! BAM! BAM! BAM! BAM! BAM! BAM! BAM! BAM! BAM! BAM! BAM! BAM! BAM! BAM! BAM! BAM! BAM! BAM! BAM! BAM! BAM! BAM! BAM! BAM! BAM! BAM! BAM! BAM! BAM! BAM! BAM! BAM! BAM!

Kris Solomon could barely stand the noise ringing in his ears. It was deafening! Not only did he feel violated at the core of his being with this horrendous banging but simultaneously, he could see extremely bright lights that were in rhythm with the violent sound.

BAM! Lights flash! *BAM!* Lights flash! *BAM!* Lights flash!

He was exhausted and nauseated by the constant violent, blaring attack on his ears and the blinding, strobe-like, colorful light that made his inner world a torture chamber. Kris Solomon started to question himself, "How can my beloved friend give me such a substance that causes me so much pain?!" Now this "new world" he was experiencing seemed to change with each blatant *BAM!* sound and coinciding flashing light. As far as he could see he was in an artificial machine world, not organic or natural at all. It was mechanical in its very foundation. It was cold and calculating. It was run with precision, and without mercy or empathy. This artificial realm was designed to trap people's souls in its relentless determination to capture you in its clutches by preoccupying your existence with sensory overload! This machine world was built to highjack and manipulate its captive's five senses by stealing their focus, time, attention, and Inner G. It constantly consumes, and is never satisfied until you completely submit or are utterly destroyed in the process. It uses sensory overload to rudely and unapologetically inject itself into the very soul of existence of your entire being. It uses its sensory clutter upon sensory clutter to overwhelm us with extreme sensory gluttony.

In the background of this madness, Kris Solomon could hear gears and levers of this giant machine matrix but could not see them, as they were hidden in plain sight. This artificial world seemed to change its configuration as rapidly as the sound reverberated through his head in a constant pulsating and agonizing tone. There was no up in this world. There was no down. There was no left. There was no right. Just artificial sound, light, and structures that seemed hell-bent on driving him insane.

He begged Kora to make it stop as she wiped the sweat from his forehead in an attempt to comfort him from his inner torture. Tears were forming at the sides of Kris Solomon's eyes, while Kora wiped them away as soon as they appeared. She knew that whatever it was that he was going through, whatever it was that the tea was showing him, it was for his best interest.

Finally, after what seemed like an eternity, Kris Solomon accepted this world he was in and started to embrace it as a means of blocking it out. His breathing became slower and more deliberate. All of a sudden, he could hear a faint voice in the distance amongst the clutter, faintly and desperately trying to communicate with him. *"Calm your mind. Calm your mind. Calm your mind. Calm your mind. Calm your mind."* With each repeating of the statement, Kris Solomon could hear it clearer, and the deafening sounds and lights became fainter. Gradually, the sound disappeared completely and all Kris Solomon could hear was his saving grace, "Calm your mind."

Kris Solomon was now in complete darkness, solitude, and quietness. All he was focused on was his own breathing.

Instantaneously, Kris Solomon seemed to be shot out of a cannon! He zoomed past an army of Yayvou soldiers gnashing their teeth and clawing at him as a last, fatal attempt to keep him from escaping their torturous world. He discovered that it was the Yayvou that controlled and ran this artificial simulation he now called Hell. Kris Solomon felt like he was traveling in a wormhole through many galaxies, through this ultraviolet, transparent tunnel. So many distant memories flashed around him as he was spiraling through space and time.

Then, all of a sudden, it stopped! He was left in his thick, suffocating, dark surroundings that felt heavy on all sides of his being. He could not moved. Was it because he was paralyzed with fear, or was there something physically constricting his movement? Kris Solomon inhaled and exhaled to calm himself, but soon realized he had taken his last breath. He could not breathe; it was as if he had been buried alive.

He started to panic, as he could not inhale any air. The black matter around him had swallowed him up and left him to die in this darkness all alone. His lungs started to ache and his heart started to pound out of his chest, desperately searching for air. He tried to scream for help but no sound exited his mouth.

Just when he thought he'd left one torturous world, he landed in another one that was just as traumatic! Soon he came to the realization that losing consciousness was inevitable. He calmly prepared himself for his fate.

Suddenly, Kris Solomon felt a hand from above push through the thick, dark matter and grab his left wrist. Its grip was so intense and strong but gentle as it pulled him out of his black grave and left him on a sparkling lapis lazuli floor gasping for air like a fish out of water.

When Kris Solomon regained his composure, he looked up to see the goddess Nekhebet standing over him with a slight smile on her face. Kris Solomon realized for the first time that he was really Sutol, Nekhebet's personal bodyguard and daughter. He started to sob uncontrollably. His eyes overflowed with a constant reservoir of tears and his nose instantly became plugged as streams of mucus poured out. Kris Solomon was in a state of intense gratitude and overwhelming appreciation as it poured out of his heart. He couldn't help repeating to the goddess Nekhebet, "You found me! You found me! You found me! I was all alone, buried alive, not knowing who I was, and you found me! You took the time to search for me when others had forsaken me. You found me! You found me! You found me! You saved my life when others didn't see my value!" Kris Solomon could barely contain himself as the goddess Nekhebet just nodded and gently fondled his head as streams of tears poured from his eyes. He collapsed into a heap again on the floor, crying profusely with love and gratitude that someone felt him worthy and would not give up on him. For seeing his value and finding him worthy of being saved.

Kris Solomon closed his eyes once again to try to get rid of the endless tears that were streaming down his face. He could not see clearly through the watery, blurry vision that came from his eyes. As he opened his eyes again, he found himself in the same black and heavy prison he was just pulled out of! Once again Kris Solomon could not breathe and was suffocating. He felt all the same familiar characteristics as he did before, as if he was buried alive. Just as he was about to pass out again, the goddess Nekhebet once again raised him out of his pitch-black grave. Now Kris Solomon found himself gasping for air once again but this time on a polished jade floor. He was overwhelmed again and started to wail uncontrollably with gratitude, appreciation, and humility. Once he took that first gasp of air, he returned to being buried alive and the process started all over again. One thing that did not change was every time the goddess Nekhebet saved him, he felt and displayed extreme emotion, like it was the first time he was experiencing this.

Kris Solomon was exhausted as he went through this process for another four hours! The only thing that changed was the crystal floor he landed on after each resurrection. It went from hematite, to carnelian, to aquamarine, to malachite, to amethyst, to onyx, to turquoise, to alabaster, to agate, to citrine, to kyanite, to sodalite, to obsidian, to jasper, to aventurine, to tiger's eye, to schungite, to smoky quartz, to rose quartz, and ended with him sprawled out on a pure diamond floor.

Kora continued to wipe the tears and mucus from Kris Solomon's eyes and nose. She was just as exhausted as Kris was but was dedicated to seeing him through his journey, not knowing what he was perceiving. She had gone through three boxes of tissues already as Kris Solomon purged all those things that did not serve his higher good, as his journey was exposing his truth.

Kora couldn't feel her legs anymore because they were numb from the lack of circulation from sitting in that position for hours supporting Kris Solomon's head and shoulders, but she didn't mind. Kora noticed his chest rise and fall more than usual as he seemed to drastically change his breathing pattern. His eyes remained closed as they darted around under his eyelids.

As Kris Solomon was resurrected for the final time, he was left sprawled out on a solid gold floor in a sobbing heap. As he wiped the tears from his eyes, Nekhebet was no longer present.

He was startled to not see her as he looked around frantically, turning 360 degrees in search of his goddess. Upon his observation, he discovered that he was in a giant, sacred temple of some sort. The temple was so humongous, Kris Solomon must appear to be the size of an ant compared to this massive megalithic structure.

As his vision started to become clearer with each blink, he realized he was under an enormous altar and in his sight were giant, ancient Kemetic gods that were administering some type of sacred ceremony. There must have been at least 12 of these giant beings eagerly preparing for some type of ritual.

Just then, one of the giants, who had the body of a muscular human and the head of a black dog, spotted Kris Solomon under the table. Kris was terrified that he had been seen. He could not help but think how similar this intimidating god looked like his beloved puppy, Pu. The giant, dog-headed god spoke with a booming, deep, rich voice. "We have been waiting for you. Please come so that we can initiate you into the House of Sacred Harmony. You will forever be one of us, the protectors of the gods and goddesses of the realms of time. You will be assigned to the goddess Nut. The goddess of the sky that swallows up the sun at night only to give birth to it in the day. How powerful you must be if you are assigned to protect a goddess of such power and stature! From this day on, know your power and from this day forward, walk like the giant you are among all of us giants initiated into the House of Sacred Harmony. You will take the oath and if need be, sacrifice yourself in the service of the sacred feminine."

Just then, Kris Solomon started to grow. Incredibly, he reached the astronomical height of the other gods. The gods all lined up on either side of Kris Solomon as he lay on his back on the glistening, solid-gold floor. All the gods reached out with both hands so their left palm was facing up and their right palm was facing down, hovering over Kris's body. As they alternated the position of their palms, they all started a familiar chant that seemed to follow Kris Solomon wherever he went, from this realm to the next and back. "Ahh Ma Ra Ahh Sa Da Ahh Say So Ho. Ahh Ma Ra Ahh Sa Da Ahh Say So Ho."

The chant went on for quite some time as they reversed their position of their hands faster and faster. Kris Solomon felt a warm sensation enter his body from the bottom of his feet to the top of his head. It started to get even hotter as it now pulsated through his veins. His breathing became heavier and heavier with each passing moment. Kris Solomon felt like he couldn't contain all this Inner G radiating through him as it got more intense with each beat of his heart.

Now he was more seething than breathing. He clenched his fists tighter and tighter and involuntarily clenched his toes at the same time. Just when he thought he could not stand it anymore for fear of exploding, he opened his eyes and mouth and screamed from all the power surging through his body.

Kora let out a gasp as the once dark bedroom now became illuminated with ultraviolet light erupting from Kris Solomon's eyes, nose, ears, and mouth. Kora remained calm as she supported Kris Solomon's head and shoulders but sheltered her eyes with her other hand from the blinding light escaping Kris Solomon's head.

Just as soon as it started, it suddenly stopped. Kris Solomon's eyes were still glowing an ultraviolet light color and he was still seething as he breathed in and out with enormous intention. He slowly and powerfully lifted himself up and stood over Kora, taking in deep breaths, trying to control all the Inner G that was brewing inside of him like a nuclear power plant. He had to fight to control it as the human body was not made to contain this vast amount of Inner G.

He slowly and deliberately grabbed Kora's waist with his left hand and lifted her completely off the ground so that he could see her eye to eye. Still seething from his heavy breathing, he spoke for the first time in the seven-hour ordeal. "They do not know what they have awakened."

Kris Solomon set Kora down to the ground softly. He looked up toward the sky and passed out in Kora's waiting arms. Kora gently put a pillow under his head and grabbed a blanket from her bed. She snuggled on the outside of Kris Solomon's back and lay the covers over both of them while they lay in the copper and crystal circle she laid out for them. Kora wrapped her arms around her "sleeping giant" as if to protect him. She knew her mission had been fulfilled and her friend must leave her in the morning. She fell asleep with a smile on her face.

Simultaneously, Pu quietly lay down on the outside of Kora's bedroom door, eavesdropping on the whole ritual the entire time. She knew that there are some journeys that her master must go on by himself.

Chapter Eleven:
Buried Alive

Indigo greeted Kris Solomon and Pu with and open heart at her front door. "Welcome, King. My sister has told me sooo much about you and your wonderful companion, Pu. I am so excited to meet the two of you. I hope the journey up here was not too strenuous, as I know my place is off the grid. Welcome to my humble dwelling. Make yourself at home. What's mine is yours. Please feel free to have access to anything you like."

"Thank you, my sista," Kris Solomon answered. "It seems like it's been a lifetime journey to finally meet you. Thank you for your hospitality. Whatever Pu and I can do to help you, please do not hesitate to ask. We are all yours as well."

"I appreciate you, King," Indigo replied. "The first thing you two can do is get acquainted with the property. There are miles and miles of unexplored wilderness out here waiting for you to discover. But before you go off on your own adventures, I want you to explore this one trail that circles the property. It outlines the perimeter of my land. After you are familiar with the boundaries, then I would say it is safe to venture out farther. But only after you get familiar with the main trail."

"Sounds good, Indigo. Pu and I can't wait to explore, just show us our room so we can put our bags up and we would like to head out after that," Kris Solomon excitedly responded.

After they stored what little gear they had, Indigo walked them out the back door and they headed to the first trail marker. "Okay, Kris Solomon, the trail makes a six-mile loop around my property. Please stay on the trail, as one can easily get lost if they venture off the trail even a few yards. Promise me you won't venture off. Cell phone reception is virtually non-existent up here and you have about six hours of daylight left so please, be careful," Indigo pleaded.

"No worries, mama," Kris Solomon responded. "You forget, I have my trusted guardian angel with me, so we will be fine. See you in a few hours, Indigo. Thank you again for letting us stay with you!" Kris Solomon hollered back as the excited duo were eager to hit the trail and start their new journey.

Fifteen minutes later, Pu and Kris Solomon came across a swarm of butterflies in the middle of the trail headed directly toward them. They are everywhere. The only way of escaping them was to jump off the trail and take cover. Kris Solomon hastily ducked around a tree and put his arms over his head for protection to avoid being bombarded with this flying mass of colorful wings and pixie dust.

Two minutes later, as the colorful cloud dissipated, Kris Solomon opened his eyes, stood up, and gathered himself as he stepped foot back on the trail. In the distance, he noticed Pu chasing a lone, stray butterfly up the trail. "Pu!" Kris Solomon called out. "Come back!" Pu paid Kris Solomon no attention. She was hell-bent on catching this flying straggler as she banked to the left off the trail and disappeared into the woods.

Kris Solomon finally reached the point in the trail where she jumped off. Before he chased after his friend, he called out to her, taking heed of Indigo's demands that they stay on the trail no matter what. Pu did not respond, so Kris Solomon reluctantly stepped off the trail in pursuit of finding his friend.

Kris Solomon searched for Pu but to no avail. There was no sign of her anywhere, as seconds turned into minutes and minutes turned into hours. Kris Solomon plunged deeper and deeper into the pristine, overgrown woods that engulfed him completely and before he knew it, he was lost.

Finally, in the distance, he saw Pu curiously sniffing around at what appeared to be a four-inch-wide, rusted metal pipe buried in the forest floor protruding out conspicuously two feet above the ground. This pipe seemed out of place in the middle of the overgrown forest. When Kris Solomon got a closer look, he put his ear to the opening of the pipe and could hear a faint whirling sound, like a fan, and sounds resembling distant whimpering.

Kris Solomon instinctively stood erect and was deadly silent. He looked around to see if he could see anybody observing him in his close proximity. All he could hear was nature's soundtrack of branches gently rustling in the wind and birds occasionally chirping above. When he believed they were all alone, he hunted for a big stick to dig around the pipe and further his investigation.

After about an hour of digging, as Pu had joined in to help him, Kris Solomon's makeshift digging stick made a resounding thump as he thrust it with all his might into the soil around the circumference of the buried pipe. Kris Solomon wiped his brow, pouring down with sweat, with the palm of his hand as his eyes burned from the salty liquid assaulting his eyes. It appeared that his excavation had discovered a metal plate buried some three feet underground. When he struck this metal object again with his stick, it reverberated as if it was hollow inside. Kris Solomon put his ear up against the opening of the pipe once again. He could now hear faint, little girls' voices wailing, crying, and moaning words he could not distinctively make out.

Suddenly, Kris Solomon could hear what sounded like an ATV or quad runner rumbling up to the area from a distance. He could hear it getting closer and closer with each moment. He instinctively ducked down as the motorized vehicle got louder and louder in his direction. He quickly put his left index finger up to his lips and looked in Pu's direction. Pu instinctively suppressed her bark with all the strength she could muster, but out of her tightly closed jaws came a low and faint growl. Kris Solomon frantically put some fallen branches and dirt over the hole he had just dug. He picked up Pu, holding her snout, and ran behind a nearby tree to hide and observe the approaching vehicle.

The man got off his ATV and parked it near an open clearing. He proceeded to hide the ATV under a camouflage tarp he had stashed behind a nearby tree. Kris Solomon found it peculiar that the man looked like he just stepped out of a meeting on Wall Street. He was very well-groomed and clean-cut. He was Caucasian, about five feet ten inches tall, and 185 pounds. He was clean-shaven and had short, well-kept hair gelled back. He was wearing a tailored suit with patent leather oxfords. He seemed to be in excellent shape and was toting an over-packed backpack and carrying in each hand what appeared to be two full plastic grocery bags.

He walked over to a pile of brush on the far end of Kris Solomon's newly dug hole and put down his bags, then started to remove the brush from the immediate area to expose a hidden trapdoor underneath a giant boulder. With all his might, the man proceeded to roll the rock out of the way. He then methodically unbuttoned his top shirt button and loosened his silk tie and pulled out from under his starched shirt a key that was dangling around his neck attached to a dog tag necklace.

Kris Solomon and Pu were fixated on what they saw. Could this be the man that was responsible for all the latest kidnappings of the young Black girls Kris had been seeing on the news and media these last three months? Kris Solomon believed the latest missing girl count must be at least up to four by now.

The man opened the trapdoor to expose the top of a large trailer that had been buried three feet underground. Pu let out another grunt, this time even louder. Kris Solomon immediately grabbed Pu's mouth to make sure she didn't let out anymore primordial sounds of rage.

The man stopped what he was doing and glared in the direction of Kris Solomon and Pu, scanning the area for any signs of movement. Kris Solomon and Pu stayed in their crouched position behind the tree and Kris closed his eyes with all his might, as if this would somehow make him invisible.

One of the girls in the buried trailer started to cry even louder. Her wailing got the attention of her captor and he immediately threw his bags down the trapdoor, looked around one last time, and scaled down a makeshift rope ladder that dangled to the floor of the underground prison. There was a rope attached to the inside of the trapdoor and he grabbed a hold of the rope and the trapdoor was pulled shut with a resounding thump, closing off the ominous, buried tomb from above.

Once the trap door closed, Pu and Kris Solomon let out a big sigh and started panting heavily. Kris Solomon just now realized that he had been holding his breath the whole time. He knew that he couldn't leave the area for fear of never being able to find it again, let alone trying to find his way back to the farm, as the sun was setting and night was approaching. Pu and Kris Solomon would have to camp out somewhere close by so as to not be detected by this psychopath.

Kris gingerly walked over to the ATV and lifted the camouflage tarp. He carefully unloosened the gas cap, took off his left shoe and sock, and dipped his sock into the fuel. He put the gas cap and tarp back on and headed up a hill about 100 yards away to set up camp for the night and make a fire to keep them warm. He found a place hidden behind a collection of giant rocks.

Kris cleared an area and laid out his magic kente cloth on the forest floor. He proceeded to gather some scrap wood, brush, twigs, and branches to start his makeshift campfire, as the night temperature had started to plummet. He placed his pile of brush in an open area behind the rocks and close to his kente cloth and laid his gas-soaked sock on bottom of the kindling pile. He took out his lighter and ignited the sock. There was a big gush of light and heat from the ignited sock that engulfed the brush and it settled into a nice, warm fire.

Pu and Kris Solomon lay down next to the fire, mesmerized by the events they'd witnessed that day. Kris Solomon realized that he had collected enough wood to last him three days, let alone one night. Under the clear, starry night sky, Kris Solomon dozed off wondering how in the world he could rescue those helpless girls from that monster, and where they would go once he got them out.

Goddess Mother Nekhebet visited Kris Solomon in the woods that night after he dozed off. *"My dear Sutol, I am so proud of you, my daughter. You have followed your heart and have found me amongst the distractions of this prison planet and the personal cell you call your physical body, like I trusted you would. You have secured a new home for our beloved Temkaay people. There is only one thing left to do. Unbeknownst to you, I have been training you all your life for this exact moment. All that is left for you to do is sacrifice your own life for a cause greater than yourself. That is the only reason you have incarnated into this dimension. This is your only purpose in life.*

"Once you have completed your task, I will be saved from my torturing captors and we will once again be reunited together in peace, love, and harmony. Our people will then once again rise from the ashes and resurrect a new future for our beloved Temkaay in this dimension.

"Have no fear, my young princess warrior. You are stronger than you can ever imagine. Remember, the world that you

reside in is the illusion; my world from which you came is the truth that you seek. I miss you, beloved. It is time. It is time. It is time..."

Kris Solomon woke up from his slumber and sat up straight as an arrow in a cold sweat as he tried to regain his bearings. He could have sworn that he was just having a conversation with a beautiful being right next to him by the fire. He asked himself, "Why did she keep referring to a female?" He asked himself the question, "Time for what?"

His sudden movement startled Pu, and she also became wide awake. "Pu," Kris Solomon said, "I have a sudden urge to go back to the buried trailer tonight. I just want to look around real quick and I will be back. I want you to stay here, ok? I will be back in an hour. Do not make a sound and stay put. I know I can trust you to be good."

Pu turned her head away as if disgusted by Kris Solomon's words. She thought they were a team until the end, never to separate from each other. In her obvious disappointment, Pu reluctantly crawled under the kente cloth, lay down, and didn't make a peep or move in her repugnance of Kris Solomon.

Kris Solomon realized the terrain looked very unfamiliar at night, and he didn't know which way to turn. There were no landmarks he could recognize as he searched desperately to retrace his tracks back to the buried trailer. He realized that he'd just made a complete circle in the dark and was standing back at his makeshift camp where he started from.

Pu came out from under the kente cloth and saw her friend standing there in frustration. She gave him an "I told you so" look with a smirk on her face. Kris Solomon rolled his eyes at his companion and directed her to get back under the kente cloth. Finally, he threw his head up in frustration searching the vast, clear sky for any clues as to the whereabouts of the buried trailer.

Just then, Kris Solomon saw a shooting star streaking across the sky overhead, lighting his path directly to the buried dungeon. He followed the light.

When he arrived at the buried trailer, he realized the ATV was gone. He must think quick. Should he take this opportunity to rescue the girls? What if the man came back when he was down there? Where would he take them if he could get them out? He didn't even know where he was located. What if he was still there and had just moved his quad runner somewhere else? What if he had a gun? What if the girls were too weak or too terrified or too drugged to escape?

In the midst of his panic attack, a calming voice in his head kept repeating, *"It is time. It is time. It is time..."*

Kris Solomon took a deep breath and went over to where the trapdoor was located and started to remove the brush that was hiding it. The large boulder on top of it was already moved out of the way. Kris Solomon knew that there was a possibility the kidnapper was still down there.

"It is time...."

Kris Solomon paused, took another deep breath, and swiftly swung the trapdoor open and looked inside. His nose was immediately accosted with warm and stale air that smelled of feces, urine, body odor, decomposition, rotting food, and hopelessness. When he looked down, all he could see in the trailer was a bit of moonlight that had penetrated the darkness of the trailer. It was only about a three-foot-square bit of light that illuminated the inside of the dungeon.

Kris Solomon paused again to see if anyone revealed themselves from the shadows. After about a minute, no one appeared. It was deathly silent in the underground dungeon. Kris lowered the rope ladder from the top of the trailer opening, just like he saw the white man before him do. It fell to the floor of the trailer. Kris Solomon looked around one last time to make sure the coast was clear before he cautiously lowered himself inside the makeshift tomb.

As he descended down the rope ladder, he heard the cries and muffled moans of little girls reverberating throughout the pitch-black darkness. Kris Solomon took a few seconds to adjust to the darkness of the trailer so his eyes could recalibrate to relieve his temporary blindness. Gradually, Kris Solomon started to made out fuzzy images in the darkness, and he forcefully widened his eyes to see clearer.

As he felt around in the dark, he bumped into what felt like cold, metal fencing on his left that extended along the length of the trailer. The fencing went all the way up to the ceiling of the trailer. Every three feet or so was a metal gate with a padlock on it. From his count, Kris Solomon could feel four locked padlocks. He remembered the key dangling from the white man's neck and came to the conclusion that it was the key for these locks. How would he ever retrieve the key from that monster?

The stench was almost unbearable, and Kris Solomon held his breath between breathing through his mouth to avoid the attack on his nostrils. As his eyes adjusted, he could make out even more objects. There were four pens or kennels for dogs on the left side of the trailer. They seemed to be three feet wide by four feet long. Each kennel contained two buckets. One of the buckets seem to contain water and the other one seemed to be used as a toilet. Each kennel had a pack of baby wipes. There were dog bowls in each pen that contained some type of slop in them. There was a pallet in each pen covered by a thin wool blanket. Under the itchy wool blankets on each pallet was a small body, each curled up in the same fetal position as the next one in the adjacent pen, lined up in a row. Each of the bodies in each pen were shaking uncontrollably; partly from the cold, wet environment they were exposed to and partly due to the fear, abuse, and trauma they had endured.

Kris Solomon investigated even further in the darkness. On the other side of the trailer was a twin bed with soiled sheets. Above the bed, by the protruding pipe that led outside that Kris Solomon discovered on the outside of the trailer, was a hanging box fan whirling in fresh air from aboveground. Kris Solomon also noticed another three-inch pipe with a box fan attached in front of it, blowing stale air out. He sensed the fans were probably used as ventilation so the stagnant air in the underground trailer could circulate.

Sitting next to the bed was a small desk. On top of the desk was an open case of bottled water, a box of trash bags, a bag of plastic spoons, duct tape, rope, a small video camera, and a laptop. There was a pull-out drawer under the desk. Kris Solomon carefully slid it open to reveal a bottle of blue pills, a shot glass, a half-full bottle of Crown Royale in its purple felt pouch, scissors, some type of lubricating gel, and some baby wipes. Adjacent to the desk was a large cooler. Kris Solomon reluctantly opened it, not wanting to reveal its secrets. Inside was a bed of ice. Laying on top of the ice was a two liter bottle of Coke, a half-eaten loaf of bread, jars of peanut butter and jelly, and a plastic bag containing several glass vials with a clear substance in them and syringes.

Just then, Kris Solomon was startled by a familiar sound coming down from the trapdoor of the trailer above him. When he looked up he saw Pu yipping frantically. Kris Solomon instinctively knew that the kidnapper must be returning. "Pu!" Kris Solomon cried out in a loud whisper. "Good girl. I know the man is coming. Go hide by the tree. Go now, I will be okay, Li'l Mama. Hurry. Now go. Hurry!" Kris Solomon stumbled over the ice chest in his haste, spilling its contents all over the trailer floor. He dove over the upturned ice chest to grab the rope to close the trapdoor with his fingertips in the nick of time. The trailer turned black instantly with the sudden thud signaling the closing of the trapdoor. The stale, thick air returned like a noose around his neck and started to choke him almost instantly.

Meanwhile, Pu used her mouth to drag the last of the branches Kris Solomon had removed to expose the trap door. Hopefully, the darkness of the night would cover up any telltale signs that the tomb's entrance had been disturbed.

Pu quickly dashed to the familiar tree they hid behind only hours before and quieted herself, crying a soft whimper, worrying about her master's safety.

In the darkness of the trailer, Kris Solomon could faintly hear the muffled sound of the quad runner rumbling right above him. All of a sudden there was deadly silence as the man cut the engine to his ATV. Kris Solomon knew he must hide; but where to go? He looked around frantically. Amidst all the spilled contents of the cooler, Kris Solomon squeezed himself under the disgusting twin bed mattress and the trailer floor. He positioned his head so he could see the man's feet when he entered the trailer in case he had to leap to his feet in self-defense.

The trapdoor suddenly flew open as it was ripped off its hinges and rattled the whole trailer. Kris Solomon heard a distinct and familiar hissing sound from the opening of the trailer above him, but dared not to moved. His heart started to beat out of his chest. The figure over the trapdoor leapt from the top of the trailer and made a loud thud when he landed on the trailer floor, shaking the trailer like a 7.0 earthquake. The four girls who had been drugged were awakened by all the commotion. As each one of them slowly gained consciousness, they saw the figure coming into focus from their sleepy eyes. They all let out a bloodcurdling shrill. Kris Solomon peeked from under the stained mattress and saw the giant, white, scaly, claws with four-inch-long, razor-sharp, shiny black nails.

It was Commander Ammut.

Chapter Twelve:
The Seeding

Indigo paced frantically back and forth in her living room, on the phone with the authorities. It was past midnight, and her two friends had not come home from their hike earlier in the day. Indigo told the dispatcher on the line, "They were only supposed to be gone for a few hours and now it's going on nine hours since they left." Indigo was worried sick.

The police dispatcher heard the stress level in her voice and tried to calm her down. "Ma'am, the police will get in contact with the local park rangers first thing in the morning and send out a search party at the break of day. Please try to get some rest tonight. I am pretty sure they are okay. It is a mild night tonight and not too cold, so I am sure they will be just fine where they are. This happens more often than you think, and almost always ends on a happy note."

Indigo gave the police dispatcher a description of Kris Solomon and Pu. Once they had all the information they needed, the police dispatcher promised the search team would be there in the morning to start their search in the area they were last seen, then asked Indigo to end the call, per police protocol.

* * *

"I know you are here, you sssniveling coward. Ssshow yoursself and quit hiding like thessse pathetic little femalesss or I will ssstart biting off their headsss. You have been running away from me long enough. Fight me like a male speciesss or I will thrash you like that pathetic little girl who failed to protect her queen."

Kris Solomon suddenly recognized that familiar, eerie voice. Could it be Commander Ammut back again to try to kill him? Kris threw the mattress off himself and landed on his feet in his patented Sutol war pose, ready for battle. He was in a squat position with his right hand outstretched and his left hand over his heart.

To his astonishment, he didn't see Commander Ammut. He saw the white man who had abducted these four traumatized little girls. Kris Solomon exclaimed, "Leave these innocent little girls out of this. They have nothing to do with this. This is between me and you!"

Ammut's attention immediately focused on the frightened little girls and he abruptly headed toward the kennels where the terrified young girls were being held captive. Kris suddenly noticed Commander Ammut had the same key that the white man had around his neck. It had to be the key to the locked kennels. Kris realized that Commander Ammut had shape-shifted into the kidnapper's body. He must find a way to get the key off of him so he can open the kennels to free the girls.

Instinctively and without hesitation, Kris jumped on the back of Commander Ammut, putting him in a choke hold. Instantly, Commander Ammut shape-shifted back into his original reptilian form. The nine-inch, jet-black, razor-sharp, venomous spikes that grew from Commander Ammut's spine returned and consequently impaled Kris's chest and stomach. He howled in pain. Kris collected himself and with all his might, stabbed the side of Commander Ammut's neck with a sharply splintered fallen tree branch that dropped into the trailer in all the commotion.

This act sent Commander Ammut reeling in agony and just before he retreated to gain his composure, Kris snatched the necklace from around his neck that contained the key.

Kris was flung to the other side of the trailer where the girls were being held and hit the side of the trailer with so much force the trailer partially collapsed on one side. Kris was broken up from the inside out, and blood gushed from his wounds. He gained his composure and managed to draw enough strength to reach the cages the girls were locked in.

As Kris desperately tried to open the locked enclosure that imprisoned the first kidnapped victim, he nervously dropped the key and fumbled around to pick it up in the faintly lit buried trailer converted into an underground tomb. In the background, Kris could hear Commander Ammut snarl and wail in agony and pain, trying to pull the makeshift wooden spear out of the side of his neck while he swung wildly about like a mini Godzilla, destroying everything in his path.

Kris Solomon suddenly stopped and calmed himself in the midst of all the chaos. He quieted his mind and blocked out Commander Ammut's yelps and screeches. Kris was now in his own world. Everything seemed to be in slow motion for him now and he could not hear a sound. He calmly approached each cage and with the precision of a surgeon, unlocked each lock smoothly and efficiently. The girls ran into his arms and he directed them to the makeshift rope ladder to climb out of their underground torture chamber.

The first girl he freed had a hard time getting to the rope in the midst of all the destruction. She finally made it to the rope but lost her grip as she tried to rush too fast to escape the horror. She tried again and lost her balance on her second attempt too, still groggy from the mind-altering drugs she was forced to take.

Suddenly, she looked up at the opening of the buried trailer and saw Pu barking at her, waiting for her. With Pu's encouragement, she mustered enough strength to compose herself and pulled herself up to safety. Pu bit the back of the girl's shirt and pulled her up aboveground. She was showered with Pu's tongue kissing her all over her face.

Kris has just unlocked the second girl's cage as the first one hoisted herself up to safety. The second girl made a beeline to the rope and jumped on the ladder and handled it like a champ. She had no false steps, and scampered up the ladder in no time at all. Pu greeted her with all the kisses she could stand.

Just then, Kris stumbled to the ground on his way to the third girl's cell. He had to crawl to her cage, as he had lost a lot of blood and was getting progressively weaker. Somehow, with all his strength, he opened the girl's cage. She also found her way to the rope ladder and started to tentatively climb up.

Commander Ammut gathered himself and swung his tail wildly. The tail whipped the rope ladder and cut down one half of it. Halfway up, the terrified girl clung to the rope with one hand in an effort not to fall back onto the trailer floor to her doom. When she looked down, she saw Kris and Commander Ammut engaged in a fierce fight to the death.

Because of the large pools of blood, water, and ice from the spilled ice chest, the floor of the trailer was a death trap. Commander Ammut had trouble getting on his feet, and he kept losing his footing.

The girl was paralyzed while she hopelessly dangled on the rope for dear life, spinning in midair. She was terrified by Commander Ammut and could not take her eyes off of this ferocious-looking creature.

Pu barked hysterically at the girl. She finally snapped out of her stupor and redirected her focus on Pu and found enough strength to climb out of the trailer in the nick of time.

There was one girl left. Unfortunately, she was paralyzed in fear and was frozen in a fetal position and could not move. Kris painstakingly maneuvered his way between the girl and Commander Ammut, encouraging her to get up and get out of there. She was not responding. Kris exhaustedly fell to one knee, pleading with the little girl to get up.

Commander Ammut finally pulled the splintered wooden spear out of the side of his neck and let out a bloodcurdling shriek.

Kris Solomon rose to his feet and could barely assume his familiar warrior stance. He did not know how long he could hold Commander Ammut at bay. He must summon all of his energy to make one last-ditch effort to free the last innocent victim. Kris Solomon took a deep breath and belted out his warrior cry. He lunged toward Commander Ammut. He faked like he was going to strike Commander Ammut's head as he gathered up speed, like a heat-seeking missile. Suddenly, he ducked down at the last second and narrowly slid between the small gap of Commander Ammut's legs. He rose behind him in one motion and kicked him in the back of his right knee, instantly shattering Commander Ammut's knee.

Once the commander was on one knee, Kris jumped on the back of Commander Ammut and put him in a choke hold, as Commander Ammut's spikes pierced Kris's chest and stomach again, going ever deeper as he tightened his grasp around his neck. Kris could barely stand the agonizing pain of opening those fresh wounds once again, but knew what he must do in order for the last girl to escape.

Commander Ammut thrashed wildly about inside the trailer in desperation to get Kris Solomon off of him and catch his breath as he was being choked out.

At the top of the trailer opening, Pu was now foaming at the mouth, barking, trying to get the last girl's attention to escape, but to no avail.

Commander Ammut backed up with all his might against one of the trailer walls to impale Kris Solomon even more with the spikes going down his spine in an effort to kill him before he lost consciousness. Kris Solomon let out another bloodcurdling scream but did not loosen his grip around Commander Ammut's neck in an effort to choke him out before he himself succumbed to his injuries.

Finally, Commander Ammut dropped to one knee and started to lose consciousness. Kris Solomon didn't know how long he could hold on, as he started to get weak from losing so much blood, but somehow, he refused to let go.

Commander Ammut finally dropped to both knees but was struggling with all his might to stay conscious.

Kris Solomon's eyes started to roll in the back of his head but he stayed steadfast.

Finally, Commander Ammut's tongue dangled from his mouth as he took a faceplant straight to the floor and lost consciousness. The force of the fall flipped Kris Solomon head over heels and he crashed into the metal kennels across the trailer. Kris Solomon gathered himself. He placed his hand over his stomach and chest area and felt the warm, wet, sticky substance pouring out of his body. His mind was not on his mortal wounds but on the task of getting the last girl out of the buried dungeon.

He steadied himself as he stood up gingerly with the help of the metal fencing. He made his way to the girl and told her it was time to go home. All she could do was jump in his bloody arms and cling to him for dear life. Kris Solomon gingerly made his way to the makeshift rope ladder and saw that it was barely hanging by a thread. He wanted to climb out with the frightened girl in tow but it would not support him.

He summoned Pu from above and told her to lay some soft branches and leaves around the trailer opening and that she needed to back up, as he was going to try to toss the girl out of the trailer.

Pu didn't hesitate. She gathered the organic, soft material and backed up as she waited for the last girl to appear. Kris Solomon backed up as far as he could inside the trailer amidst the water, ice, blood, and debris. Commander Ammut was laying directly under the trailer hatch. Kris Solomon's plan was to get a running start with the girl straddling his shoulders. He would then jump on Commander Ammut to give him an extra boost. At the same time, he would throw the girl from his shoulders out the trailer hatch to safety.

Kris Solomon told his young friend that she was going home and to not be scared. He was feeling his wounds suck the life out of him as he was losing masses amounts of blood with every breath. Finally, Kris Solomon gathered himself, as he was in a now-or-never moment. He took off yelling at the top of his lungs. He reached Commander Ammut's massive body and stepped on him as planned. Kris Solomon pushed off the body with all his might and got airborne. He lifted the young girl off of his shoulders with two hands and pushed her with all his might.

Just then, Commander Ammut woke up and raised his arm to clip Kris Solomon's left ankle. Kris Solomon belly-flopped over Commander Ammut and nose-dived back into the trailer wall.

The girl, now in the air, had gained enough momentum and with just enough force to lift her high enough where both of her hands reached the edge of the trapdoor opening, she clung to the side of the open hatch. She was screaming as loud as she could in terror for fear of falling back into that hellhole with that monster.

Pu appeared at the top of the hatch. She bit one of the girl's sleeves and helped to pull her up in the nick of time before she fell to her peril. Pu looked down into the trailer and saw Kris Solomon and Commander Ammut crawling at each other, trying to fight with their last breaths while they lay beside each other, dying. Kris Solomon called out to Pu, "You gotta go now, Pu. Get the girls to safety. I will be right behind you. You have to leave now before he escapes and kills everybody. Now go!" Kris Solomon didn't want Commander Ammut to trace his way back to the campsite in a last-ditch effort to get his revenge.

Pu hastily corralled all the sobbing girls together, got their immediate attention, and barked at them to follow her. One by one, the traumatized girls found enough strength and trust and followed Pu through the dark night in the terrifying woods to the safety of the camp 100 yards away, hidden amongst the rough terrain. Pu guided them to the makeshift camp by the warm fire and laid-out kente cloth, which they used as a blanket. As the last girl found her way to the safety of the camp, Kris Solomon told Pu not to come back and that he would meet her at the camp with the girls after he had defeated Commander Ammut.

The four girls found safety and comfort under the kente cloth and warm fire as they huddled in each other's arms. One by one they dozed off, leaning their heads on each other's shoulders for support in a huddled mass. They found safety in being in such close proximity to one another. They also seemed to find a sense of peace petting and hugging on Pu while facing the warm fire.

As they each dozed off one by one, the kente cloth worked its healing magic and radiated a warm, glowing, ultraviolet light coming from underneath it. By the time they woke up at dawn, they would have forgotten all of their hellacious days in the underground dungeon. They would have no memory of the horrific things that were done to and seen by them. All of their physical and emotional scars will have been healed. They would be able to return to their lives before their kidnapping as if it never happened. They could resume their lives as innocent, provided for, and protected little girls ranging from 10 to 14 years of age and embrace their innocence once again. They would not be eternal victims to those horrible circumstances and would grow up to have healthy and balanced relationships with all the men in their lives.

* * *

Happening the same night...

Janus finally found a man who would treat her like the queen she is. She met him at her church, of all places, a few months back. It was his first time attending services and he was dressed to the nines. She wasn't initially attracted to him but he pursued her relentlessly with many unwanted advances. All of the women in the church were mesmerized by him, except Janus.

Eventually, she broke down and went out on a date with him and the rest is history. Since that date, they had been inseparable. Even when they are not together, they can be seen texting each other constantly, and they can't get enough of each other. She was in love once again.

This new man catered to her every need. He couldn't get enough of her cooking. He adored her and clung to her every word as he listened to her attentively. He was a true gentleman in every sense of the word. He opened and closed her door. When they went out to eat, he positioned himself at the table facing the door, just in case he spotted trouble and needed to get Janus to safety. He listened to Janus's goals and dreams and supported her in any way he could to manifest them. Every night before she went to bed, he rubbed her feet until she fell asleep. The first thing she felt in the morning was his soft and gentle kiss to greet her with the rising of the sun on top of her forehead. Some mornings she was awakened with the smell of bacon and eggs and freshly squeezed orange juice being brought to her to have breakfast in bed.

This night marked their three-month anniversary from the day they first met at the church. Her knight in shining armor had a surprise for his queen this special night. When Janus walked into the house after a hard day's work, she was greeted by the soft, glowing light of what must have been one hundred white candles flickering throughout the house. Her mystery man greeted her at the door wearing his black Hugo Boss fitted suit and a white, button-down shirt. He was barefooted. He put his fingers up to Janus's lips as if to tell her, don't say a word. He immediately grabbed her briefcase and purse and placed them on the table right next to the front door. In one motion, he swept Janus off her feet and started to carry her to the bedroom.

The hallway was littered with red-and-white rose petals scattered throughout the floor. The smell of roses was intoxicating.

In the background, Janus could hear some classical jazz music setting up the theme for the night; divine, passionate, explicit, vulnerable, and deserving indulgence of love. They entered the bedroom and to Janus's surprise there was a fresh bowl of fruit and assorted chocolates on one nightstand. On the other nightstand was a warm bottle of massage oil, chilled champagne with two glasses, and a freshly rolled blunt. Janus saw the lighting had changed in the bedroom. There were candles flickering, but her man had changed all the light bulbs in the room to black lights. Everything was illuminated in a glowing, purple hue, and certain pastel colors were glowing in the dark. There were still rose petals all over the floor and on top of the bed but they were glowing fluorescent teal and purple in color.

The Black knight gently lowered Janus to the bed and removed her shoes. He grabbed her a plate of fruit and started to feed her. He took one of the chocolates and put half of it in his mouth. He moved towards Janus's mouth and she instinctively devoured the other half of the chocolate, then they both devoured each other's tongue in a passionate kiss of primordial ecstasy.

The Black savior commenced to pour her a glass of champagne. Just as he handed it to her, he started to undress himself slowly in front of her. After he was fully naked, he started to free Janus of her binding clothes that had been restricting her all day long at work. He gently got in the middle of the bed and turned on his back, totally exposing his manhood which was ready, willing, and able.

Janus raised her eyebrows in anticipation of his raw masculinity. The Black messiah whispered in Janus's ear, "Baby, I want you to get on top so you can get yours first, okay? After you are fully satisfied I will dick you down for however long you want and put you to bed. Okay, Queen? I am here to serve you and you alone."

Their hearts started to pound and race in unison, intermingling and vibrating at a rate where shared Inner G infused into one divine song. His heart was pressed against her chest, trying to get as close as possible to his reflection, which yearned to be acknowledged. Similar to a child pressing his hands and face against a toy store window, yearning and dreaming of possessing the toy that he had always wanted, so his heart lay upon hers as he made his intentions known. With all his heart and soul, he held this thought at his center.

Janus locked her feet around the outside of his ankles so he could not escape her blissful bond. She opened her mind, heart, soul, and legs to give him full access to the most sacred place known throughout the entire universe. Janus had turned herself completely inside out in a ritual of divine manifestation. She had courageously expressed to him through her vulnerability the depths of her powerful life force. To do this phenomenal feat took the courage, strength, and trust that only a woman can possess.

The opening to all that is, was now awaiting his entrance. With full awareness of the depths that lay before him, he plunged further into the sacred, with every last drop of his being. His head started to prepare for the initiation into the gateway of infinite possibilities. His thoughts started to sway to and from this dimension to the next, from the seen to the unseen, as their souls danced, played, and swirled above their heads.

He got an intense, cold sensation moving like a wave submerging his body. It began at the bottom of his feet and steadily climbed up his ankles, then his inner thighs. Janus sighed in his ear. It felt like a butterfly had gently landed on his earlobe to told him its most sacred of all secrets. This was her way of giving him permission to emancipate his masculine spark in the form of ultraviolet liquid gold. His main purpose of existence is to give life at the expense of his own, if need be. As the feeling of inevitability involuntarily possessed his body, he converted his essence into liquid sunshine that flowed into the gateway, leaving behind the human shell that imprisoned his soul.

As he swirled inside the dark matter, he was tossed wildly about but found bliss and purpose in the chaos that bombarded his new definition of reality. He finally let go and relinquished his ego to a power greater than himself. He would succumb to her completely. He was her servant to do as she wished. She guided him through the dark matter like a leaf floating down a running brook. He was helpless to her grasp, so he didn't fight or try to escape. He was totally defeated, but somehow joyous in acceptance of being conquered. So he continued the process without any preconceived notion of where he would finally arrive with his destiny.

Suddenly, he was in a tunnel with a blinding-white light at the end of it. The light warmed and comforted him in his liquid blanket of ecstasy. As he neared a giant golden throne, he felt intrigued by the power emanating from the entity that occupied its space. The presence demanded his respect, submission, and allegiance. He was awestruck by the brilliance of light and overwhelmed with emotion for what he was about to see. He witnessed two child-like figures occupying the space on the throne, designated for divinity. The throne was on top of a hill with lush, lavender-colored grass, and the scent of jasmine and honey filled the air. There were purple, teal, and indigo curtains surrounding the walls of the temple. On the ceiling of the temple were diamonds and crystals of amethyst, lapis lazuli, jade, and gold flakes that were illuminated and sparkled like stars on a clear night sky.

Nekhebet and Sutol were the babies that were sitting on the throne in the temple in Janus's womb. They seemed to be back in Nekhebet's majestic temple on Temkaay. They were playing patty-cake while chanting the Transcending Song. Janus's mate had been teleported inside Janus's womb when he released himself during their sexual encounter. Janus's womb had now been converted into Nekhebet's temple once again. The baby Nekhebet took an illuminated bead from her left earring and pinched it between her tiny little index finger and her thumb. It burst into a white light and like illuminated glitter, fell in between the two of them as they faced each other on a golden throne sitting Indian-style. The glitter started to liquefy and coagulated into a luminous, ultraviolet egg that divided itself at an alarming rate and started to grow exponentially. The two baby girls seemed amused and resumed their game of patty-cake while chanting the Transcending Song through their giggles and laughter.

They laughed at their newly arrived visitor, who was in utter shock at what he was witnessing. Nekhebet instructed the man for the first and only time, "Your mission is to serve Janus and the children she will have. You must give them your love and your light to protect and provide for them. A part of you must die in order for your goddess to thrive. If you serve me, you will know wealth beyond your wildest imagination and nothing will be impossible unto you."

Baby Nekhebet dismissed the man back from whence he came with three consecutive claps from her tiny hands. Baby Nekhbet and baby Sutol returned to their game as the man's soul was instantaneously snatched back into his physical body down the long tunnel. He reemerged and found himself back in a world that he was familiar with, on top of Janus and out of breath.

He was still in a panic and disbelief. Janus looked at him in terror and asked him if he was okay. The man shook it off and assured Janus all was well. He was speechless for about five minutes and his eyes were in a fixed gaze staring into space.

Suddenly, he released a big smile and kissed Janus lovingly on the cheek. Janus let out a sigh of relief and pondered to herself, what is this man hiding behind that silly grin? but dared not to inquire any further. "Just hold me, baby, and never let me go," Janus pleaded to her partner.

"I got you, Boo G. I got you," the man replied. Then he whispered under his breath, "Or should I say, I got us?"

Janus turned her head sharply at Red as if to say, "What did you say?" but let it go. Janus had learned the hard way that some things are better left unsaid.

Bright and early the next day, four rescued girls were awakened out of their deep slumber by the recently deployed park ranger search party. The girls cried uncontrollably as they clung onto the rangers in the brown-and-green uniforms with the funny hats with the small chin straps. They all tried to speak at once but no one could understand their words through their sobbing.

When the park rangers asked them where they were held, they all pointed to Pu to show them the way. Pu excitedly led them back to the buried trailer but before she went, she retrieved the red kente cloth in her mouth to take with her.

When they got there, Pu saw the mangled entrance to the buried trailer and looked down into it. She saw Kris Solomon's lifeless body spread out on the trailer floor in an awkwardly painful-looking position. But he had a peculiar smile on his face. Next to him was a bloody, decapitated white Kimono dragon's body and the head was nowhere to be seen.

Pu quickly flung the kente cloth down the door opening and it landed flush over Kris Solomon's body. It took the park rangers approximately thirteen minutes to climb their way down there. During all that time, Pu was staring at her friend's body, hoping for any signs of life or movement. Kris Solomon's body never moved.

When the park rangers finally made their way to the bottom of the trailer, they checked Kris Solomon's vital signs and their worst fear was confirmed. Kris Solomon was not alive. It seemed like Pu was too late bringing him his magical kente cloth that saved his life and many others so many times before. Pu slowly backed out of the crime scene undetected, in the midst of all the commotion, with her tail between her legs. She whimpered softly to herself. Pu quietly and inconspicuously disappeared into the thick of the woods, never to be seen again.

Chapter Thirteen:
Metamorphosis

(Three Years Later)

We see Janus's and Red's triplets—Hershel, Empress, and Amethyst—playing at a neighborhood park. Red and Janus are holding hands with their fingers interlocked, snuggled close to each other on a park bench overlooking the play area. They are obviously very much in love and happily married. They are snuggled up watching their children play in awe and admiration. The girls are still playing patty-cake every chance they get as they spin around in the center of a merry-go-round singing their special song. Their little brother, Hershel, is pushing them as fast as he can as he laughs uncontrollably, spinning his two sisters around and around, faster and faster. No doubt all this kinetic energy is creating an unseen, spiraling vortex above them that is opening up cosmic gateways that only the two sisters can traverse and comprehend.

Red signals to the children that it is getting late and time for them to leave the playground and go home. The children beg their father to stay just a little bit longer but before Red can give in to their request, Janus steps in and puts her foot down. She tells them they will be back tomorrow if they are good. Hershel looks around and grabs his loyal, beat-up, red-and-white Nerf football that never leaves his side. Amethyst hastily does a perfect cartwheel and in one motion she retrieves her "Wakanda Forever" spear that lights up upon contact and assumes her warrior squatting pose, letting out a piercing yipping sound. They both hurriedly make their way to their parents' arms in the direction of the park benches.

Empress, on the other hand, runs the other way as fast as a three-year-old can go into some neighboring bushes. Red immediately calls out to her and chases after his daughter. He yells back at his wife, Janus, "There she goes again! I swear that girl has a mind of her own. Empress! Empress! Wait for Daddy!"

When Red catches up to her, he finds her sitting down in the dirt amongst the bushes with her legs crossed over each other, caressing what appears to be a cuddly, black ball of fur in her lap. Empress and the fluffy, black bundle look up at her father simultaneously, each having big, puppy-dog eyes. Red's heart melts instantly.

"Can we keep her, Daddy? Please?" Empress begs her father.

"Baby girl, he might belong to someone. Do you see a collar on him?" Red inquires.

"No, Daddy, she is all by herself with no one to love her and she is a girl, silly."

Red is amused by his young daughter's perception and knowledge of gender at such a young age. "Okay, precious, you are right. She is a girl; Daddy's bad. This is what we will do. We will take her home for now, but tomorrow we will be back to put up flyers all over the park that we found a lost puppy. If no one claims her, we will continue to take care of her. How does that sound?"

"We get to take her home, Daddy? For real?" young Empress exclaims, not registering anything else her father told her.

"Yes, Li'l Mama, we can," Red replies to his overwhelmed daughter.

Empress makes a beeline to her siblings as fast as she can to give them the great news, with the puppy clinging onto her for dear life. "I gotta pup-peee! I gotta pup-peee! I gotta pup-peee! And her name is Pu!"

www.ingramcontent.com/pod-product-compliance
Lightning Source LLC
Chambersburg PA
CBHW071905220626
47052CB00002B/214